MERIEL WAS FA...
MAKE UP HER O...

HER SISTER SYD...

Clearly Meriel was far too inexperienced in the w...
the world and the wiles of men to choose among suitors
like the mysterious Edward Trevillion, who bedazzled her
in a whirlwind courtship only to leave her bewildered
when he disappeared . . . or the almost too-handsome
Morgan Leighton, whose seductive skills had sharpened to
a near-irresistible edge through association with the loveliest ladies of London . . . or Sir Max Westbook, who was
far too sure of his own position to stoop to conquer Meriel
no matter how beneficial it would be for both of them.

Clearly it was up to Sydney to guide her younger sister to
the right choice—even if it meant losing her own chance at
love. . . .

THE
PERFECT MATCH

The
Perfect Match

by
Norma Lee Clark

①
A SIGNET BOOK
NEW AMERICAN LIBRARY
TIMES MIRROR

NAL BOOKS ARE AVAILABLE AT QUANTITY DISCOUNTS WHEN USED
TO PROMOTE PRODUCTS OR SERVICES. FOR INFORMATION PLEASE
WRITE TO PREMIUM MARKETING DIVISION, THE NEW AMERICAN
LIBRARY, INC., 1633 BROADWAY, NEW YORK, NEW YORK 10019.

SIGNET TRADEMARK REG. U.S. PAT. OFF. AND FOREIGN COUNTRIES
REGISTERED TRADEMARK—MARCA REGISTRADA
HECHO EN CHICAGO, U.S.A.

SIGNET, SIGNET CLASSIC, MENTOR, PLUME, MERIDIAN and NAL BOOKS
are published by The New American Library, Inc.,
1633 Broadway, New York, New York 10019

First Printing, September, 1983

1 2 3 4 5 6 7 8 9

PRINTED IN THE UNITED STATES OF AMERICA

1

The two red-caped figures in matching high-crowned bonnets squelched and slid their way precariously along the muddy road in their high wooden-soled pattens, trying to avoid the water-filled ruts and holes in the mire of the road. They giggled and gasped and called warnings to one another, each holding in one hand a cloth bundle containing her indoor slippers and a library book, the other hand clutching up her skirt as far from the mud as modesty allowed.

When they came to a stile they turned aside without consultation, waded through the wet grass of the roadside, and climbed up to sit on the steps. This was clearly an accustomed and much-welcomed resting place. Though dressed similarly, it did not take any close inspection to see that they were very different. Even at a distance one girl could be seen to be nearly half a head shorter and much fairer than the other.

"Lord, Syd, why you would not ask Papa to put the horses to, I cannot imagine," gasped the taller girl, turning up her face to the watery June sunshine.

"It would only upset him and make no odds in any case, for he would not take the chance with the road in this state."

"Well, the donkeys, then—at least we could have ridden."

"Oh yes, and have them digging in their heels every few feet and having to get down and try to pull *them*. No, I thank you. I prefer to have only myself to pull through this."

This was said decidedly, as one used to always knowing her own mind, but with the greatest cheerfulness in the world. In fact, Sydney looked about herself with evident satisfaction. She was clearly not in the least discomposed by their undignified progress. "After being mewed up in the house for four days, I declare I could happily walk twice as far," she added.

5

"We shall be all mud splashes to the knees," observed her sister.

Yes, these were sisters, though there was little to inform the casual observer of their relationship. The more discerning would have seen a similarity in the shape of mouth and, at times, an expression that was very like. The elder, Sydney, was smaller, with pale, smooth ash-blond hair, grey eyes, and a delicate pink-and-white complexion that was her best feature. She had never been considered a beauty, though the sum of her parts pleased, when a summing up of the components should not have been calculated to do so. Her nose was undistinguished, being too short and turning up at the end too pertly, her forehead was round and high, her chin a trifle too long. There was also evidence that she was not in the first flush of youth, there being lines at the corners of her eyes and beginning to deepen about her mouth. But the grey irises ringed with black were compelling and her smile revealed even white teeth behind a firm, well-shaped mouth, and her figure was neat and trim, her movements precise and graceful.

Her sister, Meriel, was in every way her opposite: tall and willowy, ebony and ivory. Her nearly black hair curled riotously about the perfect oval of her face, her black eyes were almond-shaped, her profile a clear-cut cameo, no line of worry evident. Nor should there have been, for she was but seventeen to Sydney's twenty-seven.

Presently they set off down the road again and came after some twenty minutes into the small town of Upper Chyppen. They had come at the invitation of Mrs. Maplethorpe to take dinner with her, but they had left early to give themselves time for several small errands in the town before they must present themselves to Mrs. Maplethorpe. There was a packet of cinnamon to purchase for Cook, ribbands for the refurbishment of last summer's Italian straw bonnets, and nibs for pens commissioned by Papa. Last, but most important, they must visit the circulating library where they had a subscription and exchange their books. They ordinarily read aloud to each other every evening after supper, but the four days of rain that had kept them indoors with a great deal of extra time on their hands had forced them to finish their books more quickly than was usual. This had been particularly irksome to Sydney, for they had already finished her own book and she had had to sit through Meriel's choice, *Alphonsine* by Ma-

dame de Genlis, which Sydney had disliked excessively and had considered not at all suitable for a seventeen-year-old girl, dealing as it had with an unconsummated marriage and a wife who finds consolation in the arms of a page in the household.

When they entered the shop, Meriel wandered away at once to inspect the shelves, while Sydney handed over their books.

"Oh, Miss Armytage, did you like your choices this time?" cried Miss Twoomy, the shop's owner.

"I liked Miss Burney's book very well, but I did not feel Madame de Genlis proper reading for my sister. I would appreciate it if in the future you could in some way advise me in advance if the subject matter is too . . . er . . ."

"Oh, indeed I will, Miss Armytage. My word, I had no idea it was . . . I had not read it, you see . . ." Miss Twoomy looked flustered but interested, and Sydney was amused to note as she turned away that Miss Twoomy whisked the book under the counter instead of returning it to the shelves.

The sisters began taking down books and consulting one another, reading a few lines here and there to sample the style of first this book and then another. They were both great novel readers, though their tastes were somewhat at variance. Meriel preferred Gothic horrors by Mrs. Radcliffe, or dashing romances with a great deal of swooning and sword play, while Sydney preferred Maria Edgeworth's Irish stories or, best of all, the work of Jane Austen. Even Papa would stay to hear them read aloud anything by Miss Austen.

"Miss Twoomy, do you . . . ?" Sydney turned and then stopped short as she saw that Miss Twoomy was engaged with a customer, a tall, well-dressed gentleman. "Oh, I beg your pardon."

The gentleman turned as she spoke and now smiled and bowed. "Please continue. Miss Twoomy and I had concluded our business," he said with great courtesy.

"Thank you, sir. I was going to ask, Miss Twoomy, if Miss Austen's new novel had come in as yet."

"Ah, you mean *Emma*," exclaimed Miss Twoomy, "though I am sorry that I do not have it for you, my dear. Oh, Miss Armytage, allow me to make you acquainted with Sir Max Westbrook. He is newly come into the neighbourhood and we must all make him welcome."

Sir Max removed his tall beaver hat and bowed again. "Charmed, Miss Armytage."

"Welcome, sir. Do you plan a long stay in Upper Chyppen?"

"I have taken Lades Hall for a year."

"Ah, a charming manor with many pleasing prospects. I am sure you will be very comfortable there, will he not, Miss Twoomy? Meriel, do come and meet our new neighbour."

Meriel looked up startled from a book she had already begun to read with such engrossment she had been entirely lost to what was transpiring around her. She closed the book over her finger to mark her place and came across the room at once, however, at Sydney's summons. Sydney decided she must scold her for this when they were alone, for it seemed rude to treat an introduction as only a momentary distraction for which one was unwilling to lose one's place in a book. Besides, a new face was not an everyday occurrence in their small neighbourhood.

Meriel saw Sydney's tiny frown of displeasure, and guessing its cause, hastily dropped the book on the counter and performed a very pretty curtsy to Sir Max as Sydney introduced them. She stood demurely before him, not at all discomposed by his rather astonished stare, for she was already accustomed to this kind of reaction from almost every male she encountered. She was not in the least a vain girl, but nor was she stupid, and she had heard too often that she was pretty not to have understood by now that she was so.

What Sydney blessed her for was her apparent ignorance of her quite astonishing beauty. To know oneself a pretty girl was no bad thing, to Sydney's way of thinking. She herself had enjoyed being called pretty when she was young, and thought the burden of plainness an unfair one for any girl just reaching the difficult threshold of womanhood. But the knowledge of being a raving beauty would be just as much a burden, she thought, and could create an unwholesomeness of character.

"There, now, Sir Max, was I not telling you Upper Chyppen was filled with charming people?" chirped Miss Twoomy.

"Indeed you were, Miss Twoomy, though I fear you did not go nearly far enough in your encomiums. Are we truly neighours, Miss Armytage?"

"Well, not to say *near* neighbours, sir," replied Sydney.'

"I am devastated. Where do you and your sister reside?"

"Quite on the other side of Upper Chyppen from Lades Hall. About two miles out from town."

"Only a step, in fact," he replied firmly. "I shall certainly take advantage of it to call at the first opportunity—with your permission, of course."

"With pleasure, sir, and I am sure my father would be happy to make your acquaintance also."

"I will bid you good day, then. I must hurry home at once and write to my agent directing him to extend my lease."

This avowal caused both girls to laugh. He bowed to all of them and took his leave. Meriel at once picked up her book and found her place, while Sydney turned once more to the shelves and absentmindedly hunted for something for herself. Her thoughts, however, were not on her work, but upon Sir Max Westbrook. Specifically, Sir Max in relation to her sister, for she had been much struck by the handsome picture they made as they had stood together just now before her.

She had been worrying a great deal about Meriel for some months. To be exact, ever since Meriel had made her first appearance at the Upper Chyppen Assembly in pale rose gauze and a wreath of fresh pink roses and silver ribband on her piled-up black curls. The effect had been devastating, and her entrance into the Assembly rooms had created as near a sensation as had ever been seen in that staid establishment. The stunned silence of those nearer the door had spread slowly over the entire room until every head was turned in their direction. Then there was a concerted quiver over the audience, a rising hum of whispering as head bent to head in question and comment, then an abrupt rush of young men towards them who formed an elbowing crowd from which Sydney at last managed to extricate herself, laughing and pleased.

Since that evening there had been a stream of young men making their way to the Armytage door to pay their homage, giving rise to the worry that had begun to beset Sydney. For, gratifying as it was to know that Meriel aroused so much admiration, it gradually began to seem to Sydney that there was not one among these young men who was truly worthy of her. Her loveliness and sweet good nature would be wasted on these awkward red-faced youths. She lived with a dreadful apprehension that Meriel would develop a *tendre* for one of

them, though as far as she could judge there were no signs of any such thing so far. Meriel accepted her success calmly, as though it were all part of putting down her skirts and putting up her hair. Sydney, however, was not sanguine, though she recognized that she was prone to needless worry on Meriel's behalf.

This had been so since her sister's birth, when a ten-year-old Sydney had taken the newborn infant from the lifeless arms of the mother who had just died giving birth to her second daughter. In that instant of racking grief there was roused in Sydney a fierce protectiveness for this baby sister who would forever be deprived of the love and tenderness of her own mother. Added to this was the guilt Sydney was always to feel at having had ten years of her beloved mother's care while Meriel had had none. She vowed in that long-ago moment to make it up to her sister by devoting her life to mothering her. She had begun by interfering so much in the baby's care that after three months the nurse had packed her bags and left. Sydney had had no trouble persuading her grief-stricken father that she was competent to take care of Meriel without help. And so she had proved. Meriel had been, fortunately, a sturdy, healthy baby, and with the help of Mrs. Willowes, the housekeeper, Sydney had served very well as substitute mother. She had only recently begun to see that there was more to the task than she had ever suspected—that worry for a child continued, in some ways became more intense when childhood fevers and falls were over, especially if that child was a girl, and beautiful, and had reached the age when one must begin to think of losing her.

Sydney hoped she would be sensible about that, but she had noticed a tendency in herself to look upon all Meriel's swains and find them sadly wanting in all those qualities she thought her sister deserved in a husband. Not that Sydney was mercenary, though she hoped of course that whoever won Meriel's heart would be sufficiently endowed with this world's goods to ensure Meriel a life of comfort. What she did want for her, more than wealth, was a man of some sensitivity and understanding and culture. The young men who flocked around now, while good enough creatures in their way and all sons of minor gentry, were nevertheless somewhat rough in their manners and tended to talk a great deal of horses and hunting and to fall asleep in their chairs during the music after a

dinner party. Not one knew anything of literature or art, and would not have admitted it if he had done so, and seemed to have no interest in anything that happened beyond a day's ride from Upper Chyppen.

If only, Sydney mourned, Papa could be persuaded to give Meriel a Season in London. She would set the whole world on its ear, and surely make a very fine marriage. Sydney began to dream of her sister as Lady So and So, driving out in her own fine carriage, entertaining a glittering assemblage to dinner, appearing gorgeously gowned at the Queen's Drawing Room. Ah, surely not so wild a dream?

But she knew in her heart she was being ridiculous. Though they lived very comfortably, there was no way Papa's income could be stretched to include something so wildly expensive as a London Season, even had there been a single female relative, or even a close friend, in Society who could sponsor Meriel. Though Sydney had reluctantly given up this dream, the shreds of it still floated in her mind.

Now, the moment Sydney had seen her sister standing before Sir Max Westbrook, the idea had instantly occurred to her that here was the very image of all that she had ever thought of as gentlemanly. He was tall and well-made, with a fine, bony face, clear, warm brown eyes, and a firm, well-shaped, generous mouth. Altogether as well-looking a gentleman as she had ever seen, she thought, and though taking Lades Hall for a year did not promise great wealth, it must mean his pockets were not entirely to let. She thought he must be between thirty and five-and-thirty, and halted her racing thoughts briefly to consider whether this was too old for a seventeen-year-old. Pooh, she thought at last, brushing it aside, it is the perfect age for a man to marry, and better for a very young girl really. He would be a calm, steadying influence for her.

It was not until Mrs. Maplethorpe's manservant had opened the door to their rap that a thought occurred to Sydney that caused her to stand rooted, staring at the man as though she had seen a ghost. What if Sir Max were already married!

"Sydney?" whispered Meriel, nudging her gently.

"What? Oh! Good afternoon, Porterman."

"Good afternoon, miss," he replied imperturbably. "Will you step in?"

He helped them exchange their pattens for their slippers,

then they trod across the hall in his dignified wake and were much gratified when he threw open the drawing-room doors to announce them grandly, just as though he had not known both of them in their swaddling clothes.

Mrs. Maplethorpe, a large, imposing-looking woman with a very kind heart, swam across to embrace them warmly. "My dears, we have not seen you this age. Has not the rain been dreadful? I wanted Maplethorpe to send the carriage for you, but he was too fearful of the state of the roads. You must be exhausted from your long walk. Will you not step upstairs to lay aside your bonnets and refresh yourselves?"

While they were shepherded above stairs and fussed over by Mrs. Maplethorpe, Sydney allowed her mind to revert to the thought that had startled her so on the doorstep. Of course Sir Max must be married. Such an attractive man could not have reached his age without being snapped up long before this. How idiotish I am, she thought wryly, to have got him and Meriel all the way to the church door after five minutes of conversation without once considering such a possibility. I hope I am not turning into one of those scheming mamas who thrust their marriageable daughters at every male who appears on the horizon.

Having been used for so long to think of herself as Meriel's mama, there seemed no incongruity to her in naming herself so. She continued to caution herself in that frame as she smoothed her hair and washed her hands, assuring herself that it was still some years before she must needs truly concern herself about an eligible *parti* for the child in any case, and she was only being foolish and doting, and she must be alert in future to these tendencies in herself, and other warnings of a like nature. However, in spite of all of them, another thought came unbidden into her mind: it was, after all, perfectly possible that Sir Max was *not* married.

She went down to dinner in a much lighter frame of mind.

2

Dinner with the Maplethorpes was very much like many such dinners that had preceded this night, for they were a small community of not more than fifteen families of Quality, who had been accustomed to entertaining one another in various combinations for many years. They were tolerant of one another's crotchets, as indeed they must be if they were to keep up any sort of social life, and though there were inevitably small quarrels and disagreements, they were, for the most part, short-lived.

Tonight the Armytage sisters were to dine with Squire Dobbs and Mrs. Dobbs, the curate, Mr. Fortescue, and Mr. Claiborne Cole and his sister, Arabella Cole, as well as the Maplethorpes and their daughter, Cassandra, a young lady of eighteen years. Mr. Armytage had also been included in the invitation to his daughters, but since the rains had reduced the roads to a quagmire, he would not take out his carriage and he declared if his daughters wanted to walk two miles to eat their dinner and make the agreeable to a set of neighbours they had known all their lives, they were welcome to do so; as for him, he would take his mutton at home.

The numbers were not even, but most Upper Chyppen hostesses had long since given up attempting this for there were always fewer gentlemen available than ladies. In this case Mr. Maplethorpe led in Mrs. Squire Dobbs and Sydney, Mrs. Maplethorpe followed with Squire Dobbs, Mr. Cole offered an arm each to his sister and Meriel, while Mr. Fortescue came last with Miss Cassandra.

Miss Cole was not best pleased with this ordering of things, for in her opinion she should take the precedence over Sydney Armytage, though the Coles were not a more prestigious family than the Armytages and Sydney was the elder. Nevertheless, Arabella Cole felt that a baronet by marriage in

13

her family and the fact that she had had a Season in London entitled her to more distinction than Sydney. Why she should imagine this to be so was unfathomable to her neighbours and they very firmly ignored her pretensions, though they privately found them amusing.

She conveyed her displeasure with a frosty aspect for the first few minutes, but when the company persisted in pretending they did not notice anything out of the way, she finally unbent and joined in the general conversation. She was a young woman of some three-and-twenty whose regard for herself was somewhat more elevated than either her looks or her birth supported. She was not ill-favoured, but there was something disagreeable in the tight, thin set of her mouth and something hard in the pale blue eyes. She had blond ringlets that she always wore dressed in the latest fashion and a plump figure always dressed à la modality. The elder Coles being long deceased, she and her brother kept house together in the family home in Upper Chyppen, with a tolerable degree of comfort. Her aunt had married a title, lived in London, and had provided the much-vaunted Season, which had occurred several years previously; and since Miss Cole was still unmarried, it was evident she had not "taken."

She made great use of her Season, however, larding her conversation with "At my come-out in London we . . ." and "As Lady Castlereagh said to me at my come-out in London . . ." A more frequent reference, however, was to "my aunt, Lady Boxton." Indeed, poor Lady Boxton's ears must have been beset by a continuous ringing if the number of times her title and relationship to Miss Cole was brought up in her niece's conversation was anything to go by. Miss Cole's acquaintances were wont, at times of social indecision, to wonder slyly: "What would Lady Boxton recommend?" Never if Miss Cole were at hand, of course, for they were seldom truly malicious regarding one another.

Her brother resembled her closely, being blond, portly, and rather pop-eyed. He had a tendency to pomposity, but was on the whole not offensive, though considerably under his sister's thumb. His ideas on any subject could always be traced directly to her, but he seemed perfectly content to allow her to do his thinking for him. He had been much struck by Meriel at the Assembly dance, and showed a tendency to moon about for several days, but Miss Cole had soon put an end to it. She spoke disparagingly of schoolgirl gawkishness and cow eyes, and then encouragingly of how a gentleman of his looks and birth could no doubt find an heiress for himself if he cared to, and presently he began to look down condescendingly upon Meriel as though she were rather beneath his notice, though of course one must always be courteous.

"By the by," said Mr. Maplethorpe as they were finishing their soup, "I have a choice bit of news. Lades Hall has been taken at last and we shall have an addition to our little circle this summer."

"*How* exciting," exclaimed Mrs. Dobbs. "It always gives things such a nice lift when there are new faces. Who is it, Mr. Maplethorpe?"

"Chap from London, name of Westbrook. That is the extent of my knowledge. Heard of it from Porterman, as a matter of fact, who said his nephew is going as footman."

"Oh, I do hope it is a nice family," exclaimed Cassandra. "It would be so pleasant to have more young . . . er . . . people." She blushed, for she was sure everyone must think she had been going to say "young men," as indeed she had. She was a sweetly pretty young girl, somewhat shy, who had been bosom bows with Meriel since their childhood.

"I hope they will not be the sort of high-in-the-instep Londoners who will look down on us as provincial," said Mrs. Dobbs.

"Westbrook? I no doubt met them if they are from London. I must write and ask my aunt, Lady Boxton, who they are," Miss Cole said.

"We met him this afternoon at Miss Twoomy's," announced Meriel calmly.

"What!" This came as a concerted gasp from several mouths at once, and every eye was riveted on Meriel.

"What a sly boots you are, child, never to have mentioned it till now," reproached Mrs. Maplethorpe.

"What was he like, Meriel?" demanded Cassandra eagerly.

"Why, he seemed agreeable. An older gentleman. You really must apply to Sydney. She spoke more with him than I."

Immediately all eyes turned to Sydney. "He is very nice indeed, and not old in the least," she said, and paused to cast a quelling look at her sister.

"Do go *on*, Sydney," pleaded Mrs. Dobbs.

"There is little more I can tell you, Mrs. Dobbs. He is a well-spoken man, most courteous and pleasant, and told us only that he had taken Lades Hall on a year's lease."

"Is he a well-favoured man, dear?" Mrs. Maplethorpe wanted to know.

"Why, I think he could be called so."

"But you must have heard the rest of his name, Sydney. Surely he was not introduced simply as Mr. Westbrook?"

"Oh, of course—he is Sir Max Westbrook."

"Not . . . not *Max* Westbrook?" Miss Cole exclaimed dramatically.

"Yes. Do you know him, Miss Cole?" asked Sydney.

"We were . . . acquainted . . . in London. He was . . . we were . . . but I must say no more—please do not ask me."

The company obliged her, though she made a great business of fumbling in her reticule for a scrap of lace, which she touched, not too surreptitiously, to an invisible tear in the corner of each eye. Her brother stared at her in great surprise, but the rest of the guests felt it would be a breach of good manners to notice this untoward display of emotion, and deliberately turned away to allow her time to recover. They all felt her remark had been in bad taste in any case. If there had been something between her and Sir Max, she should never have mentioned it in company.

Their interest in him was not lessened, however, and they carried on with eager speculations about him: was he wealthy? who were his people? where were they from? was there a Lady Westbrook? if so, were there children?

"Was he married when you knew him in London?" Cassandra was unable to resist asking Miss Cole.

"Of course not, my dear. Surely you do not think I am so lost to all propriety as to encourage the attentions of a married man?" Miss Cole looked saddened that Cassandra could have such a low opinion of her standards of conduct.

"Oh no, Miss Cole, certainly not," protested Cassandra, "but I had no idea . . . Was he a suitor, then?"

"Ah"—Miss Cole looked mysterious—"it was thought so by many."

"How exciting," breathed the innocent Cassandra. "Is he dark or fair?"

"Oh . . . well . . . I suppose one could best describe him

as medium in colouring. But you must not embarrass me with this inquisition, child.''

"Oh, it is the most romantic thing in the world, Miss Cole. Please tell us what happened?''

"Happened?'' Miss Cole was beginning to look uncomfortable under the interested gaze of nine pairs of eyes. Even Mr. Fortescue and Squire Dobbs, notorious trenchermen, had arrested the continuous motion of fork to mouth as they awaited her answer.

"I mean . . . well . . . between you,'' persisted Cassandra.

"Really, Miss Maplethorpe, I must protest,'' chided Miss Cole, casting a reproachful look at Mrs. Maplethorpe.

Reminded of her duty, Mrs. Maplethorpe called her daughter to order and reluctantly changed the subject. The dinner flowed on through a boiled duck with onion sauce, crimped salmon, and a damson pie, followed by a savoury of roasted cheese. The ladies then withdrew, leaving the gentlemen to their wine for a time. When they rejoined the ladies, Sydney and Miss Cole were persuaded, as usual, to favor the company with a few selections on the pianoforte, and, as usual, most of the gentlemen used the occasion for a nap to digest their dinners.

When the tea tray was brought in, the conversation reverted to Sir Max Westbrook inevitably, his advent being an exciting event in the rather circumscribed lives of all of them. They were, after all, minutely informed of nearly every circumstance of one another's lives, and were bound to fall avidly upon any new event.

Mr. Fortescue opened with, "I wonder if Sir Max will be in need of more servants? Mrs. Crumb's daughter must find work.''

"Well, he is taking Porterman's nephew, so he cannot be bringing all his own servants down from London. In fact, I should think he would not bring any of them. One knows these London servants. They are never happy in the country,'' encouraged Mrs. Dobbs.

"I shall make it a point to call on him at once, then,'' declared Mr. Fortescue. "The Crumbs are in a desperate case. Poor Mrs. Crumb is now completely bedridden.''

"Well, of course, we must all call on the newcomer,'' said Mrs. Maplethorpe.

"Not before the roads dry up, you won't, Mrs. Maple-

thorpe,'' declared her husband, "for I'll not take the chance
of miring the carriage or breaking an axle.''

"Will you call on him, Miss Cole?'' Cassandra wondered
irrepressibly, still caught up in what she thought a tragic love
affair.

"Well, I hardly think that would answer, Miss Maplethorpe,'' returned Miss Cole loftily.

"Perhaps he will call on you,'' offered Mrs. Dobbs helpfully.

"Why, that would not be proper at all,'' protested Mr.
Cole—this so unexpectedly of him that everyone looked up in
surprise. "I mean to say . . . well, I don't believe it would be
. . . after what has happened between them . . . would it,
Bella?'' He met his sister's icy stare, flushed uncomfortably,
and buried his face in his teacup, not entirely sure what he
had done wrong now, but unable to mistake the look of
censure in his sister's frigid eye. Suppose there will be the
devil to pay when we reach home, he thought glumly. Should
have told me all about this fellow before now anyway, he
thought, beginning to build his defense. I am her brother,
after all. Some fellow toying with her affections, why has she
not confided it to me? Call the rascal out, by God. Why, I
might have met him in the High Street and brought him home
to dinner in all innocence! She wouldn't have cared for that,
I'll be bound. He began to feel distinctly put upon.

Sydney and Meriel soon rose to prepare for their departure,
since they had the long walk still to make before darkness fell,
or Papa would worry. After bidding the company good night,
they repaired upstairs to resume their cloaks and bonnets;
then, in the hall again, Porterman helped them change their
slippers for the pattens, their wooden soles set on iron rings,
and they went clumping off down High Street in the nearly
horizontal rays of the setting sun.

"Sydney,'' began Meriel after a long, companionable silence,
"is it not fascinating about Arabella Cole and Sir Max?''

"Fascinating,'' agreed Sydney dryly.

"What do you suppose happened?''

"Why, nothing apparently, as she is still Miss Cole.''

"But that is just it! Do you suppose he pursued her with
his attentions and then callously broke her heart by not
proposing?''

"The sort of novels you read have sadly distorted your
imagination,'' observed Sydney.

"Oh, Sydney, it is all very romantic, do admit!"

"Tell me first what about it you found romantic."

"Why, all of it. She said . . ." There was a long pause while Meriel tried to remember. "Actually, it was more what she did not say, I think."

"Exactly. She *said* nothing definite, really, though she allowed us to infer a great deal. The only solid fact she admitted to was that he was neither dark nor fair, but medium in colouring. Sir Max, if you will recall, has very dark brown hair and eyes and is rather brown-complected. Would you describe that as medium?"

"Nooo. . . ."

"Nor would I."

"Oh, Syd, do you suppose it was all untrue? That she has never met him at all?"

"Ah, well, I suppose she may very well have done, for all I know, though I must say she has retained only a very hazy memory of him if so. I should not think he was a gentleman one could forget so easily."

"Would you not? I must say he made no great impression on me. However," she added hastily at Sydney's amazed stare, "he seemed perfectly pleasant and I am sure I hope that if there is a Lady Westbrook she is one of those jolly sorts who like to entertain. Mrs. Maplethorpe says Lades Hall has a good-sized ballroom."

Sydney consoled her hopes by telling herself that Meriel could not be expected to be struck all of a heap at a first meeting, and besides, she was definitely not going to push her sister into marriage with the first eligible man to come along. Especially as the man might prove to be quite *in*eligible.

Just the same, came the reassuring thought, I for one do not think he is married. Sir Max Westbrook is the sort of gentleman who would be bound to mention his wife if he had one when he spoke of paying a call on us.

3

Elmdene Grange was a square, solid, grey-stone mansion set atop a slight rise, from which the grounds sloped gently away around it in a spread of green lawn dotted here and there by trees in a pleasingly unplanned manner. A giant, centuries-old cedar spread a wide circle of welcoming summer shade to one side of the house. On the other side the drive swept around to the stables. Beyond the stables the land leveled off towards a generous-sized pond.

Several generations of Armytages had made their home here, content to live the quiet life of country gentlemen, marrying daughters of other comfortably off country gentry who could contribute a good dowry to the general welfare of Armytage living, raising their families and engaging in gentlemanly pursuits. They had been fortunate in always having a son to hand over to, and the present incumbent was no exception, though his son, two years older than Sydney, had broken with tradition by going into the Navy. His mother's family had been Navy people and boasted of at least two admirals, so it seemed not unnatural for Mr. Armytage's heir to be drawn to such a career. His father knew he loved Elmdene and would always return to it, and, when the time came, would make it his home and do his duty by it.

Mr. Armytage was a mild man of sanguine temperament, slight, grey-haired, and of retiring habits. He was not a recluse by any means, but was rather more inclined to his own fireside than that of anyone else. He was content to tend his estate, raise his daughters, work on his *History of England*, a work which had occupied him for the past twenty years, and make what improvements were necessary to his property. One of these had been the rebuilding of the boathouse. What had once been a small thatched shelter for a rowboat, he had enclosed to house the boat in winter, the other an open pavilion where the family could sit and read or talk on hot summer days.

He had also had a small landing stage on pilings built out into the pond, where the boat could be tied up, and it was here on the day after the Maplethorpe dinner party that Sydney was seated, legs dangling over the water, fishing pole in hand. Mr. Armytage kept the pond well stocked, and the girls enjoyed trying their hand at fishing. Not, perhaps, in the ordinary way, an activity one would associate with well-bred young ladies. In the country, however, with long days to be filled, one learns to take what amusements lie to hand.

Three good-sized carp floated already in a pail beside Sydney, recovering from their ordeal. She was attempting to take one more, which would be enough for dinner. If she proved unsuccessful, she intended to grant a stay of execution and release her catch back into the pond. It was a warm, perfect June afternoon, and the air seemed literally to pulsate with the energy of growing plant life all around her. From time to time Meriel called out from the hedges on the far side of the pond, where she was searching out wild strawberries.

They had received two young gentlemen after breakfast, whom Meriel had treated with her usual unruffled equanimity. When they had taken their departure, the girls had quickly changed their gowns and escaped to the pond. There were no engagements for the day, which now stretched placidly before them with, at its end, a good dinner of fresh fish and strawberries, if they were both fortunate in their pursuits.

It took Sydney nearly an hour to land her fish, but she was patient and there was plenty of time. By the time she cried out triumphantly and pulled in her catch, Meriel had been sitting for some time in the summerhouse, a full basket of berries beside her, taking a sketch of Sydney with her fishing pole, sitting in the dappled sunshine of the landing stage.

Sydney was delighted with the drawing and declared it was very like. She sat down immediately to try one of Meriel holding the basket of strawberries. It would not seem to come right, however, and there was much rubbing out and redrawing, accompanied by annoyed exclamations. Music, not art, was her métier, whereas Meriel seemed able to catch an impression with a few swift lines, and her watercolours were prized gifts in the neighbourhood.

"Tcha!" Sydney exclaimed finally in disgust at her

ineptitude, and threw aside her pencil. "I only make it worse! Is it warm enough to bathe, do you think?"

"Oh, Syd, do let us. I have thought of nothing else. It was so very warm in those hedges."

Sea bathing had been gaining in popularity for some years and was now all the rage, but the Armytages had been accustomed to make use of their secluded pond for bathing from childhood on. Sydney's brother had taught her to swim by the time she was seven and she in turn had taught Meriel. Now they laid aside their straw bonnets and repaired to the closed boathouse, where the loose, long-sleeved woolen gowns they wore for bathing hung in readiness for their whim.

They waded out, and shrieking with shivery pleasure, immersed themselves in the cold water, carefully keeping their heads up so their hair would not get wet. After swimming about for some time, they climbed out to sit in a patch of sunshine on the landing stage to dry off.

Meriel lay back lazily on the wooden staging and closed her eyes. "Oh, divine day. I wish it could go on just like this forever."

"You would soon grow bored if it did so, I make no doubt."

"Not so. I am never bored."

"That is because things continually change. You would not like it if there were no dinner parties or picnics or dancing."

"Oh, I meant to include those things in the 'not changing' part."

"You mean, then, I suppose, that you want to remain seventeen and have eternal summer and dance and dine out and swim and be lazy."

"Just so."

"But then you would never grow up, never marry, never have children or grandchildren. You would not care to miss all that, I vow, would you, now?"

"I am not so sure. I am very content just as I am."

"That is just the problem. You will not remain just as you are. Next year you will be eighteen, and two years later twenty, and so on. And what seems delightful at seventeen can hardly be as satisfactory then, when your mind will have grown and your ideas will have changed."

"No doubt you are right, Syd, as you generally are, but

this is all too deep and serious for such a day. Ah"—she yawned hugely—"how sleepy the sun makes one."

Sydney took this broad hint and remained silent. Meriel was not much given to philosophizing and was rarely inclined to be inward-looking. She was a good-natured girl, of placid, imperturbable temperament. For the most part a gentle, biddable soul, she yet managed to be very firm when she truly wanted something, and obtained her way by a quiet refusal to be swayed rather than by tears or tantrums.

When the sun, which had seemed to hang stationary above them for so long, at last gave up its apparent intention to stay and edged over to the west, they retired to the boathouse to change back into their simple cotton round gowns. Then, tying on their bonnets and gathering up fish, berries, and sketching pad, they strolled slowly back to the house. They entered through the kitchen and left their day's booty with Cook to deal further with and went through to the front hall. There Sydney found a parcel on the hall table that proved to be addressed to herself. Much mystified, she unwrapped it to find inside a copy of *Emma* by Miss Austen. On the inside cover it bore the inscription: "To a fellow Austenite. Max Westbrook."

"Why . . . for heaven's sake! How very kind! Meriel, do look. Is this not astonishingly kind of Sir Max? How did it come here, do you suppose?"

"The best way to find out is to ask Lizzy."

Lizzy was the downstairs maid who cleaned those rooms and answered the front door. The upstairs maid, Lutie, took care of the bedrooms and helped the young ladies to dress. These and Cook were the only indoor servants Mr. Armytage employed.

The girls returned to the back of the house, found Lizzy, and were told the gentleman had brought it himself when he came to call.

"What! Sir Max came to call? But why did you not come to fetch us, Lizzy?" cried Sydney.

"Why, miss, your papa came out of his study and carried him off to the drawing room while I was taking his hat. They have been there since, and I served them wine and biscuits not a quarter of an hour ago."

"Do you mean to tell me he is still in the house? Oh, why did you not say so? He might have come out into the hall and found us in all our dirt. Quickly, Meriel, up the backstairs. Lizzy, send Lutie up to help us change—in fact, do you come also so we can be quicker."

Sydney pushed Meriel ahead of her up the backstairs. "You must put on your new rose-sprigged muslin, Meriel. Lutie can brush your hair out loose and tie it back with that length of rose ribband I have—I must look it out—now, where did I put it?—I am sure it will go perfectly with your gown."

"What will you wear, Sydney?"

"Oh, I have not thought. My blue, I suppose—it does not matter. Do hurry, child!"

"Why should it not matter for you? I cannot see why I am to be decked out, and not you. In fact, I cannot believe we are not perfectly fine as we are. There is nothing wrong with this gown. I have a great partiality for it."

Fearful that too much protest would only cause her sister to take one of her stands, Sydney laughed and began unbuttoning the back of Meriel's dress. "Well, of course, I did not mean I do not mind what I wear, dear. I had already decided on my blue without realizing it, I suppose. For of course we cannot shame Papa by appearing in the drawing room before his guest in gowns we wear to scramble through the hedges and go fishing in. Now, please don't be difficult, darling. Here is Lutie to brush your hair. I must go change myself."

In Sydney's own room Lizzy waited to help her out of her old gown. Then she washed her sun-flushed face and hands, unpinned her hair, brushed it smooth, and coiled it back into its usual knot on top of her head before stepping into the blue muslin Lizzy held ready. It was made with a low, rounded neckline, the sleeves short and puffed in the French fashion, and fell from its very high waistline just beneath the bosom to a wide flounced ruffle at the hem. Meriel's was similar in cut, but the white sprigged muslin had been varied with three rows of narrower ruffles at the hem and an edging of lace around the neckline.

The girls met in the upper hall and Sydney thought her sister had never looked lovelier, even the night of the Assembly, than now with her ivory skin rose-tinted over the cheekbones and her black curls falling about her shoulders.

Mr. Armytage and Sir Max rose to greet them as they entered the drawing room. "Sir Max," Sydney cried out at once, "this is a pleasant surprise! And how very kind of you to bring us the book."

"Miss Armytage, Miss Meriel . . ." He smiled, bowing over their hands in turn. "I could not resist bringing it when I knew how much you liked her work."

"But how had you it?"

"I had brought it with me from town and read it on the way. Not even the jolting of the carriage could keep me from it. I hope you will enjoy it as much as I have."

"Of course we will. Why, even Papa admires her. Papa, Sir Max has brought us Miss Austen's new book."

"That was most thoughtful of you, sir. You have provided us with many evenings' entertainment."

Sydney glanced significantly at her sister, and Meriel hastily added her gratitude to the rest with an entrancing smile that caused Sir Max to stare speechlessly for quite fifteen seconds.

Mr. Armytage, inured by seventeen years of such smiles, turned back to his chair, saying, "Well, well, let us all be comfortable. You were telling me of the improvements you have wrought at Lades Hall, sir."

Sir Max started out of his trance and hastily turned to his host to resume their interrupted conversation. He met Sydney's eye for a look compounded of ruefulness and amusement at himself, and it seemed to her it was the sort of look most often exchanged between two people who knew each other's minds so well they are confident of understanding without words. That look one notices sometimes between lifelong friends, close relatives, or husbands and wives. It warmed her heart to think he felt trustful enough of her understanding to share with her his appreciation of Meriel's beauty and his amusement at himself for his schoolboyish reactions. Oh yes, she thought contentedly, this was indeed a man worthy of her sister. She noticed that Meriel appeared to be listening with something more than her usual placidity to the conversation and began to hope that his thoughtful gift and a second meeting had animated her thoughts to a more open reception of his qualities.

She was also aware, as would be any woman in charge of a household, that dinner, following the country customs of early hours, must soon be ready. She remembered the four fish—how propitious!—mentally checked the rest of the menu, and made her decision. At the first opportunity she said, "Sir Max, could we possibly persuade you to stay and take dinner with us? It will be nothing elaborate, of course, and only ourselves."

"You are very kind, Miss Armytage, but I could not presume so much on your hospitality."

"But indeed you could, sir, if you but say you will and give us all the greatest pleasure."

Sir Max cast a glance at Mr. Armytage, "Sir, I—"

"No, no, you do not require my invitation. My daughter makes all such decisions and tells us all how we are to go on. If she has set her mind on having you, you had best give in, sir. There! That is the best advice I can give you."

Sir Max laughed and Sydney blushed a little, but she did not make any false protests at her father's charge. After inquiring if she were sure she would not mind his sitting down to dinner in his riding dress, and being assured it was a matter of no consequence, he accepted the invitation and Sydney excused herself to give orders to Cook.

When the fish made its appearance after the roast chicken, Meriel impishly informed their guest that his hostess had caught them herself that very afternoon.

"Do you tell me so, Miss Meriel?" He turned an astonished eye on Sydney. "You quite amaze me, Miss Armytage. Do you also hunt your own game?"

"I would if I could persuade Papa to teach me how to handle a gun," she replied, laughing. "Do you remember when I used to beg you to let me accompany you, Papa, when you took out a gun for pheasant?"

"Oh, dear me, yes. She was always quite intrepid, Sir Max. A mere scrap of a thing she was at the time, too."

"Is there much good fishing in the neighbourhood, Miss Armytage?"

"Not much that I have heard of. These fish are from our own pond that Papa keeps stocked."

"Now, there is an idea. I wonder if I could introduce such a thing at Lades Hall? There is a stream on the property I believe could be dammed. I must see your pond, Mr. Armytage and have your advice on the subject."

"So you shall, sir. We will walk down there after our dinner. I am a great believer in gentle exercise after a meal. I have never understood this craze for sitting about in a drawing room after a heavy meal listening to music. So soporific.''

"Indeed it is, at least for gentlemen, I have noticed. The fashion here, Sir Max, is for gentlemen to be played to while they sleep off their dinners,'' said Sydney with some asperity, for this was a sore point with her.

"Perhaps if music were more of a required accomplishment for gentlemen, they would be playing and we would be sleeping,'' answered Meriel, causing everyone to laugh, and, Sydney noted, Sir Max to look at Meriel admiringly. His compliments when the fresh wild strawberries accompanied by thick cream were placed before them, and Sydney explained they had been gathered by Meriel that afternoon, were even more gratifying. The visit was turning out more successfully than she could have hoped, and everything, she felt, was progressing most promisingly.

4

That same day after the Maplethorpe dinner party, while Meriel and Sydney were receiving their callers before noon, Arabella Cole was still lying in her bed sipping her chocolate. She seemed to be gazing emptily into space, thinking of nothing in particular, but her mind was busily occupied planning her costume. For her mind was made up. She was going to pay a morning call on Sir Max Westbrook.

It was imperative that she do so at once, before he could meet and perhaps be interrogated by anyone else in Upper Chyppen. She had no doubt the story of her interesting history with him would have spread all over the town before the day was half over, and she imagined, with a shudder of horror, the look of bewilderment, even denial, with which he might greet a reference about herself. There were those in Upper Chyppen who threw all propriety to the wind in their determination to ferret out gossip.

However, if he *had* already made her acquaintance when questioned, all would pass off well enough. He might be puzzled if reference were made to their having met before in London, but would no doubt let it pass as a misunderstanding. Due to the state of the roads, she had every reason to believe that few would make the effort to call on him today. Therefore, *she* must go today—now!

She set aside her chocolate with resolution, and flinging aside the coverlet, rose and rang for her maid. A half-hour later she sailed into the breakfast room, her plump figure resplendently encased in a mustard-yellow pelisse richly embroidered and befrogged with gold braid down the front. On her blond ringlets she wore a confection of Italian straw, towering white plumes, and a lavish amount of ruched bronze ribband.

Her brother, in the process of demolishing a large beefsteak, said somewhat thickly, "Oh, I say, Bella, you are in full fig this morning. Monstrously smart!"

"Please try not to speak with your mouth full, Claiborne. It is disgusting. Finish up quickly and come along. I have ordered the carriage brought around."

"The carriage? But why—?"

"We are calling on Sir Max Westbrook," she answered impatiently. "Now, do come along."

"Are you mad? You cannot travel on the roads today."

"Nonsense."

"No, it ain't nonsense at all. It won't do, Bella, won't do at all. We might make it on horseback if you are determined to go."

Arabella, however, who knew perfectly well she was not at her best on the back of a horse, nor did a riding dress become her, brushed this suggestion aside. Telling him not to waste any more time and to come along at once, she turned aside. Claiborne reluctantly laid down his knife and fork and rose. There was never any use in arguing with Bella when she had the bit between her teeth.

As he might have predicted, they were not more than half a mile outside Upper Chyppen before the first problem beset them. Claiborne, who was driving, drew rather too close to the verge, and the back wheel slipped over. Fortunately, the mud being so treacherous, they had been travelling very slowly. Claiborne quickly pulled up the horses and jumped down to assess the damage. Arabella, perched precariously on the tilted seat, helpfully berated him for carelessness. Since he had no real defense against her charge, he contented himself by muttering beneath his breath about the stupidity of females who insisted on having their own way against all advice.

He avenged his outraged feelings by insisting that she would have to get down, since the carriage could not be moved while she was in it. When he had finally convinced her that no further progress could be made until she had complied, she grumpily allowed him to assist her down, to stand gingerly on a clump of grass, issuing orders and directions for the best way to set about extricating the carriage, while he slipped about in the mud and at last urged the horses to drag the carriage back into the road. She then declared she could not possibly walk through the mud to the carriage, as it would quite spoil her slippers, and he was forced to carry her, which did nothing to improve his temper.

Some mile farther on, the road dipped into a shaded hollow and the horses, attempting the slope out of it, kept slipping back, while the temporarily stationary carriage sank slowly deeper and deeper into the mud, until it was at last caught fast.

Cursing, Claiborne climbed down again and attempted first to pull the horses up the slope and then to push the carriage from behind, while Arabella sat staring straight before her, lips tight over her unspoken criticism. This self-restraint was of no avail, however, for after sweating and straining uselessly, Claiborne finally declared she would have to get down again.

"Oh, for heaven's sake, Claiborne! I shall have strong convulsions!" Arabella exclaimed exasperatedly. "If I had any notion that you could not handle things better than this, I would have had Rowland drive us."

"Well, and so I wish you had done. What is the point of having a driver if one does not use him? It was you who said that I must drive."

"Well, you know how servants gossip, and I did not want anyone to know where we were going."

"Why *are* we going, in any case, I should like to know? I cannot approve it at all, Bella. Damned if I want you having anything further to do with the fellow after his shameful behaviour to you."

"Oh, try not to be so ridiculous, Claiborne," she snapped. "I have never met the man."

"But, I thought—"

"I cannot be responsible for what you thought. Will you please do something useful for a change and stop yammering away like this."

"Then you will have to get down," he returned peevishly. Since he could not be swayed, she was forced to obey, though she insisted he must carry her to a stone wall, where she sat watching him in outraged majesty.

After further fruitless effort, Claiborne finally declared that he must find help, and went stomping off down the road. Presently he returned and with the help of a farmer and a bale of hay laid over the mud, they were free and on their way again.

They reached the gates of Lades Hall and turned with immense relief down the gravelled, tree-lined drive. Disdaining her brother's assistance, Arabella climbed haughtily down from the carriage once again and marched up to the front door, which opened at once to her peremptory rap.

However, Bolton, Sir Max's manservant, regretfully informed her that Sir Max was from home and he was unable to state with any certainty when he might be expected to return. Unwilling to admit defeat at this stage, Arabella grandly announced that she would wait.

Bolton greeted this decision with grave courtesy and respectfully requested them to follow him into the drawing room, where he offered them some refreshment. She accepted and he withdrew. The Coles seated themselves, not speaking, since both were still out of charity with each other. Presently Bolton returned, followed by a footman bearing a tray with wine, lemonade, and biscuits.

"Thank you," said Arabella, graciously accepting a glass of lemonade. "I presume Lady Westbrook accompanied her husband?"

"Sir Max is unmarried, madam," replied Bolton.

"Ah," murmured Arabella, and sipped daintily at her lemonade.

When the servants were gone she looked about with great interest, noting that the room had been furnished with good taste and at obvious expense. Her interest in Sir Max sharpened.

A well-favoured man, Sydney Armytage had said, and also, it was clear, a man of means.

Claiborne, having finished all the biscuits, drank off his wine and rose to pour himself another glass, ignoring his sister's disapproving stare.

"The trip out was difficult enough," observed Arabella tartly. "Our return will not be made easier if you are flown with wine."

"Now, see here, Bella, this is ridiculous. We must leave."

"We have been here but twenty minutes, and remember, the longer we wait, the drier the roads will be."

"But damme, the man may be away for hours. Do you propose we spend the day here waiting?"

"Please do not swear, Claiborne. If you were capable of the least sensibility, it would be apparent to you by now why it is imperative that I make the acquaintance of Sir Max without delay."

"Well, it ain't. If you haven't met the fellow, I can't think why you wanted to tell such a clanker last night."

"Because it irritates me to have that bossy Sydney Armytage always trying to be first in everything in that pushing way of hers."

"Don't seem pushing to me. Always amiable, and a fine-looking girl."

"Girl!" Arabella laughed scornfully. "On the shelf any-time these past six years, and you call her a *girl?* As for fine-looking, I would not admit any such thing. Skinny and washed-out, *I* would call her."

"Oh, now, see here, Bella—"

"Oh, *never mind!* If you intend to be so disagreeable, I suppose we might as well leave, for it will never do to expose Sir Max to your sulks. Never mind how important anything is to me." She rose to shake out her skirts, having realized they could not with propriety wait any longer, and sailed out of the room, her spirits somewhat raised by having had the last word and shown up her brother as selfish.

He followed her guiltily, and the return journey was painfully and stickily negotiated, though without any of the accidents that had plagued their coming, and once safely home, Arabella ordered Claiborne to stroll about the High Street in search of the elusive Sir Max, and, if encountered, to waste no time, but bring him home with him at once. He stumped off bad-temperedly to do her bidding, while she changed into her most becoming house gown and ensconced herself in the drawing-room window with her embroidery frame, where she could keep an eye on all passersby. It would have been interesting to know whether, had he passed, she would have rushed out to drag him into the house. However, since her vigil was fruitless, we shall never know.

The Armytages and their guest strolled down to the pond after dinner as the sun was sinking into the horizon, flinging long streamers of shadow across the grass in farewell. The pond and the boathouse were inspected and damming methods were discussed at length, and Mr. Armytage was congratulated on his design for the pavilion. Then Meriel, an expert with the oars, surprisingly offered to take Sir Max for a row on the water, which he accepted at once without any protests about being allowed to take the oars himself. They stepped down into the boat, arranged themselves on the seats, and Sydney untied the boat. As Meriel backed away, Sydney and her father went into the pavilion and made themselves comfortable. They sat in silence for a time, enjoying the fineness of the evening, the smell of water and greenery, the frog concert just beginning to tune up.

"A good sort of man," said Mr. Armytage presently, which from him was an accolade of high order.

"I am happy you like him, Papa. I think he is a pleasant addition to our community. He seems much taken with Meriel."

"Do you think so? I cannot say I noticed anything out of the way myself. Meriel is far too young for anything of that sort, in any case."

"She is seventeen. Our mother was seventeen when you married her."

"*She* was not too young at seventeen. Meriel is."

Since Sydney was not prepared to dispute this point, she said nothing more. They sat companionably watching the sun sink behind the hedges on the far side of the pond, making a silhouette of the couple and the rowboat. When Meriel saw Lizzy and Lutie coming across the grass with the tea tray, she turned the boat and rowed back.

When they were all served, Mr. Armytage asked Sir Max from where in England the Westbrook family came.

"Oh, from Dorset, but I make my home mostly in London

now. I am the eldest and inherited the estate, but my brothers are still at home. My mother remarried some years ago, and as I wanted my brothers to be raised in their own home, I persuaded my stepfather to remain there. He is a good chap and has been a good father to my brothers, but he and I do better apart."

"That was certainly most generous of you, sir," commented Mr. Armytage.

"Somewhat selfish, also, I fear. I wanted to live in London and could not have done so had he not been agreeable to staying. He is a far better manager than I, and likes that part of the country."

"And what do you find to do in London?"

"Why, I am in commerce."

"Commerce! Surely you did not go into trade, Sir Max?" Mr. Armytage's tone expressed his disbelief that a gentleman could so lower himself.

"Well, in a way." Sir Max laughed. "I invested in sugar cargoes, you see."

He proceeded to tell them about all this, and it began to sound a very romantic business, with his talk of exotic faraway countries.

"But how do you come to be in so prosaic a place as Upper Chyppen, Sir Max?" Meriel asked.

"Oh, that is easy. I happened to mention to a fellow I know that I would like to find a place of my own to get away to—you know, right away from London, especially for the summer months. Well, he mentioned Upper Chyppen as a pleasantly situated town, and as I knew of nothing else, I came along to see for myself. I found Lades Hall standing empty and settled on the spot that I would take it. This was some three months ago. When my agent wrote that it was ready for occupancy, I came straight down."

"Why, then, it *must* have been someone from the neighbourhood who told you of it. What is his name, sir?" demanded Meriel. "We must surely be acquainted with your friend."

"Why, he is Morgan Leighton, though he said he had no family here and had himself left some ten years ago, so . . . ."

Sydney felt a swift frisson pass through her nerves at the name, and Sir Max's voice faded, while the teacup she was just raising to her lips remained frozen for an instant in midair. Then she set the cup carefully back onto its saucer and leaned back in her chair, grateful for the uncertain twilight in which they sat.

She was glad to note that her heart was not thumping, nor were her pulses racing, as a result of hearing Morgan's name leap out of the past at her in that way. The reaction she had experienced had been unpleasant, certainly, but over quickly and not in the least painful. She became aware of Sir Max's voice again.

". . . so I will write to him and thank him for putting me in the way of finding such a nice property. Perhaps I can persuade him to pay me a visit."

"You mean you will persuade 'them,' do you not, Sir Max? For surely he is married," Sydney heard herself saying.

"Ah, poor chap. He lost his wife about a year ago. Very sad thing. Yes, I *will* write to him to come. I shall do so at once. It will do him a great deal of good, and I feel sure you will all like him very well. Do you remember him, Miss Armytage? Miss Meriel says that he tutored her, but your father says he does not remember him."

"Yes," she said faintly. Then, more strongly, "Yes, I remember him."

5

If ever a young woman is inclined to be romantic, seventeen is surely the age when romanticism reaches its peak. It may begin earlier for some girls, but surely all, by seventeen, have reached their romantic apogee. Some girls, of course, are never so inclined, while some have only very short seasons, and again, there are those who never recover.

Even at seventeen Sydney had belonged to the first category, for though she had read all the required fiction to put her into the proper frame of mind, and had quite fancied herself in the role, her common sense and humour had always damped any pretensions she might have entertained of aspiring to the role of romantic heroine. Try as she might to picture herself as the star-crossed lover of a tall, dark-browed lord, the picture had always become blurred by practical questions of why, or how, or why not, until she had only been able to imagine herself, had she been so foolish as to give in to inclination, as a figure of fun, amusing her friends and family by enacting Cheltanham tragedies for no discernible reason. For the sad truth was that the elements required for a romantic heroine were sadly lacking in her life: a castle, a handsome, titled hero, an ogreish father, or at least uncle, and a passionate, volatile temperament. (Beauty, she had felt, could be dispensed with, provided one were passably pretty, but a volatile temperament was a necessary requirement.)

It had seemed to her that any two reasonably calm and intelligent people of the opposite sex who were inclined to a partiality for one another might work out some means to effect a marriage and happy life for themselves without undue stress upon themselves or their relatives and friends if they set about it in the proper spirit. So it was that when she met Morgan Leighton she was able to greet him without losing countenance, assess him as a pleasing young man, and, eventually, to lose her heart to him without experiencing any great emotional storms to overset her.

She had decided, when Meriel was seven, that her own mathematics and knowledge of geography were inadequate to properly teach her sister. As her father seemed disinclined to take on this task himself, she made inquiry in the neighbourhood for someone suitable. She learned that a family newly arrived in the county, the Smythe-Burnses, had three little boys being tutored at home. She wrote to the Smythe-Burnses asking if it would be at all convenient for her sister to attend sessions in the required subjects with the young Smythe-Burnses.

A very civil response to this inquiry was soon received, and after a further exchange it was settled that Sydney would deliver her sister to Burns Hall twice a week at ten in the morning for the lessons, for which she would recompense the tutor directly.

Burns Hall was situated some three miles by road from Elmdene, but by making their way more directly across the fields, the trip could be cut to two. In any event, the distance was no great objection, for both girls enjoyed walking.

Norma Lee Clark

Mr. Leighton, the tutor, had received them with every courtesy, and the three little boys with much elbowing and giggling until called to order. Mrs. Smythe-Burns had come in and professed herself pleased to meet her young neighbour and had borne her off for a long coze about the other families in the immediate vicinity while the lessons went forward.

On the walk home Sydney had had the leisure to think how pleasant a young man was Mr. Leighton, and how handsome. He was slim and not above middling height, with light brown curls falling with attractive carelessness over his brow, small, neat, extremely regular features, and bright hazel eyes. His hands were small and fine, as indeed was everything about him, projecting an indefinable delicacy. In her brief interview with him she had been able to assess little beyond his physical appearance and his good manners, but her impression was certainly favourable. When applied to, Meriel allowed that she had enjoyed her lesson in figures tolerably well, but that she did not think she would like it so well as geography; that she found Mr. Leighton a nice man; that she thought his face much more suitable for a girl.

Sydney was shocked into laughter by this last remark, and while she could not but see the reason for such an observation, was still inclined to find him a most prepossessing young man.

As the lessons had progressed, so had her acquaintance with him, as he seemed to find it more and more necessary to spend some time discussing Meriel's progress before each class and similarly some time after in outlining future lessons. His manner in these conversations was so charming she found herself nearly mesmerized by it. He would bend his head down to her and speak earnestly, his hazel eyes gazing steadily into her own with great warmth, then attend her replies with equal attention, his manner suggesting that her every word was precious and inconceivably interesting to him. It did not take long for her to discover in herself a decided partiality for Mr. Leighton's company, and when he began riding over, as though casually, to Elmdene, she was constrained to believe he had a similar liking for her own.

They never met socially, only at the Smythe-Burnses' or at Elmdene, so the neighbourhood was never aware of their acquaintance, which was just as well, as things turned out.

Their friendship improved to a very particular regard, and

at last to mutually avowed love. For some time Sydney went about holding her bubble of happiness shyly within her, content to keep it to herself for the time being. Then one day he came in great excitement to tell her he had just received news that an uncle had died leaving him heir to a shipping concern in London. She naturally rejoiced in his good fortune until he informed her that he must leave at once and permanently for London. Her eyes filled with tears at this news, and he seized her hands and declared that she must come with him. When she protested that he had not even spoken to her father yet, he passionately urged her to elope with him at once and they would marry in London.

Now her heart was torn, for her instinct was to agree to anything he asked of her, but her mind told her she could not do so. Not only would such a course of action cause grief to her father, there was Meriel. Her head hanging miserably, she confessed that her duty to her little sister made it impossible for her to contemplate leaving her home for at least five year. He kissed and comforted her charmingly, begging her not to cry, and telling her she was a silly little thing, and that of course she was not obligated to do any such thing. But no amount of cajoling could persuade her, and at last he became angry and said she did not truly love him.

Then it was her turn to comfort and reassure him. She said her heart would always be his, and that five years was no time at all, since they were so very young, and that by the time they could marry they would be better acquainted and so better able to adapt themselves to the serious business of marriage. He did not agree with her by anything he said, but he allowed himself to be placated, and they parted at last without anything being definitely settled, but with many protestations of love and promises to write daily, which indeed they did for a month. He had no friends in London and was lonely, and apart from this, somewhat frightened by the welter of business responsibilities falling so suddenly on his inexperienced shoulders, and he poured all of this out in his letters. Her answers were filled with love and pride and eager confidence in him.

Then his letters began to come with less frequency. Two months after he was gone, they ceased altogether. Throwing pride away, she had written several increasingly cool letters, which remained unanswered, before she realized that her romance was over, that she had lost him.

She did not go into a decline, for she was not the sort of girl who would do so, and her responsibilities were too great to allow it, but her heart was very sore for many months. Then, as gently as she had fallen in love, she got over it and slowly but inexorably time began to erase his memory, until she rarely thought of him at all. She had never regretted her decision not to leave Meriel, for it gradually came to seem to her that a truly honourable man would have understood and approved her obligation to her sister and would not have tried to dissuade her from her duty in order to gratify her own wishes, and a truly constant man would have been willing to wait for her. She was finally able to forgive him and herself for youthful folly, for after all, had she not forgotten him as well after a time?

She had, when she thought of it at all, assumed him to have married long ago, which had prompted her inquiry of Sir Max, and she wished very much that *she* were married, for she could not like facing him, a spinster still, and having him think she had cherished his memory too much to look at another, or, worse, that she had never received another offer, which she had not. She had met several young men who had appealed to her fleetingly, though never long enough for an attachment to form on her part. She felt assured, however, in her own mind, that it was only her less-than-enthusiastic reception of at least two suits that had prevented offers being made. Certainly she had always supposed that she *would* marry, but for the past several years she had come to accept that it was now unlikely. She consoled herself that she had not also had to forgo the joys of motherhood, having had Meriel to raise from birth, and that, except for that brief time after Morgan left, she had never been other than happy and content with her life.

All of this did not prevent her, however, from tossing sleeplessly that night after Sir Max's startling announcement. She had dissembled before all of them, not willing to enlarge upon the subject of her acquaintance with Morgan. She had been grateful for the near-darkness that covered her blush.

Fortunately, her father, who feared the evening damp so near the water, urged a return to the house. Soon after, Sir Max had taken his leave, and nothing more was said on the subject. She was much agitated, however, and sleep continued to elude her as the night passed, until she reminded herself that there was little she could do to change matters now. She could hardly alter events that had taken place ten years previously, nor could she have prevented Sir Max's friend from being Morgan Leighton. It was equally impossible for her to go to Sir Max and ask him not to invite his friend to Upper Chyppen. There was nothing left to do then but accept whatever was in store for her, without continuing to fret herself. It was always possible, in any case, that he would be unable to accept Sir Max's invitation. This thought was soothing enough to allow her finally to fall asleep.

"Syd," said Meriel suddenly as she sat dreamily over her morning chocolate, "was not Mr. Leighton a very pretty young man?"

"Good heavens, Meriel, what an expression to use," exclaimed Mr. Armytage, looking up from his plate. "I cannot help feeling there must be a better one."

"I do not see why it is necessary when it conveys the impression properly, and the only other expression I could think of was 'handsome,' which I did not remember thinking him, for I have never cared for that sort of look in a man. In any case, if one may call a woman 'handsome,' why cannot one call a man 'pretty'? But am I remembering Mr. Leighton correctly, Syd?"

Sydney, who had become extremely interested in the arrangement of the butter on her toast, replied, "He had a certain smallness of features that might be des—"

"Exactly! The very man! Imagine my remembering all these years. I suppose it was because I had never met such a dainty-looking man that he made such impression on me."

"Really, Meriel, Papa is right. Your vocabulary is most peculiar. Now, do finish up your chocolate or we shall be late. Did you order the carriage brought round, Papa?"

"Yes, yes. Run along and fetch your bonnets."

The girls rose from the table at once and went upstairs for bonnets, shawls, gloves, parasols, and prayer books. They were soon off to Sunday-morning services in Upper Chyppen. When the weather and the roads permitted, they went in the carriage; when one or the other failed them, they walked; but always attended unless illness prevented it. They were sure to meet there every family of their acquaintance, and all were sure to greet one another with cries of surprised pleasure, just as though they had not met at least once during the preceding week, or "as though they are surprised that the rest are doing their Christian duty," said Mr. Armytage dryly.

In the churchyard after the service was over there was invariably a great deal of milling about as conversational groups formed and reformed. In one such group there came together on this day Mrs. Maplethorpe, Mrs. Dobbs, Arabella, and Sydney. As they exchanged greetings and courtesies, they were joined by Sir Max, who bowed over Sydney's hand and asked how she did.

Sydney returned his greeting and proceeded to make him known to Mrs. Dobbs and Mrs. Maplethorpe. When she came to introduce Arabella, she said with mischievously twinkling eyes, "Oh, but of course, you already know Miss Cole, do you not?"

"I have not had the pleasure," he replied.

"Oh, Sir Max, in London! Can you have forgotten?" chided Arabella archly, hoping to retrieve the situation by counting on his good manners not to deny her.

"Certainly not, Miss Cole. If we had met, I could not have forgotten it," he said with prompt gallantry, "but I am sure I am very happy to correct that sad omission now."

The two older ladies in the party very carefully refrained from looking at one another or making any signs at all at this definite proof that Arabella Cole sometimes exaggerated the truth, though each of them showed a certain pent-up look at this restraint. They were not so virtuous as to refrain from looking at Arabella, however, and she was forced to muster up a vivacious smile and say, "Oh, men are the most dreadful creatures alive! I vow we poor women must always suffer for their forgetfulness. But since it is Sunday, I shall have to forgive you, I suppose. You may show you are properly contrite by escorting me home, Sir Max."

"It would give me a great deal of pleasure to do so, Miss Cole, if it were possible. However, I have just persuaded Mr. Armytage to accompany me to Lades Hall to advise me about my stream, and he commissioned me to fetch Miss Armytage to the carriage."

Sydney was delighted to join this expedition, and took the arm he offered her and bid her friends good-bye. Sir Max raised his hat to the other ladies, and they walked away.

Miss Cole's smile, which had become somewhat fixed during his speech, faded completely as soon as their backs were turned, to be replaced by something less pleasant.

"How very perverse men can be, do you not think, Mrs. Dobbs? How short are their memories," said Mrs. Maplethorpe.

"You are so right, dear Mrs. Maplethorpe. But you must not mind it, Miss Cole. I feel sure he cannot truly have completely forgotten so close an acquaintance as was between you. No doubt it will all come back to him in time," consoled Mrs. Dobbs.

Miss Cole ignored this. "How very inspiring, is not it?" she inquired, her accents sugar-encrusted. "Why, I am sure I should never have so much courage as darling Miss Armytage."

"What can you mean, Miss Cole?" inquired Mrs. Dobbs, almost a tiptoe with excitement, for it was clear Miss Cole was about to make some shocking statement. She glanced wide-eyed at Mrs. Maplethorpe to reassure herself that her friend was fully aware of it. Mrs. Maplethorpe evidently was, for she was leaning eagerly forward to make sure she missed nothing.

"Well, you must surely see as well as I that after all these years on the shelf, Miss Armytage does not despair of matrimony. To entertain such hopes at her age, when youth and beauty are past, takes a great deal more courage than I should ever be able to summon were I in the same case."

"Oh, never say so, Miss Cole. I am convinced that you will be able to," offered Miss Dobbs bracingly.

"Dear Mrs. Dobbs," said Miss Cole, laughing, an edge of shrillness betraying her anger, "how droll you are. I do assure you I love a sense of humour above all things in the world. But I must protest, for surely you cannot think my courage will need calling on, for I assure you I shall be married long before I reach such a great age."

"Not so great an age as all that, Miss Cole," protested Mrs. Maplethorpe loyally, for she was very fond of Sydney. "Sydney Armytage can be no more than seven-and-twenty. Only four years older than you, actually, is not she?"

"Is that all she is? I am sure I thought she was much . . ." Miss Cole's eyes widened in pretended dismay at the dreadful thing she had been about to say. She looked about with an affectation of confusion and saw her brother, who was a few yards away in conversation with Squire Dobbs, and said,

"Oh, there you are, Claiborne, I have been looking for you this age. Come along, do. Good morning to you, ladies." She took her bewildered brother's arm and pulled him firmly away.

Mrs. Maplethorpe and Mrs. Dobbs exchanged a long look. Mrs. Maplethorpe raised an eyebrow; Mrs. Dobbs's lips twitched. It was enough, for it expressed unspoken volumes that each good lady was too kindhearted to put into words. It was a great comfort to each to be able thus to communicate and share their enjoyment of such little comedies, without being forced into ungenteel, vulgar gossip. They parted with the mutual satisfaction of knowing that Arabella Cole was going to provide them with a tolerable amount of entertainment this summer.

6

Nothing could have been more felicitous than the visit to Lades Hall, nor more promising for Sydney's secret hopes. Naturally a major portion of their time was spent inspecting the stream and the various glades and grassy banks along it that recommended themselves as ideal sites for creating a pond. Mr. Armytage's every word was attended to with the most deferential attention by his host, and he expanded under this attention to near-joviality. This caused Sydney's heart to warm even more towards Sir Max, for nothing could have pleased her so much as to see her dear papa enjoying himself, and she congratulated herself for having judged Sir Max's character correctly.

All of this did not preclude many opportunities for him to speak with Mr. Armytage's daughters, and it seemed to Sydney that he most often turned to Meriel to consult her artistic judgment, for he had seen and greatly admired her watercolours and drawings hanging on the walls at Elmdene.

Meriel followed where the others led, taking Sir Max's or

her papa's arm when necessary, with equal impartiality, and, to Sydney's anxious eye, with a disquieting tendency to treat them both with the charmingly respectful indulgence of the well-mannered young towards the elderly. She told herself that this was after all only their third meeting, and Meriel was perfectly capable of realizing Sir Max's worth by herself without any prodding from her sister, for Sydney was well aware that her sister was more observant than her air of abstraction would seem to promise.

When the question of the pond had been settled to both gentlemen's satisfaction, Sir Max suggested they might like to view a small cottage *ornée* the owner of Lades Hall had had built as a retreat for himself from his wife's relatives.

"It is beyond that belt of Scotch fir, just over there," he said, "and the path is quite dry, I assure you, no dirt at all to fear for your slippers."

This was agreeable to everyone and they set off, Sir Max leading the way with Meriel, and Sydney was gratified to note that no lover could have been more bent on pleasing his companion than Sir Max seemed to be with Meriel. He pointed out especially pretty trees, bent to pick violets and wildflowers for her, and seemed set on entertaining her. Meriel's reaction to all this was not apparent, since her straw poke bonnet completely obscured even a glimpse of cheek should she have turned her head. Meriel, however, was never an animated sort of girl. Her smile was sweet rather than brilliant, her speech studied rather than lively, and in movement she was slow and languid. She resembled her dead mother to a remarkable degree, which endeared her all the more to her sister and father, even though they sometimes experienced some exasperation at her lack of attention to what was going on around her. She seemed wrapped in a dream most of the time, her eye fixed on some inner horizon.

She and Sir Max had emerged from the firs into the sunshine, and Meriel suddenly stopped. "Oh!" she gasped rapturously. Sydney and her father hurried forward and saw before them the cottage *ornée* with its ornamental chimney stack, patterned brickwork, and thatched roof, the Gothic windows with tiny diamond panes and the walls creeper-covered. It was a charming pastiche of a building, protected on one side by the widespread branches of an enormous oak, while over the minute porch rail a rambler rose had flung a blanket of blossom.

"Oh, oh," Meriel whispered breathlessly, "I . . . I *must* take a sketch of it!"

"Of course you may, dear child, and at once. I will just step back and have some materials fetched out to you—"

"Oh, dear me, Sir Max, I cannot allow you to give yourself so much trouble on any account," protested Mr. Armytage.

"Indeed not, sir, you must not think—" Meriel began in great agitation.

"Nonsense, it is but a matter of a moment. Do you go ahead and look about the interior—the door is not locked— and I will rejoin you in a moment," replied Sir Max, and hurried away before they could protest further. After a moment, as they all stared after him in dismay, Mr. Armytage said that as Meriel had not spoken with any intent to put him to such bother, and that obviously they could not now prevent him from carrying out his intentions, the only thing left to do was inspect the cottage as he had suggested and thank him graciously. They proceeded into the house and walked through the rooms, all small, but well-proportioned and comfortably fitted out, and presently they were rejoined by their host, who conducted them up the miniature staircase to see the bedrooms above. By the time they had descended again, they could all see, through the open front door, menservants setting up chairs and a table in the shade of the firs, and Meriel hurried out at once. The rest followed in a more leisurely way, and by the time they reached the trees, she was already seated, the sketching block in one hand, a pencil in the other, studying the cottage with narrowed eyes.

"Will you sketch also, Miss Armytage?"

"No, I thank you, sir, my talent with a pencil is not one I would display publicly." Sydney laughed.

"Perhaps you will enjoy strolling through the trees while your sister works, or will you prefer to rest?"

"Oh, do let us continue our walk, the shade is so delicious."

"Well, I for one shall take advantage of this comfortable chair to rest my legs. You two go along," urged Mr. Armytage, sinking into the seat with a sigh.

Sydney took the arm Sir Max held out to her, and they walked back into the trees. "This is such a lovely property," said Sydney, "I wonder the Wilmots could give it up so completely."

"You were acquainted?"

"Only vaguely. Mrs. Wilmot never cared for the neighbourhood—much too provincial for her tastes. It is true she had a host of relatives who were forever visiting, so I suppose her poor husband had need of a place to which he could escape. Eventually, I heard, she insisted on moving to London when their children were grown, and the place has stood empty till now. I hope you will find us more congenial."

"Ah, I hope the neighbourhood will find *me* so, for I like it here more with each day that passes," he replied, smiling down at her with such warmth that she became flustered and looked away.

"Have you no desire to live elsewhere, Miss Armytage?"

"Elsewhere? Good heavens, no. I am a country mouse through and through, I fear. I have been to visit in London and Brighton and Bath, and once visited a friend in Scotland for some weeks, but I am never so contented as at home."

"That is very refreshing to hear. I find most people vaguely discontent with their lot, always wanting to travel, to have more money, a new carriage, more prestige or attention."

"Or more food, a better home to live in, warmer clothes in the winter, a better education for their children," she added gravely.

"Oh, you speak of real need, while I spoke of greedy discontent. The first is more distressingly common than most of us are willing to know of. The only good thing that comes from such a state of want is that it can, among the more sensitive, keep contentment from turning into complacency."

"And what of you, sir—are you content with your lot, or do you want more?"

He met her eyes seriously for a moment before he said quietly, "Why, until very recently I would have said I was well content with my life. Now, however . . ."—as they walked, they had circled through the trees and arrived back at their starting point, and before them was Meriel, a lovely picture in her white gown and straw bonnet, totally absorbed in her work—". . . I find that I do indeed want more."

Sydney followed his gaze and thought she understood very well the significance of Sir Max's words. She made no reply, and they advanced to where Mr. Armytage sat. On the table was a pitcher of lemonade and cakes, with a footman standing by to serve them. Mr. Armytage woke abruptly from a light doze when Sydney called out to Meriel to put aside her work and join them. She declared her drawing to be finished, and it was thought by all to be very fine. While they had refreshments, Sir Max engaged them to dine with him on the fourth evening from today, and although Mr. Armytage did not care for dining from home ordinarily, he was so pleased with Sir Max that he allowed himself to be persuaded to accept.

In another half-hour they were back in their carriage being driven away, happy in the knowledge that they would meet Sir Max the day after next at Mrs. Dobbs's dinner party. Meriel said she hoped Sir Max would allow her to sketch the cottage again from another viewpoint, and that in the meantime she would do a watercolour based on her present drawing to present to Sir Max in repayment for his kindness, which pleased Sydney exceedingly, and all agreed it had been an unusually pleasant afternoon and they were fortunate in their new neighbour.

Mrs. Dobbs's dinners were noted for their liveliness and for the abundance of food prepared by her very superior cook. There was generally some impromptu dancing to follow if enough couples could be persuaded to stand up, since Squire Dobbs quite fancied himself as a dancer and was always the first to suggest it. If she were one of the company, it was also, more often than not, Sydney who played for them.

The guests tonight were not averse to their host's proposal, for all had eaten, at Mrs. Dobbs's continual urgings, much more than was good for their comfort. The Maplethorpes, the Coles, the Armytages, Sir Max, the guest of honour, and four couples of young people were therefore only too eager to exercise. Servants hastily removed the furniture to the outer walls of the largest drawing room and rolled up the carpets, while Sydney seated herself at the pianoforte. As she played the opening strains of a country dance, the squire, who was monstrously fond of pretty girls, led out Meriel; Sir Max followed with Mrs. Dobbs and Mr. Armytage with Mrs. Maplethorpe, while the others formed couples as they could.

After several sets, during which Sir Max danced with Mrs. Maplethorpe, Meriel, and a blushing Cassandra, under the sour regard of Arabella, who felt she was being deliberately slighted, he at last bowed before her, and she was at once all smiles and flirtatiousness. When the dance came to an end, they found themselves near the pianoforte, and Arabella handed him her fan and requested that he ply it for her comfort.

Since the other dancers seemed content to rest for a few moments also, Sydney gratefully accepted the respite. She sat turning over the pages of some music on the pianoforte, and could not prevent herself from overhearing the conversation of the couple who stood so near her.

"Miss Armytage has a very fine musical talent, does not she?" inquired Sir Max.

"Oh, indeed. Why, I am sure if she practiced more she would become quite first-rate. My dear aunt, Lady Boxton, always said true proficiency could never be reached without daily practice, so I never fail to give myself over to my instrument for two hours at the very least every day. Oh, I quite insist upon it, I assure you."

"Do you indeed, Miss Cole? Then I can only assume *your* proficiency to outstrip all others'."

She laughed gaily. "Oh, I think I may say without unduly flattering myself that my ability is no small thing. I quite pride myself on my music."

"As of course you should do. Do you play the waltz, Miss Cole?"

"Oh, most assuredly, sir."

"How very fortunate we are, then. See here, Miss Armytage," exclaimed Sir Max, turning briskly to Sydney and taking her arm to lift her bodily from the piano stool, "Miss Cole is telling me that she plays the waltz, and you must give up your place to her, for I insist on hearing her do so."

"But . . . but . . . I . . ." Sydney began in some confusion at the suddenness of his action.

"Really, Sir Max, I cannot . . ." Miss Cole protested at the same time.

"Pooh, Miss Cole, you must not be falsely modest and deprive us, and you, Miss Armytage, must not be selfish and deny us the pleasure of hearing Miss Cole play the waltz." He had, during this speech, released Sydney, pulled Miss Cole forward, and pressed her down onto the seat. Now he turned, his eyes twinkling, to bow before Sydney. "As a consolation for having to give up playing, Miss Armytage, will you stand up with me for the waltz?"

Sydney felt a giggle bubbling up at the adroitness of his maneuvering and the look of astonishment on Arabella Cole's face. There was also amazement to be seen around the room on the faces of those who had watched this little play. They had not been privy, of course, to the conversation between Sir Max and Miss Cole, as had Sydney been, and so were unable to fully appreciate how cleverly Miss Cole had been hoist on her own petard, but they were nevertheless at *non plus* to see her seated at the pianoforte while dancing was going on. Mrs. Maplethorpe and Mrs. Dobbs exchanged lively, knowing glances, for they had often heard Arabella declare when she had been requested to accommodate dancers at other parties that only old maids played, while those who were young and popular enough to get partners danced.

With Sir Max's firm hand at her waist, Sydney was whirled away down the room, happy to find that her feet followed his without stumbling, for she did not often dance anymore.

"That was naughty of you, sir," said Sydney, allowing the giggle she had suppressed to escape.

"Why, how can you think so, Miss Armytage, when I thought I was providing Miss Cole with the opportunity to display her talent. I thought young ladies desired it."

"Miss Cole always very graciously consents to entertain us after dinner, but I fear she is not happy to serve as accompanist when dancing is going on."

"I take it you are so employed frequently."

"Well, yes, but I do not mind—to allow the young people to enjoy themselves."

"Now you are fishing for compliments, Miss Armytage, for surely you cannot expect me to think of you as older than your father or the squire, and I see they have danced as enthusiastically as any young people here."

"Ah, but they do not play, and I rarely dance."

"That must be remedied, for you dance too well to be confined to the pianoforte."

"I thank you, sir," she said, too overcome by the compliment to think of a wittier reply.

After a moment he continued, "I have good news. I have had a reply to my invitation to Mr. Leighton. He accepted most eagerly and we can expect him to be with us by next week."

Sydney faltered, nearly losing the step, but then managed to recover and said, "How . . . nice that will be for you."

He gave her a quizzical look, for he had not missed the reaction his news had caused, and wondered why it had been so. He wished she would look up at him again with those clear, shining grey eyes and smile as she had before.

Meriel, who had declined to dance in order to watch her sister, sat beside her father, whose pleasure at this unexpected event was evident on his face.

"She should dance more often," Meriel whispered to her father. "She is so light and graceful, it must be a treat for a partner to lead her out."

"Ah, she takes that from me," replied Mr. Armytage complacently. "I was always considered to be a fine dancer."

"You still are so, Papa," Meriel declared loyally.

"Well, well, I still enjoy it, though I doubt this new way of dancing would suit me."

"Nonsense, you would do it as well as any other. We shall practice at home, and the next time we are out, you shall amaze all your friends."

Mr. Armytage smiled and patted her hand, not demurring at the plan. "We shall see, child, we shall see. They make a fine-looking couple, do not you think?" He watched his elder daughter fondly, for Mr. Armytage also had secret plans.

7

As it turned out, Meriel was unable to accompany Sydney and her father to Sir Max's for dinner, for the very day after the Dobbs dinner party, a note arrived from old Lady Divers, Meriel's godmother, summoning Meriel for the annual two-week stay in Bath. The invitation was delivered by Lady Divers' maid, who arrived in Lady Divers' coach, and Meriel was to travel back to Bath with the maid the next morning. This summons always arrived unexpectedly, and the visits were always limited to two weeks, for Lady Divers suffered

poor health and was never sure when she might be up to
entertaining a visitor.

It might be more accurate to say she *enjoyed* poor health,
for her complexion was clear and pink, and she had hardly a
wrinkle or a grey hair despite her age. Her disorder was
vague, something never named, but referred to as only "my
delicate constitution," and fortunately for her it did not inter-
fere with her appetite, since her trips to her well-laden table,
carefully supported on the arm of her maid, were her only
exercise. Between these three high points of her day, life was
supported by various delicacies concocted by her excellent
cook. When not eating, she read novels and napped. Any
other exertion caused her to be laid up in her bed for days
afterwards, suffering from exhaustion. The result of all this
eating and indolence was, naturally, enormous girth, which
made activity even less possible.

Once a year, however, conscience stirred her to the effort
required to write bidding her godchild come for a visit. No
other effort was made on her part, for while Meriel was with
her she continued her life exactly as she had the rest of the
year, except that for two weeks she had the company of
Meriel while she did so. Meriel's temperament was fortunately exactly suited to this monstrously selfish old lady, for
she was perfectly content to sit quietly by the hour drawing or
doing a watercolour or reading. Her godmother's only gesture
towards entertaining her guest was to order her maid to
accompany Meriel each morning on a visit to the Pump Room
to take the waters and on the way back to exchange Lady
Divers' library book.

After the first visit, when Meriel was twelve and Sydney
had been instructed to bring her to Bath (before that, the
once-a-year letter had enclosed a five-pound note without an
invitation, for Lady Divers found children too exhausting),
Sydney was never again invited. Lady Divers thenceforth sent
her carriage and her maid for Meriel. She confided to her
goddaughter that she found Sydney exuded too much energy
for the tranquillity necessary to maintain her precarious health.
Sydney was grateful for the reprieve, for she declared sitting
about all day watching a fat old woman eating and sleeping
was not her idea of enjoyment, that the water at the Pump
Room tasted nasty, and that one never saw anyone there, in

any case, who had any conversation beyond the state of his health, a topic that bored her inexpressibly.

Meriel, while she managed to dispose of her token glass of mineral water behind a palm, being in agreement that it tasted nasty, quite enjoyed her visits to the Pump Room. She liked studying the faces she saw there, mostly elderly, and afterwards making sketches of them. She had accumulated stacks of drawing books filled with these efforts over the years, and Sydney and Mr. Armytage always looked forward to seeing them. Sometimes these studies were accomplished with a few swift, sure lines after seeing a face once, but occasionally she needed more study.

Such was the case in the drawing she was working on now, while Lady Divers snored gently from the chaise longue before the fire. Meriel had thought she had the face clearly in her mind, but she was dissatisfied with her rendering. The nose would not come right, and the more she worked at it, the less satisfactory it seemed.

It was a face that had seemed to leap out at her from the throng of strollers in the Pump Room this morning, her first day in Bath, not only because he towered over most of the people there, but because it was a youthful face, not so usual a sight in a place given over to catering to the ills of the elderly. Also, the strength of the bone structure impressed itself on her artist's eye with considerable impact. From her seat partially hidden behind a potted palm but offering a perfect view of the visitors, Meriel's eyes had followed the face as the gentleman walked slowly up and down the room, supporting on his arm an elderly lady who could only be his mother, so like were the sets of their eyes and mouths.

Now she turned over the page, determined to do no more to the sketch until she had seen the face again. Tomorrow he might be there once more, and she would concentrate on the nose.

The following morning she found herself hurrying along quite eagerly until Mabel, Lady Divers' maid, complained and Meriel slowed herself to a more decorous pace. Once she was inside, her eyes flew about the room, too sparsely populated this early to miss seeing him had he been there, but he was not. She felt suddenly flat with disappointment, and the faces she did see seemed boring, not worth studying. She and Mabel took their glasses of the water and made their way to their usual station behind the palm. After a few moments, however, her usual serenity returned as she reminded herself that it was still early in the day, and she found herself noting interesting facial features that her fingers itched to record. She always wished that she could bring her sketchbook here, but shrank from exciting the sort of attention to herself such an action would inevitably create. She had, however, armed herself with a tiny scrap of paper and a stub of charcoal pencil, for she was determined to capture that elusive nose today.

Then, suddenly, she found her eyes resting on the face she sought. He was holding his mother's glass while she fumbled in her reticule, and he stared rather absentmindedly about. Meriel noted again his height and the easy assurance of his carriage, the well-tailored coat and immaculate whiteness of his neckcloth and shirt points. Not a Dandy, but very particular in his dress, she decided approvingly, before her eyes were drawn back to his face. Yes, she had got it all right yesterday except the nose: the deep sockets of the eyes, the thickness of the lids over the dark blue eyes, the downward slant of them at the outer corners, the prominent cheekbones above the long, hollowed cheeks, the shapely mouth, the strong jawbone and chin. The nose, now—what was it that had eluded her? Ah, it was the shape of the nostrils! She withdrew her scrap of paper and charcoal from her reticule and her eyes flew for a quick moment from the paper to his face while she sketched quickly. Then she tucked both away again and her eyes moved up his face until she found herself staring directly into his own rather puzzled eyes. So deep, however, was her concentration on measuring the exact distance between his eyes and then that between his dark brows and hairline, that her gaze moved on up without consciously registering his awareness. When her gaze came down again she noted one eyebrow raised and eyes now amused. Her concentration was broken, the face in its entirety became clear in her vision, and she realized he was smiling at her. She smiled back unselfconsciously, and then his attention was recalled by his mother and he bent over her solicitously for a moment. Clearly she had requested their departure, for he immediately led her away to the door. Just before he went out, he turned and again met Meriel's eye; then he was gone from sight.

When she had returned to Lady Divers and was sitting

quietly with her sketchbook, she rapidly and without any hesitancy at all drew his face, then, turning over the page, drew with the same sure hand a full-length picture of him staring directly at her, glass in hand, eyebrow quirked, and lips curved into a smile. She sat back contentedly and sighed, for she knew she had got him exactly right.

The following morning the upstairs maid handed her her morning cup of chocolate and a message from Mabel informing her that Lady Divers was suffering with the headache and would require Mabel's attendance, so she must be excused from their visit to the Pump Room today.

"Please convey my sympathies to my godmother and tell Mabel I will relieve her this afternoon. Meantime she is not to worry her head about me," replied Meriel calmly.

When she had finished her chocolate she rose and dressed in her best walking dress of blue spotted muslin with a Vandyked flounce at the hem and a matching blue muslin pelisse. With it she wore a high-crowned bonnet of fine moss straw ornamented with velvet violets and blue ribbands to tie under her chin.

When she left the house presently there was no one to question her but the butler, who looked somewhat perturbed to see Miss going out unaccompanied, but she bade him good morning calmly and tripped so confidently out the door he held for her that he could not bring himself to question her. It never occurred to Meriel that it was not proper for a young girl to go out alone or to attend the morning session at the Pump Room unchaperoned. She had been used to going about alone most of her life, quite often walking alone into Upper Chyppen on errands for Sydney. She had accepted Mabel's company in Bath as her godmother's surrogate, and as such easily dispensed with, for Mabel, though kind, was elderly and uncommunicative.

Meriel, therefore, made her way to the Pump Room, her confidence not the least undermined by any knowledge of her impropriety. She armed herself with her glass of the waters and took up her usual position behind the palm and looked about contentedly. The room was crowded this morning, but it took her only a moment to find the face she sought. He had evidently been watching for her, for their eyes met and acknowledged one another instantly.

He then was forced to turn away as another party came up

to him and his mother and there was a flurry of greetings and compliments. Meriel looked about, noting an interesting chin here and quite the most bristling bushy eyebrows she had ever seen, but her interest was shallow this morning, her eye not truly recording. She felt sure the gentleman would eventually free himself and bring his mother over and they would all speak together, and she was content to wait.

Naturally, she was unaware of the problems inherent in her situation that would make such an event highly unlikely, for she had been very little in Society, her experiences so far limited to Upper Chyppen, and never alone before. If a gentleman at home had wished to be presented to her, he had had no trouble finding someone in the same room who knew her and could introduce them. It did not occur to her that this condition did not prevail in her present situation, nor that it was necessary. She was equally unaware of the attention she was attracting today in her lone state. She had been the subject of much speculation in the past days because of her beauty, but now there was more than admiration and curiosity in the sidelong glances. An unattended young woman, no matter how beautiful, was an affront to the proprieties, and gentlemen and ladies alike were shocked and wondered if she were quite so young and innocent as she appeared.

She sat on in placid unawareness of all this, waiting for the gentleman to break away and come across the room to her. When he did bow and move away, however, it was toward the door, and except for again turning to exchange a look with her, he continued on out. After a few moments she set aside the glass she had continued to hold, rose, and made her way out of the room and back to Lady Divers' house.

Meriel was not given to romantic flights of fancy about herself, so she did not experience palpitations, faintness, bitterness, or humiliation. She did not feel rejected or scorned. She, in fact, trusted this unknown man completely. She had only to remember the straightforward looks, the breeding in the bones of his face, to know he had been unable to speak to her for reasons that had nothing to do with her. When it was possible, he would do so. She would wait.

For in spite of her air of being wrapped in a dream and her predilection for highly romanticized fiction, she was in reality a down-to-earth sort of girl, with a simple, direct approach to life, who could no more imagine herself the heroine of her romances than could Sydney. Her air of abstraction was mostly the result of always looking at the picture value of everything around her, and her taste in fiction for its very otherness from her own circumscribed life. Her placidity of temperament and a life so far free of anxiety enabled her to face any situation with equanimity and confidence that what one desired would no doubt come to one without any need for undue fretting. What she desired, in this case, was to know better the gentleman with the interesting face.

The next morning Lady Divers had recovered and was assisted out of bed and into her normal daytime position of reclining on her chaise longue, so Mabel was free to attend Meriel again, and they set off for the Pump Room together soon after breakfast.

The first thing she saw as she entered the room was the young man, who was stationed just inside the door, patently watching for her from the way his face lit up at her entrance, and he was alone. He started forward eagerly when she appeared, checked when he saw Mabel, then came forward determinedly.

"Good morning!" he said with enormous élan, as though he were greeting an old friend. "I was beginning to despair that you were not coming today and I would be forced to drink my glass alone, but now we can share the unhappy experience and give each other courage. It takes a great deal of resolution, I find, to drink it up, but with the support of a fellow sufferer it becomes easier to bear. Perhaps your maid would prefer to sit down."

Meriel, not the least flustered by this familiar address, turned to Mabel and said it was quite all right for her to sit down, since she was sure her knees must need the rest after their walk. Mabel was convinced by the little charade just enacted for her benefit, and her knees were aching something fierce, so with only the least hesitation she went away and took up her usual station. The pair left standing regarded one another for a long moment.

"I am Edward Trevillion," he said at last.

"And I am Meriel Armytage."

"Well, Miss Armytage, I am very happy to make your acquaintance at long last."

She laughed. "But it has only been three days."

"Is that all, truly? Astonishing!" He held out his arm.

"For appearance' sake, we should each take a glass of this abomination."

Glasses in hand, they strolled about for a few moments without speaking. "Now, Miss Armytage, I must tell you that young ladies who stare fixedly at strange gentlemen are bound to be forced to entertain the attentions of their subjects whether they care for them or not."

"It was your nose," she said simply.

"My . . . nose?"

"Well, of course not just at first, but then it would not come right—your nose, I mean."

"I continue bewildered. No doubt I am but a slow-top, so perhaps if you explained it to me in more detail . . ."

"It was for my sketch. The nose wouldn't come right, but the next day I brought paper, only the tiniest piece, and drew it right there, and it came right the next time."

"Oh, I see, you are an artist." He sounded somewhat disappointed, as though he would have preferred being stared at for his own sake than for her drawing.

"Well, not really," she said with genuine modesty, "but it is the thing I like to do most. Sydney likes music better."

"Sydney? Your brother?" he hazarded.

"No, my sister. It is odd, I know, but it is a family name."

"And where is Sydney? Does she dislike the waters here to such an extent that she refuses to set foot in the place, even if it means you must come alone?"

"Well, it is true she does not care for it, but no doubt she would accompany me if she were here. She is at home."

He thought over this statement for a moment, then managed to untangle it and pull out the relevant thread. "And where is home?"

"Upper Chyppen, in Middlesex. I come every year to visit my godmother, but she does not care for Sydney to come with me. She says Sydney upsets her. Sydney does not care for sitting about much, and my godmother does not care for going about."

"May I call upon your godmother?"

"Good heavens, no!" she exclaimed, horrified at the very idea of announcing to Lady Divers that a gentleman would be paying a morning visit. Then, seeing that he looked slightly affronted by the shocked vehemence of her tone, she added hastily, "She is an invalid, you see, and never receives visitors. Why, even the suggestion would send her to bed with the headache."

He burst out laughing and she was compelled to join him. "I begin to see the entire picture, and understand poor Sydney's exclusion. And what of you, little one, in such a household?" He studied her face. "No, I see. That serenity. Nothing there to send her into fits."

"Oh, no. I quite like being quiet. I work best when no one speaks to me. Conversation spoils my concentration."

"What do you draw?"

"The faces I see here in the mornings."

"I should like very much to see your drawings. Now, let me think how it could best be arranged. Perhaps I could call for you in the morning and we could go for a drive. You would bring your maid, of course, and your sketchbook."

"I would like that very much," she replied, without the least trace of artifice or coquetry.

So it was that the next day he called for her and she and Mabel were driven to Lansdown Hill and her drawings were inspected and admired, and on every succeeding day for the remainder of her stay they drove about Bath instead of attending the Pump Room. Since they were driven by Edward's coachman and attended by Meriel's maid, there was little to take exception to, though they roused considerable gossip. Lady Divers, informed by Mabel of the situation, inquired if the man were a gentleman. On Mabel's assertion that he very definitely was, Lady Divers allowed the matter to rest. No doubt, this would have been condemned by all the righteous ladies of Bath had they known of it, but any other course of action would require that Lady Divers receive the gentleman and pass on him herself, and that was too fatiguing to contemplate. After all, Mabel approved the man and was with the child every moment.

Actually, Mabel, being old and arthritic, was not with them all the time. They were within her sight, though, and she was satisfied with this, grateful not to be required to do all that walking. She had never known such people for walking! She and the coachman discussed this at great length, for it was the young couple's habit to stop the carriage and get down whenever a pleasing walk presented itself, and while strolling about, speak out of earshot of their servants.

They talked of their likes and dislikes, their relatives, their lives, where they had been in the world, art and literature. They carefully refrained from any discussion of themselves in relation to one another, in unspoken but mutual agreement that this was a matter too momentous to be approached with other than great circumspection, and at some time in the future.

Quite often, Edward insisted that Meriel bring her sketchbook because he was taking her to a particular vista he felt she would want to draw. She demurred at first, convinced nothing on earth could inspire her to it while she was in his company, which always put her into a state of euphoria, a sizzling sort of excitement that left her oblivious of everything around her. He persisted, however, in encouraging her to try, promising that he would not speak or distract her in any way as she worked, until at last one morning she gave in.

He had chosen a grassy plot overlooking a wooded ravine. She chose an angle with an eye that refused to be distracted even by love, which showed her a view of the ravine and opened out on one side to reveal a view of bland meadowland. At first she could feel nothing but his presence and continuously glanced round at him, her dark eyes laughing ruefully at herself for her helpless fascination with him. He sat some distance away, his back half-turned from her, reading a book of poetry, resolutely ignoring her. She began halfheartedly sketching in the setting and then slowly the possibilities inherent in the scene began pressing their claims and soon she was rapt. She did not forget his presence for an instant, for she found he did not distract her as she had feared. Instead she found the warm, steady glow of his encouragement inspired her in a way she had not experienced before.

In her drawing the ravine took on a dark, brooding, almost tormented romanticism that contrasted sharply with the serenity of the small bit of sunlit meadow beyond.

She finally laid aside her chalk and sighed, and he turned at once. When he saw that she was finished, he rose and came to her. He studied the drawing for so long in silence that she became worried.

"I was working very fast, of course," she began apologetically.

"No . . . no! It is perfect. My God, Meriel, you must surely know as well as I that it is . . . is . . . perfect. It is . . ."

He broke off to stare about, running a distracted hand through his hair. "I must consult with someone knowledgeable—someone who will know what will be the best thing to do next. Perhaps some study in Italy—"

"Italy! What are you saying, Edward?"

"You must study, my dear. So much talent cannot be let go by the way. I will consult Mr. Thomas Lawrence when I return to London."

"But I do not want to go to Italy!" she cried in alarm. "I could not bear to be alone in a strange—"

"Little one, do not imagine for a moment that you will be alone," he said, smiling down into her eyes in a way that caused her to become quite dizzy with joy.

8

Sydney had had little time to miss Meriel, though she had at first been inclined to be cross that Lady Divers was taking her sister away at just this time, with Sir Max's dinner party the next day. It had irritated her that the woman's total disregard for anyone's convenience but her own threw everyone's plans into disarray. Then she had sighed and accepted it as inevitable and as something that must just be borne with. After all, the visit must be paid and was best got out of the way now. It was, thank God, limited to two weeks, and she supposed Sir Max would have other dinner parties.

So she had informed Meriel of her fate, spent the entire afternoon upstairs choosing clothes for her to take, and packing her cases. She had dashed off a hurried note to Sir Max to inform him of Meriel's departure and inquiring if he would prefer to postpone the dinner until her return, and sent Tom, the coachman, off to deliver it. He had returned shortly with a reply from Sir Max saying that he wished Meriel a good journey and assuring Sydney that he would look forward to seeing her and Mr. Armytage at his table the following evening.

She had been surprised at how gratifying she found this response. So gracious, she had thought, the very soul of courtesy, just as she had known he was. Her crossness with Lady Divers had evaporated. After all, she had reasoned, the poor soul is old and ill, and even she, despite her indolence and greed, must feel the need of company sometimes; and Meriel's absence might only whet Sir Max's interest. He certainly would not see anyone in or around Upper Chyppen who could compare to Meriel in beauty or sweetness of manner. She had listed to herself all the girls in the neighbourhood who might give her cause to worry, and found it reassuringly short. The prettiest girl next to Meriel was Cassie Maplethorpe, but she had so little presence it would be unlikely she could attract him. There was Arabella Cole, who could not be discounted, no matter how much one disliked her manner.

Of course, it was possible he was on the lookout for an heiress, and his family, good looks, and money certainly entitled him to one, but if this were so, Meriel would not interest him in any case, for while her dowry would be respectable, it was a far cry from making her an heiress. There were some who hinted from time to time that Lady Divers, being so partial to her goddaughter, might leave her money to Meriel. Sydney, however, was aware that while Lady Divers was childless, she had a number of nieces and nephews, and that when it came to money one tended to want to keep it in one's own family, even if the members of that family were never allowed inside one's door while one was alive.

Sydney felt it was to Lady Divers' credit that she had never so much as hinted at such a possibility as an inducement to assure herself of Meriel's company. In fact, if the truth were known, Sydney surmised that it had never occurred to the old lady that she needed to offer such an inducement, so complete was her selfishness. She probably felt she was conferring a favour on them by offering Meriel the treat of a visit to Bath.

Somehow, though, Sydney could not picture Sir Max as a

fortune hunter or a man whose pride in his lineage demanded a great marriage. And she remembered vividly the look on his face when Meriel smiled at him that day he had brought them the book, and the tone of his voice when he had said that now he thought he wanted more from life.

So she waved Meriel on her way the next morning with a cheerful smile and spent the remainder of the day wavering between her pale lemon sarcenet evening gown and the seafoam-green muslin. She dithered in indecision, actually resorting to consulting her father at one point on which gown *he* thought best became her.

He studied her gravely for a long moment, before he suggested the lemon sarcenet as being a most attractive gown as he remembered it. In the event she wore the green with her mother's pearls as her only ornament, since that was Lutie's choice when she came to assist Sydney's preparations, and when she came downstairs her papa told her he was glad she had followed his advice.

"But, Papa, you favoured the yellow," she protested laughingly.

"Only because I knew you would be bound to decide on whatever I did not choose," he said smugly, a man who felt he understood women very well. "I have always been partial to this gown, my dear, and I must tell you you have never been in better looks."

She was told the same thing by Mrs. Maplethorpe and Cassie when they arrived at Sir Max's and she was shown into a cloakroom where mother and daughter were smoothing their hair and shaking out their ruffles before ascending to the drawing room. Sydney was very grateful for their compliments and thought perhaps the green did become her best. When the ladies were shown into the drawing room, Sir Max came forward at once, and it seemed to her there was approval in his eyes as he looked at her. He made them all welcome, bending over their hands with gratifying gallantry.

"Now, Miss Armytage. I have a pleasant surprise for you. An old friend of yours joined me today and has been most impatient for your arrival," Sir Max said, grinning in anticipation.

Sydney's heart sank, for she knew very well what his words presaged. In the brief instant at her disposal before she must face her ordeal, she managed to brace herself and take a deep breath. Then Sir Max had stepped aside and there was Morgan Leighton advancing towards her from the fireplace, where he had been in conversation with Mr. Maplethorpe and Mr. Armytage.

Oh dear, how horribly unfair, was her first thought, that he has not changed in the least and here am I showing all my years clearly. The compliments that had so buoyed her up only a moment before were erased from her mind and she was left feeling plain and old.

Morgan smiled, looking straight into her eyes, and his smile was intimate, expressing a certain rueful wistfulness, and confidence of welcome at the same time. Her lips formed into a stiff imitation. He took her hand and pressed a kiss upon her fingers for only the smallest fraction of time longer than necessary to emphasize their previous acquaintance upon the company. She was aware of everyone eyeing them with open curiosity, the Maplethorpes and Cassie having never even heard of Morgan Leighton, and her father and Sir Max to see how she would react to seeing this friend from the past.

"Miss Armytage! What a very great pleasure this is, to be sure," he exclaimed as he straightened up to face her, still retaining her hand.

She tugged at it and he released it reluctantly. She was grateful that he had not called her Sydney before all these people. "Mr. . . . Leighton . . ." she replied, unable to think of anything further to say to him.

His head cocked to one side in a well-remembered way as he searched her face, his smile insistent. "Ah, do not say you have forgotten me? I must tell you"—he turned, taking the company into his confidence—"Miss Armytage was very kind to a green young man many years ago and I have always retained a warm memory of this part of the country because of it. How is your little sister, Miss Armytage? The little girl who took lessons from me?"

"She is very well, sir," she said, wondering if it would be possible to claim the headache coming on suddenly and asking Papa to take her home. No, of course she could do no such thing, for it would be too obvious to everyone that there must be more than they thought to the story of this sudden old acquaintance popping up. Besides, was she so poor-spirited she could not face what was, after all, only a small thing? No need, really, to get into such a taking. She forced herself to smile distantly at him, and slowly opened her fan and waved it languidly before her face.

"I shall look forward to seeing her again. Do you think she will remember me after all these years? Sir Max tells me she has gone to Bath."

"Yes, so she has," she replied, glancing at Sir Max. There was something in her eyes that caused him to interrupt the reunion.

"Now, Miss Armytage, we mustn't allow you to monopolize Mr. Leighton when our other guests are eager to make his acquaintance." Max drew Morgan away to the Maplethorpe ladies and presented him while Sydney thankfully joined her father at the fireplace and took his arm. He looked somewhat puzzled by this, for he was not used to seeing his daughter put out of countenance by any situation, yet it was clear to him the meeting with Mr. Leighton had not been easy for her. Sydney turned her eyes to the flaming logs in the fireplace, trying to still her tumultuous thoughts and racing heart before she was required to converse with Morgan again. Why on earth must he needs come haring down here again the moment he received Sir Max's invitation, when he must know it could only cause her distress? Sir Max would have been sure to mention the Misses Armytage in his letter, since they had both agreed they remembered him, so he would know she was unmarried. Perhaps it was only curiosity, or perhaps only to show her how he had risen in the world. As a man with plenty of money and no ties, he could afford to gratify such whims. Perhaps he hoped to cut a swath through a society that had ignored him during his previous stay, and had nothing to do with her at all.

Well, no matter what had motivated him, she thought, good sense reasserting itself, he was now here, and must be confronted, and she hoped she was not so lacking in backbone that she could not be in the same room with him without losing her composure. He evidently felt equal to it, so, therefore, would she be. She released her father's arm and turned about to face the others, who were now joining the group by the fireplace.

She was grateful the company was so small, for it precluded any possibility of private conversation with him, though she found herself seated between him and Sir Max at the dinner table. She managed to divide her attention between them with gay impartiality, and was not a little pleased to notice Morgan looking at her after a time with something akin to bewilderment. No doubt he hoped to see me blushing and flustered, she thought waspishly, the old maid overcome with long-stored emotions, falling in a heap at his feet.

The dinner, in spite of her success in confounding what she felt must be his expectations, was a strain nevertheless, and she was glad when she could retire with the other women from the table.

"Now"—Mrs. Maplethorpe pounced as soon as they were seated in the drawing room—"tell me everything about this interesting man!"

Sydney could not help laughing. "My dear Mrs. Maplethorpe, I fear there is little I can tell you."

"But you knew him before."

"Only briefly. He gave Meriel some lessons in mathematics and geography many years ago—quite ten years, I believe— when he was tutoring the Smythe-Burns boys while they resided at Burns Hall."

"But he said you were so kind . . ." Mrs. Maplethorpe persisted.

"I expect he means because I enabled him to earn a bit of extra money by bringing Meriel to him."

"But—"

"And of course, I was polite to him when I did see him, for he seemed lonely. I believe he knew no one, and the Smythe-Burnses were a bit too high in the instep to allow themselves to become overly friendly with a mere tutor."

"Oh, yes, I suppose so." Mrs. Maplethorpe sighed, disappointed at this paucity of information. She *had* hoped for something more interesting. Then she brightened. "But there can be no question you did meet him first. I can hardly wait to see Arabella Cole's face when she learns that again you have beaten her to it."

"Why, are we in some competition, Mrs. Maplethorpe? How alarming . . . and unpleasant."

"Oh, Miss Cole likes to be first in everything," Cassie explained.

"Now, Cassandra . . ." her mother chided. "Not but what you have the right of it."

"Well, Mr. Leighton has been living in London for many years, so it is possible she met him there. No need to mention our previous meeting," she added, not very hopefully, for she was quite sure everyone in Upper Chyppen would be acquainted with all the facts by the end of the week.

"She will probably *claim* to have," said Cassie pertly.

"Now, Cassandra . . ." Mrs. Maplethorpe said automatically. "Well, I am sure it is most gratifying to have two such attractive men added to our small society. I hope Mr. Leighton plans to make a long stay."

Sydney fervently hoped just the opposite, but only said, "Yes, very nice," as noncommittally as possible.

"He has been very successful in the City, I believe," Mrs. Maplethorpe pursued. "I wonder that he has never married."

"He is a widower—so Sir Max told my father," Sydney added hastily.

"Ah, poor man. Well, he is out of mourning, so we can be as gay as we like to cheer him up," declared Mrs. Maplethorpe.

Sydney was almost relieved to have the gentlemen rejoin them at this point, and rose at once when Sir Max asked if she would not play for them.

"And I will promise not to sleep while you play," he said teasingly as he led her across the room. "In fact, I shall stand just here and turn your pages for you so that you will be assured I am awake."

"That will be kind," she answered with a demure smile, "and if the other gentlemen snore, you must sing to drown them out."

"Or wake them up"—he laughed—"but that is an idea. Do play something we can sing together, for I would like that of all things."

So they raised their voices together, to the delight of the rest, for their voices were pleasant and blended well. After a time Sydney forgot Morgan's presence and began to enjoy herself.

Then Morgan was on her other side, declaring that he too would sing.

"Of course you must," said Sydney promptly, rising at once, "and Miss Maplethorpe shall play for you. Come, Cassie dear, you must play for Mr. Leighton."

Morgan gave Sydney a reproachful look before turning to Cassie with a welcoming smile. Sydney made her way to a seat beside Mrs. Maplethorpe and sank down with a grateful sigh.

She was not to escape entirely, however, for when the tea tray was brought in, he came to her and asked if she would ride with him the following morning. Seeing a refusal in her eyes, he hastily added, turning to Mrs. Maplethorpe, "and perhaps you would allow your charming daughter to join us, and I feel sure we can count on Sir Max to make up the party." Mrs. Maplethorpe was, of course, only too happy to agree to this arrangement, and it was impossible for Sydney to refuse without spoiling her pleasure and seeming churlish.

She was so silent on the way home that her father finally asked if she was not feeling quite the thing.

"Only tired, Papa," she said truthfully.

"Did you . . . er . . . know Mr. Leighton very well before?" Mr. Armytage inquired delicately.

"Not really well. It was so brief a time," she said, again truthfully.

He digested this in silence for a time before he astonished her by saying, "You would have been seventeen, I believe, an age when young women are susceptible to a handsome face."

"Yes, Papa, you are right . . . and so I was," she replied, suddenly weary of dissembling to her papa, "but he went away very soon and I . . . recovered."

"I am glad of that. Meriel was right: he is too . . . too . . . dainty for a man."

9

Edward's mother had decided the waters of Bath did not agree with her this year, so he had been released from attending her to the Pump Room each morning. She had, however, many friends in Bath and had resolved to remain for another week to enjoy a round of dinners and whist parties. This had freed him from the fear that he would have to leave Bath before he wanted to.

He was devoted to his mother, but she had been, as he often told her, spoiled beyond saving by his father, who had given her her way in everything and spent his every waking moment trying to please her, though he had the reputation of a proud, difficult man. Not so to his wife, who had accepted his adulation and returned it. It had not turned her into an overbearing or overly demanding sort of woman, but she did tend to expect her own way, and that her son would behave to her much as his father had, which, to a great extent, he did. She also expected him to be guided by her in all major decisions, and he was only too aware that she had had her favourite goddaughter in her eye as a bride for him from the moment the girl had been born, when Edward was but four years old. She was an attractive, laughing sort of girl whom he had always been very fond of, but they had been thrown so much together by their fondly scheming mothers that they had become like brother and sister. He had been through several periods of puppy love or infatuation with other young ladies, all of generally short duration, but never at any time had he thought of his mother's goddaughter in a romantic light, nor she him. They had confided their brief loves to one another, and had often laughed together over their mothers' plans for them, both agreeing that it could never be.

He knew, however, that his mother had not given up this pet project, though he had tried to warn her that she was doomed to failure. All of this only meant that he must exert a great deal of care in the handling of her and the new situation.

Having surrendered every fiber of his being to Meriel, he knew there could be no question of his not marrying her. He was as profoundly in love as it was possible for a human being to be, and easily recognized the difference between this feeling and anything he had ever experienced with a woman before. There was no urge to simply gratify his senses or fill a boring time with a small flirtation, the chief motivation for his previous experiences. He longed not simply to possess her, but to care for her, to cherish her, to make her happy in every way. Now he knew how his father had felt, and looked with a different eye upon his mother, who had inspired the same feelings in her husband.

He spent a great deal of time reviewing all the circumstances of their meeting, still marvelling at the unbelievable good fortune that had been his in the arrangements of Fate that had brought it all about. His mother had so nearly postponed her visit to Bath this year, which would have made it impossible for him to attend her, for instance. Then Lady Divers deciding to have Meriel come to her at just this time and no other, and their having arrived at the Pump Room at the same time of day, not to speak of the miracle that she should have even noticed him! Oh, the list was endless, and equally endless were the chances that none of these fortuitous circumstances should have come about. This realization always caused his heart to jump in a spasm of absolute terror at how nearly they came to not meeting at all, and he had to spend a few moments reassuring himself with the litany: but we *did* both come here, we *did* meet, we *are* together, she *does* love me.

Oh yes, he knew that as surely as he knew of his own love for her, though no word of it had yet been exchanged between them. He knew they would speak when the moment was right for it. He could not know, but guessed, that she felt the same as he: a sort of fear at the very depth of his passion that, once released, might carry him beyond his means of controlling it. He had wanted her with a shattering intensity from the moment he had first seen her sitting so quietly and looking so incredibly, impossibly beautiful beside the palm tree in the Pump Room. How had it been possible for Nature to select, so apparently at random, from her heritage such an assemblage of features as to stun the beholder? It was even more amazing that she should be so totally unaware of the sensation she created. She was not a retiring sort of girl, nor in the least shy, but she certainly had none of the airs of a woman who knew the power of her beauty. Then, to top everything, she possessed a quite exceptional talent as an artist, though in this, as in everything, she was modest in acknowledgment of it.

But he knew, and intended to nurture that talent and give himself the joy of watching it grow. He meant to see that she had the best teachers and was exposed to the work of all the great artists, and he meant to make sure that nothing stood in the way of her art. He was seething with plans for her, but nothing could be got under way until he could speak to his mother, and the time was not right for that now. When they were home, and she was recovered from the trip and surrounded by the comfort of her own things and her own servants, he would gently inform her that he had fallen in love and meant to marry quite soon. He did not anticipate any scenes or tantrums, for that was not his mother's way, but he knew she would be deeply upset by this end to her long-cherished dream, and would not hesitate to attempt to dissuade him with any means at hand. She would come, in time, to an understanding of how impossible it would be to try to change his mind, but until then the atmosphere might be slightly strained.

She would, he knew, learn to love Meriel when she had met her, for how could she not? But the introduction of Meriel's presence in their lives now must be made in stages, with tact, to give her time to accept the idea gradually with the least hurt possible.

These were thoughts that hovered only on the periphery of Edward's mind. All that was immediate belonged to Meriel. She filled his every moment to the point of obsession and caused him to become quite absentminded and inattentive when out of her company. His mama had remarked upon it with some asperity on several occasions. He only laughed and teased her back into a good humour, though the words of confession bubbled up the back of his throat in his longing to tell someone of this miracle that had happened to him.

But he could not speak of it yet. He had not even spoken of it to Meriel herself. They had not said any words of love, no vows had been exchanged, he had not even touched her hand yet! Perhaps she did not feel the same. Perhaps he would find that it was only he who loved. . . . He started up in panic. He must go to her, speak, persuade her! But no, he calmed himself, he could not have mistaken the message in her eyes.

The days, however, were passing with frightening rapidity, and there were so few left. Yet each morning was dreamlike, seeming to go on endlessly while they were in it, but over so soon, when they must part. The partings were no cause for despair, though painful, for there was always tomorrow. It was as though the last day would not really ever arrive. They continued to drive, and walk, and stop for Meriel to sketch while he read, and they talked—endlessly.

One morning he asked her, "Have you written anything of . . . of me . . . to your sister?"

"No, not as yet," she admitted guiltily, for she knew she should have done so. But she had not liked to speak of it to

Sydney when he had not yet actually said anything to indicate his feelings. It was possible she had read into the situation more than was actually there. It could be that she had only imagined he felt as she did because she wanted so very much for him to love her as she loved him. She looked up for reassurance and their eyes met for a long moment, and she knew as surely as though he had said the words. It is all there in his eyes, she told herself. I have not imagined it, and he will speak of it when it is right to do so.

"I think," he continued, "if you will not mind it, it would be better to say nothing to anyone as yet. Do you agree?"

Her heart swelled with happiness, for those words confirmed everything. He would not have said them if he did not care for her, and she gladly agreed to what he asked. He must know best what must be done, and in any case it was all too difficult to express in a letter to Sydney. Meriel had never been good at communicating her feelings in writing. It would be better to wait and tell her of the whole thing.

Edward breathed a little sigh of relief, for he knew how quickly rumours could spread. The sister might relay the happy news to a trusted servant, who in turn would confide it to a servant in another household, who would tell her mistress, and that good lady would be happy to have another tidbit to fill out her monthly letter to her bosom bow in London. Thus the news might spread to become an item of common gossip that would greet his mother on her arrival in town. She would be unbearably hurt to learn of it in such a way, and very angry with him for allowing it.

Meriel returned to her godmother that day in a frame of mind that could only be described as bubbling.

"Did you enjoy your drive, my dear?" Lady Divers asked breathily, not yet quite recovered from an overindulgence at lunch.

"Very much, thank you."

"It is very kind of Mr. . . . er . . ." She waved a vague hand.

"Trevillion." Meriel supplied the name, unable to prevent herself from lingering lovingly over the syllables.

"Yes, Trevillion. As I say, very kind of him to be so obliging to you."

"Yes, Godmother."

"I do not believe I know any Trevillions. There are the

Devitt Trevillions, of course, though I am not personally acquainted with them. They could not be connections, I suppose?''

''I do not know, Godmother, he has never mentioned anything about them.''

''Then they cannot be connected or he would have done so. Still, Mabel says that he is a gentleman, so that is all right.'' She subsided, exhausted by this long and unaccustomed effort. Still, she owed it to the child to take an interest, though really it would be just as well when she was safely back at Elmdene Grange. Mabel assured her that there was nothing at all romantic in their attitudes that she could see, but just the same, Lady Divers did not care to take the chance of becoming involved in any complications of a romantical nature. Just before her heavy eyelids closed finally, she murmured, ''You will be returning home Saturday, of course.''

Meriel nearly leapt from her chair. Saturday! And today was Thursday. Tomorrow was their last day, then. Oh, how is it possible? Why have we wasted all these days? Did he realize that there was only tomorrow left?

Edward had not, until his mother had informed him they would leave for London on Saturday and he realized that Meriel would also be going home on that day. He was glad that it was so, for he could not have borne Bath for a single day when she was no longer in it, nor could he have been at all happy to go away and leave her there. In a way, he was glad that this phase was over and he could take his mother home and move on to the next step.

First, however, there was tomorrow, and he must work out some way for them to be alone together, if only for a few moments. He *could* not say what he wanted to say to her while Mabel looked on. He decided at last that there was a chance at Sydney Gardens, where a public breakfast was served every day in good weather.

He drove them there, settled Mabel at a table with a substantial plate of food, and led Meriel away down the path between the shrubberies. In a moment they were around a bend and for the first time out of Mabel's sight, and fortunately alone, for this particular path seemed free of other visitors. They were both very much aware of this and savoured it in silence for a time before they stopped and turned to one another.

He held out his hands and she placed hers into his trustfully, and then it seemed to her that a flash of heat shot up her arms and through her body, causing her to gasp with the pain and the pleasure of it. She closed her eyes and swayed slightly, almost overcome by an excess of emotion so totally beyond her experience or of anything she had ever dreamed as possible.

"Meriel!" His grip tightened almost unbearably on her hands, and then he had released them and was holding her close. She raised her face, eyes closed, and with something like a groan he released her. "No, no, little one, I must not—"

"Yes, you must," she whispered dreamily.

Then she was back in his arms and his lips were touching hers lightly, and then again, and once more, before they became, finally, demanding. Meriel felt her body melting into him, and for a few moments this was all she wanted. But then the pulses hammering seemingly throughout her body wanted more, and she pressed herself even closer.

Gasping, he pulled himself away and held her by the arms away from himself. Her knees were so weak that without his support she would have fallen.

"Meriel, I love you, I love you so much! You must know that," he said, his voice shaking. "You do feel the same?"

"Oh, Edward"—she smiled tremulously—"what a foolish question."

"Please tell me just the same, so that I will have the memory of the words to sustain me after today."

"I love you, Edward, my darling, with all my heart."

After that they could no more have prevented another embrace than they could have willfully stopped breathing. Their lips met again without waiting for permission, and again they were swept by a gust of passion that threatened to flame out of control, but then they heard voices. They stepped hastily apart just as two nursemaids with several young children appeared around the curve of the path. One little boy was chasing a hoop, which made its wobbly way, with the boy pursuing it, directly between them. The nursemaid scolded the boy, there was a confused babble of childish voices, and then they were gone again from sight.

Edward smiled. "This is not the ideal spot for it, but I . . . think . . . if I do not touch you, I may safely ask you to marry me without causing a scandal here. Will you, Meriel?"

"Yes . . . oh, yes!" she cried, tears glittering in her eyes.

"Thank you, darling, darling girl. I will take very good care of you always, Meriel, I promise you."

"Only love me always, that will be all the care I shall need," she said fervently. "Oh, Edward, I shall miss you most dreadfully!"

"It will not be too long, darling. I will be as quick as possible. I just need to take my mother back to London, and when she is settled down I will tell her about us. It will be best not to speak of it to anyone until I have the chance to tell her first. You understand, my love?" She nodded. "I should not be longer than a fortnight, perhaps less. Then I will come to Elmdene and speak to your father. Will he forgive me, do you think, for not having waited for his permission to address you?"

"Of course he will. Papa is not in the least a stickler for all that stuffy nonsense. You will like him enormously, and Sydney too, and they will *love* you," she cried, her hands reaching out to him, her eyes soft with her love and her need to touch him again.

He took her hands. "Meriel, beautiful girl, please do not tempt me, for I cannot answer for myself if I take you into my arms again. Dear God, how I love you! I must take you back now, for I cannot bear to be alone with you and not embrace you."

"Yes," she said simply, understanding only too well how he felt. They turned and walked back to Mabel.

10

On the morning after Sir Max's dinner party, Sydney was just mounting when the rest of the party came cantering down the drive, Cassie in a fetching new habit of bright green merino, glowing in her shy way at being part of what seemed to her a very grown-up and sophisticated riding party. Sydney felt drab in her worn and comfortable old brown habit and decided she would have a new one at once. In blue, she thought, and then was surprised at herself for this sudden interest in dress, for as a rule such thoughts were for Meriel and what would best become her.

After an exchange of greetings and civilities, the four rode off and for a time were able to ride abreast, and conversation remained general. When they left the road for a path through the trees, however, the way narrowed. Morgan held back just long enough for Max to be forced to ride forward. Cassie, beside him, followed, and Sydney was perforce tête-à-tête with Morgan.

She kept her eyes straight ahead, but was aware of his head turning to her again and again. When she would not respond to his looks he said, "This is something I have dreamed of for so long, I find it difficult to believe it is real."

"Indeed? Did you not ride in London?" she retorted lightly to counteract the freighted emotion in his voice.

"Yes, of course, but not in this way," he replied significantly.

"Ah, I understand. Nothing quite equals a ride in the country, especially on a fine spring morning."

"You are being deliberately obtuse. Oh, Sydney, my dear—"

"No, Mr. Leighton, I am neither of those things," she interrupted him briskly.

"I don't understand you."

"Now who is being obtuse? I think you understand me very well. I am neither Sydney nor your dear," she replied calmly.

"I beg your pardon. It slipped out, I fear, because that is the way I always think of you in my mind. Of course, I will not call you so publicly if you do not wish it."

"Thank you. I do not wish it," she said simply.

They rode for a time in silence before he said in a low, hurt voice, "You have not forgiven me."

She laughed. "Oh dear, *how* mean-spirited you must think me!"

"I know I am right. You have not."

"I have, you know, many, many years ago, Mr. Leighton. Now, shall we discuss something else?"

"Please allow me to speak. You need not respond, so it will not be a discussion."

"I would prefer you to say nothing more."

"I must," he replied. "I have tried for years to think what I might say to you if I were ever given the opportunity. To somehow justify my actions, more necessary to me, I suppose, than to you, since you seem to have been so little affected by it." There was something accusatory in his tone, and he waited a moment for her to deny it. When she did not, he continued, "I was very young, you see, and thrown into a situation that completely bewildered me, and I knew no one in London. My . . . my . . . ignorance about the business I had inherited was total, and I was . . . afraid. My . . . wife's father was a close friend of my uncle's. He took me in, treated me like his own son . . . told me how to run things. I don't know what I should have done without him. I. . . ."

Sydney was more moved by his confession than she had thought she could be, and hastened to say, "Please, say no more, Mr. Leighton. Truly, you need not. I understand perfectly and I promise you I bear you no ill will. Let us put all that behind us and go forward as from today."

"Friends?" He held out his hand to her.

After only an instant's hesitation she extended her own, and he clasped it, pressing it warmly before releasing it. He immediately launched into an amusing description of his activities in London, and Sydney gradually relaxed. Possibly his visit will not be so difficult after all, she thought, now that he really understands my feelings.

Morgan was well satisfied with himself, content that he had said just enough and the right thing. Not that he had not meant all he had said. He *had* been through all those things, so it was not difficult to project his sincerity. However, his motives for forcing her to listen to his "confession" had not been simply to justify his actions all those years ago. He had been all too aware of Sydney's coolness towards him, and this was not an attitude he could tolerate in anyone around him. He required that everyone look upon him with favour, and if he had done anything to bring about anyone's disapprobation, he could not rest until he had charmed his way back into that person's good graces. It was not a thing he thought about consciously and planned, but something so mechanical by now that he was no longer even aware that he did it. He was, however, conscious enough of the effectiveness of his charm to be very wary in his dealings with women, being always careful never to go so far he could not retreat.

The only truly impulsive thing he had ever done was to suggest elopement to Sydney ten years ago. Looking back at the event in the past years, he would marvel at himself, for had she agreed, he would surely have failed in London. There was no getting away from the fact that he could not have succeeded so well without Mr. Gotobed's goodwill and fatherly advice, nor from the fact that these had been extended to him as a bribe to marry Mr. Gotobed's plain, spinsterish daughter, who was as eager to marry as her father was to get her off his hands. Mr. Gotobed had hinted very strongly at what he expected from Morgan, and after a sleepless night of weighing the matter and finding that he had little choice, Morgan had proposed at once. From then on his success had been assured, for Mr. Gotobed knew the business very well and was a good teacher. If marital happiness eluded Morgan, he had not regretted it, for it was not something he had expected. As the eleventh child of an extremely impecunious vicar, he had grown up with more pressing needs, and marrying for love was so far down the list as to be nonexistent. His brief romance with Sydney had been as close a call as he cared to make, and in spite of his amazed self-approval at his own generosity in making so quixotic an offer to her, the thought of what might have happened had she accepted could still bring a cold sweat to his brow.

In the years that had passed since, he had never once thought of her with regret. She had been only an episode in his life, and he had not, in truth, been truly in love with her as she had been with him, though he had liked her better than anyone else in his life at the time and was not at all blind to all her good qualities, though he had realized as soon as he reached London and faced his problems there that she could not have been a help to him.

He had been delighted with Sir Max's invitation to come to Upper Chyppen for a visit, since he had few true friends, and none who had ever invited him to stay in their homes. He had set forth at once, though not with any romantic idea of recapturing the past. He had no wish for that, but it would be interesting to see Sydney again, and meet new people. It had not occurred to him that his arrival might be unwelcome to Sydney, for he was incapable of entering into another's feelings.

Her indifference had set into unconscious operation his need to feel her approval. It was apparent that she had long ago recovered from whatever hurt she had experienced in their relationship and he had rather looked forward to finding her exhibiting more signs of being affected by this meeting than she had. He felt that she was beginning to relent; she was actually looking at him now and laughing at his stories. Then he found that Sir Max and Miss Maplethorpe had turned back and were waiting for them to catch up.

Sir Max had decided that he had been as courteous to his houseguest as it was necessary to be. He had noticed Morgan's maneuvering to be alone with Miss Armytage and had good-naturedly acquiesced to it. After all, he supposed they would want to discuss their previous acquaintance and catch up on events since. He felt, however, that now it was his turn to enjoy Miss Maplethorpe's company. He had nothing against Miss Maplethorpe, but he had never particularly enjoyed the company of young girls, and Miss Maplethorpe was quite boringly shy. He could excuse her for it, but he didn't see why he must have more than his share of her company. It was Leighton, after all, who had invited her, so now he must take on his fair share of entertaining her.

When the lagging pair came up with them, Max did an adroit bit of maneuvering himself and presently he was riding beside Sydney, with Miss Maplethorpe and Leighton going on ahead. He glanced at Sydney, unable to hide his grin of triumph, and she laughed at him, wonderfully cheered.

"You did not mind changing partners?"

"Not in the least," she replied, with, it seemed to him, a note of relief in her voice.

"I expect you had a great deal of reminiscing to do," he hinted gently.

"Not really. Our . . . acquaintance . . . was brief, you see." Her cheeks flushed slightly at this equivocation.

Max noted it and wondered if there had been more to it than she was indicating. He hoped not, for he should not like to think he might be responsible for causing her pain by impulsively inviting Leighton here. Nor was he anxious to promote any resurrection of feeling between her and his guest, since though he quite liked the fellow, he knew Leighton had a habit of flirting with every woman he came into contact with. Being in closely related businesses in London had

thrown them together at many social affairs and so Max had
formed his opinion of him as less than serious as far as
women were concerned. Max did not condemn him for his
attitude, for he supposed with a wife as unpleasant as Mrs.
Leighton had been, the fellow deserved to find some relief
from her as best he might. He knew nothing worse of him
than this. He had never heard of him turning a girl's head so
far as to cause unpleasantness, and if he kept a mistress it was
so discreetly that word of it had never leaked out to become
common gossip. Max was not, just the same, keen on the
idea of Sydney possibly succumbing to the attentions of a
man who, Max was convinced, was only out to amuse himself.

While he did not approve of Morgan's ways, Max was
grateful to him for his suggestion about investigating the
possibilities of settling in Upper Chyppen, for he was becoming convinced as the days passed that his entire life was to be
affected by the move, and the reason for it did not lie in the
beauty of Lades Hall or the neighbourhood. His conviction
was centered around Sydney Armytage, but why this should
be so, he was at a loss to explain. After years of avoiding
entanglements with some of the most beautiful girls in London Society, it was a mystery to him that his interest had
been so caught by Sydney.

He was aware that she was neither beautiful, in the usual
meaning of the word, nor elegant, nor even young, but
nevertheless he found her compelling. He enjoyed watching
her smile, revealing her pretty teeth, and he liked the way her
lovely grey eyes lit up. He found refreshment and a sort of
peace in being with a woman who was neither shy, nor
flirtatious, nor manipulative. He had not got so far in his
feelings as to think about whether he was falling in love with
her, nor had he contemplated making any serious attempt to
attach her. For now, it was enough just to be in her company
with no plans to distract him from his enjoyment of it.

"He is . . . er . . . a charming fellow," Max offered, and
at once changed the subject. "You must miss your sister,
Miss Armytage."

"Oh yes, but I have *Emma* to keep me company, so it is
not so dreadful. Meriel will be back in two weeks," she
added, thinking to reassure him.

"Emma?" he queried, ignoring the solace she was offering.

"Miss Austen's *Emma*. We had only just started it before

Meriel left, but I could not bear to wait for her to come back before finishing it, so Papa and I are continuing. In fact, I can hardly wait to finish so I can start it all over.''

"Why, so do I—do that, I mean. Though not with *Emma*."

"Because you gave it to us before you could do so. You must have it back."

"No, no. Do not even think of such a thing. I have ordered another copy for myself. Perhaps we can read it aloud together."

"Oh yes, I would enjoy that, but I must confess I am not good at reading Miss Austen aloud. You see, I get into such whoops I cannot speak for minutes at a time, and Papa and Meriel get very cross with me, so they do the reading aloud."

They continued comparing their favourite funny scenes from Miss Austen's work, oblivious of all around them until they were interrupted by a fluting "Helloooo," and looked up startled to find the other couple beside an open carriage driven by Arabella Cole. All three were eyeing Max and Sydney curiously.

Max recovered first. "Why . . . it is Miss Cole, is it not?"

Arabella trilled out a gay little laugh. "What a tease you are, Sir Max," she chided archly, refusing to allow anyone to see her displeasure at the question in his greeting. "Now, what were you two plotting?"

"Good morning, Miss Cole," Sydney answered. "We were discussing *Emma*. Are you familiar with her?"

"Good morning, Miss Armytage," Arabella replied frostily. "I know no one named Emma. Is she from the neighbourhood?"

Cassie, who had heard all about *Emma* from Meriel, began to giggle. "Oh, Miss Cole . . . how very amusing . . . oh . . . oh . . ."

Arabella turned to eye her coldly. "Naturally, I am pleased to afford you entertainment, Miss Maplethorpe. Perhaps you will not mind sharing the jest with all of us."

"I beg your pardon, Miss Cole," Sydney intervened hastily, "the fault is mine. I should have explained that *Emma* is a novel. Do be quiet, Cassie! You are no doubt familiar with the work of Miss Austen, Miss Cole?"

"I do not read *novels*," Arabella replied blightingly.

Max interposed in an effort to spread balm upon a rapidly

deteriorating situation, "Where are you bound for so early, Miss Cole?"

She turned to him with her most fetching smile. "Why, for Lades Hall, sir, to deliver this." She produced a folded note closed with an impressive red wax seal and offered it to him. "You are so rarely at home, I could not hope to deliver my invitation personally"—she made a reproachful little moue with her mouth—"but since we are so luckily met, I will tell you also. Just a small dinner to introduce you and Mr. Leighton to some of my friends." She smiled sweetly upon Morgan, ignoring the women. Inside she was seething with fury. She had heard of Morgan Leighton's presence in Upper Chyppen only yesterday and had wasted no time in driving out early this morning to deliver her invitation and meet him, only to find him riding along with Cassie Maplethorpe, in a party with Sydney Armytage! How did that whey-faced stick manage it?

Max was somewhat discomposed by her discourtesy in not including the ladies in her invitation, in such an obvious way. He turned to glance at Sydney to find her eyes brimming with laughter. Feeling driven into a corner, he said, "Well . . . ah . . . thank you, Miss Cole, though I am not sure we—"

"Day after tomorrow, then, Sir Max. I shall expect you both. Naturally, if it is not possible, I will be happy to change the day."

"Oh"—Max cast a harried look at Morgan—"then . . . thank you very much."

"Bid you good day, then," Arabella caroled triumphantly, and with another blinding smile shared impartially between the gentlemen, she drove off with a jaunty flourish of her whip.

The four riders stared after her for a moment in silence before Max said, "What a very odd thing to do. Is it customary in Upper Chyppen to deliver invitations to a selected few in the presence of those not to be invited?"

"Certainly not," Sydney said firmly.

"Only Arabella does so," added Cassie.

"Now, now, Cassie, she does not always—"

"No, only if one is in her black book," Cassie amended irrepressibly.

To end a discussion she felt not quite proper, Sydney turned her horse away, and before Max could move, Morgan quickly moved up beside her as she trotted away. Sydney cast a quick glance back at Sir Max, trying to convey her regret that they could not continue their discussion, but he was not looking in her direction and so missed it.

When they were out of earshot Morgan said, "I knew if I were patient I would manage to capture you again. It is deuced difficult to have private conversation with you."

"Good heavens, Mr. Leighton, I had supposed we had said all we needed to say in private."

"I have not said half of what I want to say to you, I have not, for instance, told you how beautiful you are looking."

"Considering my years," she said lightly.

"Because of them," he said earnestly.

"Now, Mr. Leighton, you are bamming me for sure!" She laughed.

"Not in the least. You should know I would not do so with you, Sydney. You were a pretty girl—now you are a beautiful woman."

She turned, startled by the ardour of his voice, but only replied, "You are not to call me so, Mr. Leighton. You said you would not if I did not wish it."

"No, and of course I will not if anyone is near. But I cannot help always thinking of you as my dear little Sydney, though I know I have no right after . . . after . . ." He faltered, his voice hoarse with emotion.

Involuntarily she reached out to touch his arm. "Don't! You must not. You cannot truly mean . . ." She caught herself and withdrew her hand. "I thought we were agreed to forget the past."

"I will try. No doubt for you it has been easy to forget, but my life has been so . . . No, I must not speak of it. But remembering you, your sweetness, your softness, has sometimes been all I had pleasant to think upon." He spoke softly, humbly, deliberately looking away from her as he did so, as though to hide his feelings.

Sydney felt confused. She was too feminine not to be flattered by his words, too kindhearted not to pity him, but too sensible to believe him entirely. She watched him for a moment, but he did not meet her eyes. She could think of nothing at all to say, and so they rode on in silence.

Behind them, Cassie chattered on happily, while Max watched the couple ahead. He saw Leighton leaning towards

Sydney, speaking earnestly, saw her hand touch his sleeve, imagined all sorts of dialogues to occasion such actions, each progressively more romantic, until he became convinced there had definitely been more to their previous acquaintance than she had been willing to admit. It was not difficult for Max to imagine that Leighton, for all his libertine ways, found the same peace and pleasure in Sydney's company that he himself did; nor to believe Leighton found the older Sydney even more enchanting than the young girl he had known, possibly to the point of desiring to recapture his lost opportunity. Max had no trouble at all picturing his success, either, should he try, for he had seen the man attach and marry Miss Gotobed, that acidulous and thorny spinster who seemed to despise all men, within three months of his arrival in London.

It was equally easy for Max to see Sydney succumbing again to Leighton's good looks and charm, not to speak of the addition of his wealth. Not that he could imagine her being caught by wealth alone, but no woman was ever insulted by the fact that a handsome suitor was also the possessor of a fortune. It was also possible that, having been in love with him as a young girl, she might still be so. After all, she had never married.

Uneasiness deepened into a positive gloom as a result of all this imagining, and the day lost its sparkle and promise for him. Cassie, having received no response to her last three laboured commentaries on Nature, cast an embarrassed sidelong glance at him. His brows had contracted into a scowl, and his mouth was a tight, grim line. Convinced she had said something to displease him, she subsided into a crushed silence, wishing desperately that she could learn to think before she spoke, as Mama was always advising her to do, and that a change of partners could be arranged so that she could again exchange lighthearted badinage with the handsome Mr. Leighton, who gave one such charming compliments and made one feel so sophisticated and worldly.

11

Though Arabella had lived in Upper Chyppen all her life, as had her family for generations, she could not claim any close friendship amongst the inhabitants. Her disagreeable nature had manifested itself in early childhood and alienated all with whom she would have been likely to develop intimacy. Nevertheless, as a member of long standing in Upper Chyppen gentry, she was guaranteed entrée into local society, and her own dinner invitations were always eagerly accepted, for she entertained with good food, elegantly served by a well-disciplined if sullen-looking staff of servants, her drawing rooms were warmed by generous fires and were draught-free, and, Arabella apart, one was sure to meet one's friends there.

Then too, there was the gleeful relish with which one could launch into a recounting of the evening afterwards to one's friends who had not been there. The menu alone could consume anything up to three-quarters of an hour, after which one could savour Arabella's latest costume and her often wickedly malicious commentary of absent friends who had displeased her in some way. After which, if there were time enough, there were the tasty tidbits about Claiborne's clumsy attempts to agree with everything his sister said while treading on her pretensions in his amazingly stupid way. Oh, indeed, Arabella's parties were eagerly awaited.

For the dinner to introduce Max and Morgan, Arabella had spent an entire hour on choosing who should be honoured with her invitations. For weight and solidity she decided on Squire and Mrs. Dobbs, which meant she must also include Ursula Moppe, a purse-mouthed old-maid cousin of Mrs. Dobbs's who had lived with them for years. Then the two Misses Bidlake, unmarried sisters in their sixties whose family reached impeccably back to the Doomsday Book. With herself, this made five women and, naturally, Arabella could not be blamed for ensuring that she alone would be the belle of her own party by surrounding herself with women too old or too plain to count as competition. The men would be, besides the squire, Sir Max, Mr. Leighton, Claiborne of course, and Tristan Foxx, the only person of her acquaintance with whom she never dared cross swords, his tongue being as sharp-edged as her own and whose devastating wit she did not care to hear turned against herself. He enjoyed carving up reputations as much as she did herself, and besides could be counted upon to give hours to the discussion of gowns, bonnets, and appropriate accessories with more enthusiasm than any woman Arabella knew.

He could also be counted upon to flirt with her in company if required, though she was well aware it was done to be obliging and he expected to be obliged in return. This debt she repaid by allowing him to try on her gowns and bonnets in privacy and never revealing his strange aberration by speaking of it to anyone, not even Claiborne. She did this, not from any feeling of loyalty, but from fear of what he might reveal about her if he learned of her revelations. Among other things, he was privy to the true story of her come-out in London, for he had been witness to it all.

Far from becoming the newest "rage," being taken up by everyone, and attending several parties every day while juggling a whole circle of ardent admirers, she had elicited no interest at all in London. No morning callers clamoured to be admitted to Lady Boxton's drawing room to court her niece; only Tristan came, and he did not count, since she had known him all her life. The only invitations that arrived were to boring dinner parties and musical evenings given by cronies of Lady Boxton. Her only admirer was a dotard in his eighties, titled and of good family, but hardly a penny with which to bless himself. He thought Arabella a great heiress, and when he learned that her portion was only five thousand pounds and the rest belonged to her brother who was still young enough to marry and breed, he had lost all interest and stopped calling.

Arabella was so desperate by the time two weeks had passed and he had not reappeared, she so forgot herself as to twit him publicly when she encountered him in the Park one morning while out driving with Lady Boxton and Tristan. The old gentleman had peered about in a hunted sort of way at various acquaintances within earshot, turned a mottled and dangerous-looking purple while gobbling something about having been laid up with the gout, and promised to call. The next day he took himself off to his crumbling family seat in Dorset and was not seen again in London that Season.

Arabella's humiliation was complete. She was aware of the amused sidelong glances of those who had witnessed the event, and later of those who had been told of it. Hostesses began to acknowledge her with cold little bows in the street and eligible gentlemen to look the other way when she appeared. Lady Boxton scolded and nagged, and at last, before the Season was quite over, washed her hands of all further responsibility and sent her niece back to Upper Chyppen with the advice to look about her for some inexperienced country gentleman looking to marry up.

Tristan had returned to Upper Chyppen at the end of the Season and tactfully never referred to her experiences in London, and they began their unspoken arrangement to live and let live as far as they each were concerned. He would naturally be miffed at not being included in her dinner party, so there was no question of leaving him out. Besides, he would be sure to compliment her extravagantly before the others.

On the evening of the party, she waited for her guests with Claiborne in her drawing room, feeling assured that for once things were going the way she wanted them. She was splendidly gowned in ice-blue satin lavishly trimmed in Brussels lace, the minuscule bodice displaying as much of her full bosom as she dared, and on it her mother's sapphire necklace winked with her every breath in a way that Tristan declared, when he came tripping in before the others, to be "too absolutely riveting, my dear!"

"Perhaps it calls too much attention," she replied with a coquettish toss of her head.

"But is not that the whole purpose, foolish one?" he cried gaily.

"Claiborne says I am too young to wear such a gown," she persisted, unwisely pushing Tristan rather farther than he was willing to go.

"Too *young?*" One plucked eyebrow rose derisively. Arabella flushed. "Dear Claiborne, so droll. Do you know, Arabella, my pet," Tristan continued without lowering his voice in the least, "Claiborne sometimes has that vacuous look of a creature who has not yet discovered the function of his thumbs."

Arabella giggled sycophantishly, while Claiborne looked up blankly at hearing his name, clearly puzzling out the import of Tristan's words.

"Now, my dearest, tell me *all* about these strangers we are to meet. I must admit I am *agog!*"

"Well, Sir Max, as I have told you before, has taken Lades Hall and has apparently more money than he knows what to do with. Mr. Leighton owns ships or something and is Sir Max's houseguest."

"Oh, not *that!* Are they handsome? Are you . . . ah . . . interested in attaching them? Are *they* interested? Do they dress well?"

"You mustn't tease about my beaux," she said coyly. "As for handsome—yes, they both are that, and they seem well enough dressed to me."

Tristan, whose opinion of Arabella's taste was not high, decided he must wait and judge for himself. He looked down at his own dark wine-coloured coat with great satisfaction. The high, rolled lapels swelled out over the padded chest; the waist pinched in tightly, held in by stays. It opened over a mauve brocade waistcoat made to his own design by his resigned tailor, who had long since despaired of influencing him. He was a very Tulip of the Ton, a Bond Street Lounger, and the large pearl buttons on his coat and the twinkling paste buckles on his evening slippers had given him hours of pleasure in the choosing. He was slight of figure, his face thin and sharp, with just a touch of rouge on the cheeks to enhance the brilliant blue of his eyes, which he considered his best feature.

"And which of these creatures has taken your fancy, my treasure?" he asked, pursuing the charade as he knew she wanted.

"Ah, so difficult to decide. You shall help me to choose!"

"Both bewitched already, I make no doubt," he twitted obligingly.

"Here," Claiborne said suddenly, "what you said about thumbs. I don't care for that. No. I don't care for it at all. I am not so stupid as you apparently think."

"No, of course not. How could you be?" Tristan cooed innocently.

The entrance of the Bidlake sisters interrupted them before Claiborne had time to work out the implications of this rejoinder. They were twins, as alike as it was possible for two humans to be. Tiny, round, white-haired ladies who dressed, as they always had, identically, and always in girlish pastels. Tonight they were in pink, and they twittered and fluttered their fans, looking incongruously arch at Tristan's gallantries, before perching side by side on a sofa next to the fire, like two fat birds on a branch.

Max and Morgan were announced, and after being greeted with almost overpowering flirtatiousness by their hostess, were introduced to the Misses Bidlake and set them chirping agitatedly. They were entirely devoted to one another and had never entertained the smallest inclination to marry and part, but they were nevertheless still delighted to meet good-looking gentlemen, and, so long as they were within touching distance of one another, as capable as any women of enjoying compliments.

When the Dobbses came in accompanied by their sour-faced cousin and Arabella announced that now everyone had arrived, Morgan flicked a glance of half-amused consternation at Max, whose lips twitched in response to the message, for it certainly seemed that Miss Cole had gone out of her way to assemble an odd set of friends to meet them. He looked away to find himself pinned by the interested gaze of Mr. Foxx, who had obviously witnessed the exchange of glances and from the intelligence apparent in the bright blue eyes, had interpreted it correctly.

Tristan had indeed. Silly Arabella, he thought, thinking to become a bird of paradise by surrounding herself with wrens. *So* obvious, and more likely to bore the two gentlemen to death than anything else. In his own opinion they were both a bit above Arabella's touch, but stranger things had happened, and it was possible she might succeed in snagging herself a husband if she could be persuaded to set about it the right way. No raving beauty, poor thing, and just a shade too . . . too . . . fleshy, he thought with distaste, though of course there were men who liked that. Ah well, it should be good fun to watch her at work, and good luck to her.

Arabella sat between her two guests of honour at the dinner

table, and for a time bestowed her charms equally between them, keeping up a flow of talk filled with teasing innuendo which Max responded to as civilly as possible and which Morgan returned in kind. Midway through dinner Arabella found herself turning more and more to Morgan, leaving Max to Mrs. Dobbs, on his other side. Though she had more or less decided that she would have Sir Max, as being the more prestigious catch, she found herself unable to resist the charm of Morgan Leighton.

Forced at last to leave the gentlemen to their wine, she led the ladies back to the drawing room, where she spent a half-hour swallowing her yawns of boredom until the gentlemen joined them. Then she quickly organized a game of whist for the Dobbses and the Bidlake twins, settled Claiborne down beside Miss Moppe with orders to show her his book of pressed flowers, and seated herself across the room in the center of a sofa, intending to hold court with the three swains left free.

Morgan and Tristan obediently sat down on either side of her when Max strolled to the fireplace and stood absently staring down into the flames.

"Well, you adorable creature," Tristan began brightly, "you have surpassed yourself again. *How* I should love to lure your cook away. I never dine so well at home."

"I am sure you could if you could only learn how to instruct your servants properly," Arabella returned.

"Ah, but there it *is*, don't you see. One needs a woman to know how to handle servants. If *only* I could persuade you"—he sighed dramatically—"but I warn you, glorious one, I shall never relent. I hope, Mr. Leighton, I do not bore you with my hopeless aspirations."

"Not at all, Mr. Foxx. Any man can be forgiven for wanting a good cook."

"Oh, you naughty *thing!*" shrieked Tristan. "How you *can* tease me so, when you see I die of love for our fair one. Everyone knows of it and laughs at me for daring to look so far beyond my wildest expectations." He gave Arabella his most languishing look and picked up her hand to press it to his lips.

She rapped his wrist sharply with her fan and giggled. "Behave yourself, sir. You know well I have expressly forbidden you to speak of this to me again."

"Heartless creature. How can you treat me so? Women are so much crueler than men, do not you think, Mr. Leighton?"

"Only the beautiful ones, Mr. Foxx," Morgan responded gallantly, much amused at this little comedy being played out for his and Sir Max's benefit. He saw Max flick a contemptuous glance at Tristan before wandering away to inspect a book of prints.

Arabella signalled Tristan with her eyes to take himself off, and he leapt to his feet with alacrity and hurried across the room. "Ah, Sir Max, would you care to smoke a cigarillo with me on the terrace?" This plan seemed to meet with Max's approval, and the two strolled out the French windows.

Arabella turned to Morgan. "I hope you are not regretting that you cannot join them?" she teased.

"How can you ask?"

"Ah, I know gentlemen like to smoke those nasty things. But as you are so gallant, I must think of how I may hold your interest."

"Anything of yours would interest me, fair lady," he said significantly.

She began to tingle with anticipation. Here was a man who knew how to conduct a flirtation! "Perhaps you would care to see the conservatory? Do you care for flowers, Mr. Leighton?"

"When they are a setting for even rarer blooms, I bless them," he said caressingly.

She rose at once and led him out of the room, blind to the interested gaze of Mrs. Dobbs, who, to the detriment of her play of the hand, had witnessed the little drama. She was most disappointed to see them leave the room, depriving her of the next act.

Ordinarily, Morgan would have been too wary to go away from the rest of the party with an unchaperoned, unmarried woman, but here he felt no uneasiness. Miss Cole was apparently a woman of experience who knew the rules of the game as well as he, and was clearly as interested in some unobserved dalliance as he was himself. He found her an attractive woman, though he had to admit there was something a trifle cold in the pale blue eyes. Still, there was no denying a certain ripeness of figure that exerted its fascination.

When they arrived behind the screening fronds of a monstrously overgrown potted fern, she halted and turned to face him. She plucked the tip of a frond and ran it teasingly over his lips. "What are your favourite flowers, Mr. Leighton?"

"Blooming ones," he answered with a significant look at her bare bosom.

She pretended not to understand. "You seem interested in my necklace, sir. Do you like sapphires?"

"Perfect jewels," he replied, not raising his eyes.

She gasped, shocked and pleased at the same time. "Mr. Leighton!"

"Ah, forgive me, fairest, I must not let your . . . jewels . . . blind me to your other charms," he drawled, smiling into her eyes. "Say you forgive me," he coaxed.

She cast down her eyes with a little pout of her lips. "Well, I suppose I must not be rude to a guest, though you are very bold, sir."

"Not so bold as I should like to be, enchantress," he declared, picking up her hand and kissing each finger separately before turning it over to kiss the inside of her wrist, brushing his lips lightly over the skin there, causing her to shudder deliciously.

"Oh, sir, you will go too far," she breathed hopefully.

He pulled her roughly into his arms and they kissed hungrily, struggling frantically against one another for a long moment before she pushed him away and backed off, panting. "You forget yourself, sir."

"I could not help myself. You are irresistible! Say you do not hate me." He knew this game very well. Go so far, she protests, he apologizes, she forgives, and so on, each teasing to rouse the other. He didn't mind. He quite liked playing these games.

"I will . . . try . . . to forget what has happened," she said now, "if you promise to behave in future."

"I will behave just as you like," he promised with a meaningful look.

Well satisfied with one another, they turned and strolled back to the drawing room, where Mrs. Dobbs took note of Arabella's bright eyes and flushed cheeks and knew very well what to make of it.

So did Max, who had returned to the room in time to witness their reentrance. On the way home he said, "That was, perhaps, not very wise, Leighton."

"What, my little excursion with the eager Miss Cole?" Morgan laughed smugly.

"Too eager by half, I would say."

"Yes, a very warm-blooded lady," Morgan replied.

Max glanced at him sharply. "And clever with it, so I should watch my step if I were you."

"Good Lord! I hadn't thought! Am I treading on your toes?"

"Good God *no!*" Max exclaimed explosively.

"Oh, well, that's all right, then. Missing your chance, though. Quite a little armful, that one, and up to anything, I'd say, if you play her game."

Max made a moue of distaste. "I doubt she is playing games. She is out for a husband if I read her right."

"Oh, all women have that look in their eye until they have bagged someone. You just have to make your position very clear at the outset so they know you're not up for that."

"Not all women," Max replied firmly, and turned away pointedly to stare into the darkness outside the carriage window, unwilling to discuss the matter further. He was more than ever convinced that Morgan Leighton was a libertine and wished with all his heart he had never asked him to come here. What on earth was he to do if it transpired that *she* was still in love with this coxscomb, and Leighton decided that he wanted her?

12

Sydney sat on the dock with her fishing pole, feet dangling over the side, watching the bait on the end of her line just below the surface of the water. The sun baked down on her shoulders and through the straw of her bonnet, but it felt comforting and she was at peace with the world. Lulled by the warmth and morning quiet, her mind had slowed down to lazy, floating images, not even thoughts. It was almost like sleeping, though she was not really dreaming. Fishing was only an excuse to be able to sit here like this, alone, mind at rest, renewing itself. She never used these times to sort out thoughts or feelings, nor to solve problems. She was suddenly startled "awake" by the sound of footsteps coming down the dock toward her, and looked up to see Morgan.

"Well, well, what an unusual activity for a delicately bred young woman," he teased.

"Good morning, Mr. Leighton. How did you find me here?" she replied calmly, trying not to let her annoyance show. She did not care to have these sessions interrupted by callers, nor was she dressed to receive them. She was very much aware of the condition of her old, faded cotton gown.

"I was told by the maid that you were here, so I just found my way. May I sit with you?"

"You will spoil those fine clothes."

"Nonsense, there is no dirt at all." He lowered himself beside her. She continued to stare into the water. Sensing that she did not entirely welcome his presence, he sat quietly, only remarking, "Ah, the sun feels good."

But for Sydney the peace of the morning was gone. There was no way she could forget his presence and slip back into her semi-doze. She abandoned the attempt and, by way of making polite conversation, asked, "Did you meet some interesting people last night?"

He shrugged slightly. "The squire and his lady, a repressed-looking cousin of theirs, the Misses Bidlake, and a rather exotic creature named Tristan Foxx."

"Oh, yes, all acquaintances of mine."

"A strange assortment to want to introduce as friends," he said dourly.

She giggled, for she could picture the whole assemblage, and imagine her own dismay at having to spend an evening with them. What on earth could Arabella Cole have in mind by inviting such a boring group of people? Mrs. Dobbs was nice and could be entertaining, but her husband and cousin were both dull, while the twins were silly, and she personally loathed Tristan Foxx, with his affected manner and vitriolic tongue.

"At least if you had been there we should have something attractive to look upon," he continued.

"That is a very pretty compliment. However, I believe

Miss Cole is accounted an attractive woman, so your case cannot have been so desperate.''

"Hmm," he said, uninterested in the topic. The truth was, he could not think of Arabella now, could not even picture her. She was in a separate part of his life and would be kept there, as all the women with whom he flirted were carefully compartmented in his thoughts. This enabled him to give the one he was with his entire concentration, to exert the maximum charm to attain whatever ends he had in mind. "I believe you have a nibble."

"What?" Startled, she looked down at her line to find it bobbling gently. She swung it up quickly, and a flash of twisting silver arced through the sunlight and landed on the boards beside her. She unhooked the barb and dropped the fish in a pail of water, rebaited the hook expertly, and dropped it back into the water.

"Good Lord, how professionally you do that," he exclaimed admiringly.

"Well, so I should. I have been doing it for many years now."

"It seems an incongruous talent for a beautiful woman."

"Pooh, there is nothing to it. Would you like to try for a while?" She held out the pole.

"No, no. I would only show myself as completely inept after your demonstration. Besides, you make such a pretty picture, I prefer just to watch."

She decided to ignore these continual compliments, having decided they came too easily to his tongue to be true compliments in any case. She wondered if he was even aware he was making them anymore. She concentrated on her pole.

"It is very good to sit here like this with you, Sydney, so completely at peace," he said sometime later in a soft, dreamy voice.

She should reprove him, she knew, for breaking his word that he would not address her so familiarly, but it seemed unnecessarily contentious and foolish to insist here and now, so she said nothing.

"I have been thinking that perhaps I should look around for a country home for myself," he continued.

"Perhaps near your own family. They were country people, were they not?"

"Yes, but they are all gone from there now. My parents

dead, my brothers and sisters scattered. I do not believe any of them are there anymore. Besides, it is too far north. I never cared for that part of the country, in any case."

"You say you do not believe they are there. Do you not correspond with them?"

"One of my sisters writes occasionally—when she is in need of money," he added bitterly. "We were never a close family."

She was shocked by such a revelation. She could not imagine caring so little for one's own kin. How lonely it must be for him, and how wretched to have a sister who wrote only to ask for money. Then too, to lose one's wife, and to be childless. Her heart softened with pity for him, but she could not think of any way to express it without platitudes. No wonder he had accepted Sir Max's invitation so quickly, and expressed such warm feelings about his memories of Upper Chyppen. He must have been happy here for a time.

"I . . . I am sorry your life has been so . . . difficult," she said impulsively.

"Thank you. How good you are," he said, and reached to take her free hand and clasp it in both his own. She tried to pull it away, but he held it firmly. "Please, Sydney, do not refuse to allow me only to hold your hand for a moment. I would not wish to displease you, but surely it is no dreadful thing to hold your hand in a friendly way. We are friends, are we not?" He smiled, cocking his head to one side to look quizzically into her eyes.

She felt ridiculous, like a jumpy, nervous old maid who imagines every man is ready to attack her honour. She ceased tugging her hand and looked away in embarrassment. Again they sat in silence for a time, until he raised her hand to his lips and kissed her fingers lightly. At this she snatched her hand away, and flinging her pole onto the dock, swung her feet up to one side and rose swiftly. Before he could move, she picked up her pole and stepped to the other side of the dock, lifted the painter that anchored the rowboat, and stepped down into it. By the time he had scrambled to his feet, she had pushed the boat away from the dock. She sat down and began rowing away.

"Here! Where are you going?"

"Fishing, Mr. Leighton."

"Will you not take a passenger?"

"No. Passengers always want to talk, and that disturbs the fish. Good day, Mr. Leighton."

"I shall come again tomorrow morning," he called, but she pretended not to hear and did not answer. He turned away after a moment, his head bent as though in dejection, but he was grinning to himself. She had to run away, he thought triumphantly, because she could not trust herself! She is still fighting, but I have won just the same. I knew she still cared for me. Tried to pretend at first, almost had me fooled there for a bit, but now I see it was just pride.

Out of her sight now, he lifted his head and began to whistle cheerfully. Now, what shall I do with the rest of the day? The eager Arabella? No, better to let her fret for a time at my not coming around at once. Make her more . . . eager. His grin stretched wider.

Sydney kept rowing until she reached the far bank, but then turned away. No, she thought, someone else might come to disturb me. When she reached the very middle of the pond, she shipped the oars and lifted her pole into position. For a time she sat trying to recapture her earlier mood, but it would not come back. Too many thoughts now chased themselves inside her head.

Morgan. Was it really possible he had returned for her sake? Had he hoped, when he heard she was still unmarried, to renew his old status with her? No. Surely he could not believe she had loved him all this time. Then again, why should he not think so? It was not so unusual a thing, according to all the romantic novels of the day, but in real life . . .?

It was even less likely that his own heart had retained any feelings for her as he tried to intimate to her. After all, he had married, and surely there must have been love there at the beginning, in spite of his vague hints otherwise. The business of how desperately he had needed the help of his father-in-law. But it was not possible to marry simply for that! No, she would not believe it. The marriage may not have turned out to be a happy one, but there must surely have been love at the beginning.

Of course, he had been a widower for a year now, and if love had died out of the marriage sometime before that, it was possible he had begun, in his unhappiness, to look back upon their youthful idyll as a lost dream, one that it might be possible to recapture. Perhaps time had given that whole episode a more romantic aura than it had actually had. It had not done so for her, but she had not had unhappiness in her life to compare it to and to set it off. She did not think of herself as cynical to feel this way, but she was too level-headed not to understand that for her it had been only a green girl's first infatuation, only the lightest brush with romance, otherwise the wound of his rejection could not have healed so completely without a scar.

She remembered the way she had felt the first time he had ever held her hand. She had slipped out to meet him in the orchard after Meriel was alseep and Papa shut into his library with his *History*. The moon had been a narrow melon slice and the apple trees shedding the last of their blossoms so that they stood on a carpet of petals. One had fluttered down as she stood shyly before him, and she had reached out her hand so that it fell softly into her palm. He had caught her hand and held it, crushing the petal there. She remembered the heat from his hand moving up her arm to invade her entire body, and that her knees had begun to tremble with weakness.

Today when he had held her hand she had felt none of that; only embarrassment at being thought a prickly spinster, and a hearty wish that he would be done. When he had kissed her fingers she had had to flee because she was aware of the falseness of her position and could not endure it. She had only been feeling sorry for him and embarrassed for herself, while he must have taken her softening as something more. And he? What had he been feeling?

Here she was back full circle. And still she did not have the least inkling. She could not accept that he had loved her all these years, nor could she believe that one look at her had roused his feelings enough to cause him to make a push to engage her affections again. Why should he wish to do any such thing, when with his present affluence, youthful good looks, and charming address he would surely have no difficulty attaching any eligible young woman of good family?

Of course, her thoughts veered, Meriel was right in a way, though I didn't see it then. He is too pretty, it seems to me now. Perhaps those delicate features were more suitable for the boy than they now are for the man. Naturally, he cannot be held accountable for his physical appearance, and no doubt it is my tastes that have changed. Other women will not necessarily feel the same.

Oh, that is neither here nor there. The main thing is to decide: what are his intentions? If his are serious, what are mine? I know perfectly well that I do not love him, but that will not happen for me now surely, after so many years. Maybe it would be wise to consider the whole question without any fanciful romantic notions. I will hardly be likely to marry at all, so would it be foolish of me to refuse him a second time? Would it not be possible to marry without love?

No! She stood up suddenly and turned as though to run from such a horrible idea, setting the boat to rocking wildly. Before she could think to sit down, she was suddenly tipped over too far to catch herself and was tumbling into the water. She came up gasping and choking, clutching the side of the boat to cough up the pond water she had swallowed. When she had caught her breath she pushed her sodden hair out of her face and looked around, wondering how she was to manage to get back into the boat. Then she began to giggle, then to laugh, and the more she laughed, the funnier her situation became, until she was hanging helplessly to the boat, weak with laughter.

What an idiot she was, to be sure! On the shelf quite happily all these years, and then falling out of a boat in agitation at the thought of marriage without love—when she had not even received a proposal!

Max slept late, and when he came down to the dining room was relieved to learn his guest had breakfasted early, ordered the mare to be saddled, and taken himself off. No doubt in hot pursuit of la belle Cole, Max thought sourly. Well, let him. At least it served to divert his considerable charm from Sydney Armytage.

His spirits much improved by this thought, he ordered his matched greys to be put to his new Crane-Neck phaeton, delivered only last week from Thrupp and Maberly, and sat down to a large beefsteak for his breakfast.

He set off in high fettle, his mood matched by the greys, which fairly pranced along, tossing their heads with exuberance at the cool, scented freshness of the morning. The phaeton seemed admirable, heavier than the High-Perch phaeton, but more stable for that. Without any conscious decision on his part, he found himself on the road to Elmdene Grange and thought it would be a very good thing to stop and invite Miss Armytage to come for a drive with him.

He pulled up before the door with something more of a flourish than was his wont, for though an excellent whip, he was never flashy, eschewing all the outward symbols of the Top Sawyer, such as Belcher kerchiefs for neckcloths, crown-sized mother-of-pearl buttons on his coat, or the overlarge bouquet of flowers in his buttonhole. His inquiry brought the disappointing news that "Miss do be out fishing this morning, sir, to the pond."

"Ah, I see. Well, I will just leave my card." He climbed back onto his high-seated carriage and drove away in some disappointment. Then he began to smile. At least she was not sitting in the drawing room, wearing her best gown, awaiting morning callers, as any other woman would be doing with two such obvious admirers as himself and Leighton likely to call. She had wanted to fish, so be damned to admirers! He liked that—very much.

Cheered by these reflections, he decided to drive to Roxton and visit the lawyer who handled Lades Hall for its present owners. It would not hurt to sound him out about the possibility of purchasing the property.

He was encouraged by the barely concealed excitement with which the man greeted his query. It was apparent the owners would welcome an offer to take the property off their hands. Max clattered, whistling, down the narrow dark stairway and emerged to find himself face to face with Arabella Cole.

"Why, Sir Max! What a surprise to find you in Roxton. What brings you here?"

"Good morning, Miss Cole," he said, tipping his hat politely, "I came on business. And you?"

"Oh, Claiborne wanted to look at a mare he heard of for sale. He fancies himself as a good judge of horseflesh, though he is invariably disappointed in his choices, I fear. I came along to buy a new bonnet. Do you like it?" She preened, turning her head from side to side.

"Very fine," he replied, eyeing dubiously the concoction of Milan straw, bright cheery silk ribbands, and a riot of red roses and white plumes.

She bridled with pleasure, and felt she was indeed as fine

as fivepence in her white muslin walking dress and red velvet spencer, and was glad she had taken such pains this morning. She had come with Claiborne in the hopes that Morgan Leighton would come calling and find her out. It would do him good to kick his heels, after the advantage he had taken of her last night, she thought virtuously, ignoring the little shivers of excitement set off by the thought. So she had forced Claiborne to wait while she changed, and now see how she had been rewarded!

"Is this enchanting carriage yours, sir?"

"Yes, it is," he admitted somewhat reluctantly, for he had an intuition about what was coming.

"I made sure it was. I was absolutely riveted when I saw it, which is how you find me here. How I should *love* to come for a drive in it!"

"Well, one day we must . . ." He faltered, his mind refusing to come up with a plausible way out of this trap.

"Why, how kind! But . . . for goodness' sake, how silly of me! There is no reason—I hope you will not think me too forward—but really there is no reason why we should not drive back to Upper Chyppen together if you have concluded your business here."

Here was his chance to avoid the trap if he wanted to take it, but he could not bring himself to utter such a bare-faced lie. "But . . . but . . . your brother . . ." He faltered weakly.

"Oh"—she laughed gaily—"Claiborne can do very well without me. See, there is our landau over there. I will just step across and tell the boy holding the horses to inform Claiborne I have gone back with you."

Without waiting for his response to this, she tripped across the road and was back in a moment, waiting to be assisted into the high seat. Masking his resignation with a courteous smile, he helped her up and climbed up beside her and they set off. She opened a much-beruffled white parasol and held it over her head, looking about with shrill, nervous little cries at the height, and much laughing and chatter to call as much attention to herself as possible. They passed Claiborne and she halloed gaily and waved her parasol and then giggled at his gaping astonishment.

She calmed down somewhat as they passed out of town, but then began a most annoying series of coyly posed personal questions, starting with, "Is it possible you were seeing the lawyer with the aim of extending your lease on Lades Hall, Sir Max?''

"Ah . . . no, Miss Cole."

"Perhaps you have decided to buy. Oh, *that* would be wonderful. Have you? Do tell me."

She continued to enthuse for a time over the excellence of this plan, saving him the trouble of having to give her an answer. "Can it be you are entertaining thoughts of settling down at last?" she asked, resuming her interrogation.

"I fear I have always been a staid, settled sort of man, Miss Cole," he temporized.

"Ah, do not try to bamboozle me, Sir Max. I know all about young gentlemen and their wild oats from my experience with my brother. It is my belief that you have tired of cards and cockfights and . . . ah . . . the Muslin Company—is that naughty of me? . . . I learned it from Claiborne, you see— and now you have a mind to marry and set up your nursery."

"Heavens, how dissipated you must think me," was his noncommittal reply.

"Oh, I do not condemn you! I must admit I prefer a man to have lived, even wickedly, than to be just namby-pamby, and I am sure I have not misjudged you," she said meaningfully.

"I fear I must disappoint you, Miss Cole. I have been far too busy to be wicked, you see."

"Oh, do tell me everything about your interesting work, Sir Max," she begged enthusiastically, changing her tactics at once.

"That would take longer than we have at our disposal, Miss Cole. You see, we are nearly home."

"Oh, so soon? How quickly the time has passed, has it not? Will you not allow me to take the ribbands? I am a great whipster, I assure you, and I long to try."

"I am sorry to disoblige you, Miss Cole, but I never allow anyone to drive my greys but myself," he replied firmly.

She pouted, and looked severely ahead to show him her displeasure, but then suddenly she trilled a gay laugh, throwing back her head and twirling her parasol. He glanced around at her, startled by this sudden change, and then saw Sydney Armytage on a donkey just emerging from the gates of Elmdene Grange. He pulled up abruptly, cursing his bad luck silently, and tipped his hat. "Good morning, Miss Armytage."

"Good morning, Sir Max. What a splendid pair of greys," she replied admiringly. "Good morning, Miss Cole."

"Good morning. Is it not the most heavenly day. So perfect for driving, and so kind of Sir Max to invite me. Heavens, Miss Armytage, what a quaint mount."

Sydney felt ludicrous suddenly, like an ant being noticed by an elephant, and wished fervently that she had not taken it into her head to ride into Upper Chyppen to post her letter to Meriel. She would have preferred, also, not to have known about it if Sir Max decided to take Arabella Cole for a drive. Why on earth must he come parading her along the road before Elmdene? she thought with sudden, irrational anger.

"Yes, donkeys are quaint, are they not?" she replied with a semblance of serenity. "Well, Sir Max, you must not keep your horses standing about, so I will bid you both good day." She managed her best smile, which, however, did not quite reach her eyes, turned her mount around, and trotted off down the drive.

Max called out a farewell, which was not acknowledged, and grimly he flicked the reins and set off down the road to town as quickly as possible, wondering why he must be so plagued with bad fortune.

13

After two days of fretting, Max determined that come what might, he would ride to Elmdene Grange and attempt to tell Miss Armytage the true state of affairs regarding their unfortunate meeting. He had been in her company at two dinner parties since the day he had had the misfortune to meet her while driving Miss Cole, since every lady in Upper Chyppen with the least pretensions as a hostess had concocted an occasion to entertain Sir Max and his guest, and invitations were flooding in. These meetings had not, however, provided private moments with her to explain himself. Not that she

seemed to require one. Had she been the least bit cold or stiff
with him, he would have been better pleased somehow, but
she persisted in maintaining her usual open friendliness, meeting his eyes with a level grey gaze that showed no sort of
perturbation at all. He felt, nevertheless, that he must set the
situation to rights. He longed to tell her straight out the
circumstances of his drive with Miss Cole, but that would
sound ungentlemanly. He felt sure, however, that he could
think of a way to do it if he could only speak to her alone. It
was perfectly possible, of course, that Miss Armytage was
indifferent to him and would not care if he drove Miss Cole
out every day.

Since Leighton had not come down as yet, Max had a
hurried breakfast and set off on horseback to Elmdene. His
knock was answered by the maid, but behind her was Miss
Armytage just coming down the stairs. She smiled when she
saw him, though she did not increase her leisurely pace
with any display of eagerness.

"Sir Max, good morning," she said calmly. "Will you not
come in?"

"I hope it is not inconvenient that I have come so early?"

"Not if you will join Papa and me for breakfast."

"Oh Lord! I *have* come too early. But I hoped to get you
to ride with me this morning and I feared you might make
other plans if I left it too late."

"Then you have come in good time. My plan was to go for
a long walk after breakfast, but I would much prefer a ride."

She turned away as she spoke and led the way back to the
dining room, where Mr. Armytage sat in a flood of sunlight
pouring through the open windows, eating buttered eggs and
reading his mail. He wiped his fingers and rose to welcome Sir Max, urging him to sit down and telling Sydney to
have some breakfast brought for their guest at once.

"No, no, sir," Max protested. "I thank you, but I have
had my breakfast. I will just sit with you, if I may. Miss
Armytage has agreed to come riding with me."

Sydney's toast and chocolate were served to her and she
ate quietly while the gentlemen discussed the progress being
made on Sir Max's pond. When she finished she excused
herself and hurried upstairs to change into her old brown
habit, wishing the new one she had ordered were finished.
Dissatisfied with her appearance, she removed a set of blue

and white plumes from a bonnet and pinned them to the side of her riding hat so that they curled down to caress her cheek in what seemed to her a most dashing way. Too dashing for plain Sydney Armytage? She hesitated, then tossed her head defiantly and ran downstairs before she could change her mind.

They cantered along together, neither seeming to have much to say, but it was not an uncomfortable silence. Presently she said, "Will you mind a gallop?"

"Not in the least," he answered.

At once she turned her mount aside and flew away down a long sloping meadow. In a few strides he had caught her up and they galloped side by side to the bottom and straight on up a rise. At the top they stopped and sat smiling happily at one another.

"Lovely to gallop," she said breathlessly, "and look!" She waved her hand.

Before them the land seemed to stretch endlessly, checkered with brown squares of plowed land and green squares of new crops or pastures, broken here and there by single trees or small copses, all rounded with new leaf. There were still scraps of early-morning ground haze to lend the whole the unreal quality of a painting.

"There is a lovely mossy rock where I always sit when I come here—over there by that tree."

They dismounted and tied their mounts to the tree and sat down on the rock in the sun.

"I hope you will not mind if this becomes my favourite ride also from now on."

"Oh, no. You must come just whenever you like. Meriel loves this spot, too, and always comes here. She has painted the view several times, but is never satisfied with her work."

"Why not?"

"She says as a view it is perfect, but as a painting it is banal."

He laughed. "Possibly she is right, for it does seem to have an overly familiar look about it. I have probably seen similar scenes in paintings many times."

"Oh, Meriel is very clever, though she gives the impression of being off in a dream most of the time. Most people don't take the time to look beyond her beauty."

He changed the subject. "I am glad I caught you before you went fishing," he teased.

"Oh . . . I found your card when I came back. I was sorry to have been out when you called."

"I . . . I had come to show off my new phaeton, you see, and hoped to persuade you to come out for a drive with me."

"I am sorry to have missed the opportunity," she said evenly.

"It was a great disappointment to me. Would you have been frightened?"

"Good heavens, I hope I am not so cow-hearted as to be frightened of that!"

"Will you drive with me tomorrow? Say you will!" He turned to her urgently.

She was a little surprised by this, but comforted, which caused her to wonder why it should be so. Perhaps she had not been best pleased to find him driving with Arabella, but surely she was not so small-minded that she had been harbouring resentment against him? Now it all seemed foolish. She could not know, of course, and he would not tell her, how it had come about, but knowing Arabella Cole, it was not difficult to believe that it was she who had brought it about in some way.

"I should like that above all things," she said with pleasure. "I have always longed to ride in a High-Perch, but there is no one around here who owns one."

So it was that on the following morning, and for several mornings after, she found herself driving about the roads in Sir Max's Crane-Neck Phaeton. At one point on the second day he had suggested she might like to take the ribbands herself for a time. Not aware that this was an honour he would never have offered to any other person while his prized greys were in harness, she agreed that she would love to try her hand. She had, indeed, been itching to do so, though she would never have thought of asking him.

The greys were dreams and gave her not the least trouble, and by the third day she could feather a corner so neatly he was moved to tell her he could not do it better himself, causing her to blush hotly with pleasure.

They had at this point reached the turnoff before entering the main thoroughfare of Upper Chyppen, and before she could slow for the turn as they usually did, he motioned her to go ahead, and in a moment they were bowling along between the shops, attracting a great deal of amazed attention.

None could have been greater than Arabella's as she emerged from a shop where she had just purchased a delicious pair of lilac kid gloves. Her pleasure in them vanished slowly as she stood rooted before the store for quite three minutes, her mind unable to accept what her eyes had just seen.

Yes, it was unquestionably Sir Max, his matched greys and his new phaeton, and it was just as surely Sydney Armytage sitting beside him. But was it possible that *she* had been driving? Try as she might, the picture was too indelibly etched on Arabella's eyeballs to allow any denial. Sydney had had the reins in one hand and the whip in the other, which meant she had been driving Sir Max's precious greys, which he had so rudely refused to allow Arabella to do. As the horrible truth sank into her mind, Arabella felt such a spurt of blind rage that she seemed to see the familiar street before her through a mist of red.

She had been right all along. Sydney Armytage was setting her cap for Sir Max, she fumed silently as she stalked angrily home. How did she *dare* make herself such a figure of fun? An aging spinster ogling the catch of the neighbourhood like a miss just out of the schoolroom. And how had she managed to persuade him to allow her to drive his pair? She stopped to think about this, her hand on her own gate.

"Lost your bearings, Bella? Ha-ha!" roared Claiborne, coming up behind her. "Did you see Westbrook's rig? Slap up to the echo, eh? Prime cattle, too. Real goers. Wonder if he would care to sell 'em?"

"Be quiet, Claiborne," she hissed, nearly choking with rage.

"Make him an offer he can't refuse, eh?" Claiborne continued imperviously. "Drives to an inch, that Armytage gel. The makings of a real Top Sawyer there. Next thing you know, they'll invite her to join the Four Horse Club, ha-ha!"

"If you say one more word, you pea-brained paper-skull, I shall strike you!" Arabella managed to grind out through clenched teeth before she jerked open the gate, marched through, and clanged it shut in his face with all the force at her disposal.

Her temper had not improved when Morgan arrived for a morning call, and she slapped his face when he tried to slip an arm about her waist. He rose at once, gave her a curt bow, and took his leave. He also had witnessed Sydney driving down the street with Westbrook this morning, and while the sight had not overjoyed him, he was not unduly perturbed. She was driving very well, which meant she had been practicing. So that was where she had been the past three mornings when he had called and found her out. He had interpreted this as a sign that she was still afraid to trust herself with him and had been pleased. Now he saw it as betrayal. How could she go out when she knew he would be calling? He had distinctly told her he would do so. He felt definitely annoyed, and remembering Arabella's little scene further exacerbated his feelings. He rarely experienced such emotions for the simple reason that he rarely cared enough, nor had he ever had much trouble before in ordering events to go just as he had decided they should where women were concerned.

Then he shrugged it all away. These were minor problems. La Cole would soon come around if he gave her time enough alone to reflect. As for Sydney, he could overcome this skittishness. She was only using Westbrook, but if she thought to avoid Morgan Leighton, he would just arrange it so that she could not. Little minx, he thought with a smile. Or, no, not that, for she is never sly. A little bird, he thought, a shy little bird who will soon be eating from my hand.

He mounted and rode towards Elmdene. She would have to return there eventually, and when she did, she would find him waiting!

Unaware of the agitation their appearance had aroused, Sydney and Max made their way by various lanes and side roads back to Elmdene. At the door she handed the reins back to him with a sigh of pleasure. "*How* I enjoyed that. I cannot thank you enough, Sir Max, for allowing me to drive. Meriel will be so pleased by my new accomplishment."

He leapt down and came around to help her to the ground. As he did so, Morgan came lounging out of the open front door. "Well, there you are at last, Miss Armytage," he drawled pleasantly, nodding to Max. "Having missed you these past three mornings, I decided I must improve my timing, and you see how right I was."

"Oh . . . well . . . good morning, Mr. Leighton. We have . . . ah . . . been for a drive."

"A perfect day for it," he replied agreeably. "Nice carriage, Westbrook, and bang-up cattle, I must say."

"Glad you approve," Max answered dryly. "Well, Miss Armytage, thank you for the pleasure of your company. I hope you will honour me again tomorrow morning."

"I should be pleased to do so, and I thank you for today."

He bent briefly over the hand she extended, nodded to Leighton, and swung himself back up into his phaeton. A moment later he had disappeared down the drive.

"Fishing palled, did it, Sydney?" Morgan quizzed.

She ignored this, and wished she had thought to invite Sir Max to stay for some refreshment. Well, face up to it, she thought with resignation, and said, "Will you come in, Mr. Leighton?"

He followed her into the drawing room and watched as she removed her bonnet and gloves and ordered some wine to be brought. "The last time we met I said I would call again the next morning, but you were not here. That was unkind, Sydney."

"I am sorry if it seemed so, but I do not remember that I heard you say any such thing," she said untruthfully.

He moved close to her and bent his head near her face. "I think you are playing with me, Sydney," he murmured confidentially.

She moved away. "Please have a seat, Mr. Leighton. Ah, here is Lizzy with your wine. Will you have a biscuit?"

He was amused by her coolness, sure it was only a screen to hide her feelings. This was just her little game with him, and he was perfectly content to play it as she wanted, as he had done with Arabella. All women had their ways, each delightfully different. He enjoyed obliging them, and was always sure to have his way in the end.

Not that he had any positive end in view as far as Sydney was concerned, his only object being to bring her to heel. When he had caused those grey eyes to soften with emotion when she looked at him, he would have accomplished his entire aim.

14

When Max called for her the following morning, Sydney seemed so much more subdued that he became uneasy. Not that she was ever silly or giddy, but she was always in smiling good humour, quick to see the fun in everything. He could not help connecting this mood to Morgan's visit to her the day before. Max had not liked it in the least to drive away and leave her in Leighton's company, but since she extended no invitation to him to come in, he could do little about the situation.

Max had been more than a little disturbed to find Leighton waiting there, so much at home, so easy in his manner, so familiar, as though, Max could not help feeling, there had been much more in their former friendship than had so far been acknowledged. It also seemed that Leighton was more serious in his pursuit of Miss Armytage than Max had realized, and for all he knew, she welcomed his renewed attentions. Max knew for a fact that Leighton was also carrying on a flirtation, or perhaps something more, with Miss Cole, for the man did not hesitate to keep Max abreast of his progress in that direction, oblivious of the fact that his host did not encourage his revelations. Max was a man of the world enough to have been party to such confidences before, and had always treated them with a sort of man-to-man indulgence. They had all been, however, confidences regarding a friend's latest affair with an opera dancer or light o' love. No gentleman of his acquaintance had ever spoken of a lady in such a way. Of course, it was debatable that, if what Leighton said were true, Arabella Cole could truly be considered in that category, for surely her behaviour went far beyond what was well-bred. Still, she was Quality, and had to be treated as a lady, and only a coxscomb would speak of her as Leighton did. It was possible he was exaggerating the facts in a boastful way, but in either case it was despicable and created a dilemma for Max.

The man was a guest in his home, for one thing, and while there, must be extended every courtesy. Again, there was the unwritten code of honour that made it impossible for a gentleman to betray the confidence of a friend, and this was the very crux of the problem that troubled Max. For if, as it seemed possible, Leighton's efforts to attach Miss Armytage, if that were indeed his aim, should prove successful, what was Max to do? She would have received and accepted a proposal by that time, and Max shuddered at the thought of going to her and telling her that the man she intended to marry was a man without honour, a philanderer. He himself would appear to be a common sneaksby and gossip, and cause her pain and heartache while accomplishing nothing, for if she had gone so far as to accept Leighton, she would be bound to believe wholly in him and defend him against calumny. On the other hand, to warn her now before things could reach such a pass seemed equally impossible, even if he could think of a way to phrase such revelations, much less muster up the courage to do so. Perhaps he was only being spineless in the face of such a distasteful duty, or it might be only that his dislike of Leighton was based on his own interest in Miss Armytage.

He sighed heavily, and Sydney turned. "Such a weary sigh, Sir Max. I hope you are not exhausted by all the Upper Chyppen festivities in your honour?"

"No, no, certainly not. To tell you the truth, I have been worrying about why you seem so pensive this morning," he responded. "I hope nothing is troubling you, but if there is, I hope you will look upon me as a friend if there is anything I can do. Sometimes sharing a problem halves it, they say."

"Do they?" she said musingly, and then was silent for so long he feared he had offended her.

"I hope you will not think me unpardonably intrusive?"

"No, of course not, but it is difficult to begin," she reassured him, and then was again silent.

Since she seemed inclined to confide, he took courage for her sake and forced himself to ask, "Is it . . . something to do with Leighton?"

Her eyes flew to his, wide open with astonishment, and for one horrible moment he thought he had ruined everything that might have been. But, surprisingly, she said, "Why, how on earth could you have guessed that?"

"I . . . er . . . really cannot say for sure," he said cravenly. "But if it is so, I feel in some way responsible, having brought him here. I had thought to give you and Meriel the pleasure of renewing an old friendship, and now it seems I have only been the source of worrying you in some way."

"Yes . . . well, I suppose it has worked out that way, though I do not hold you in any way responsible. It is really nothing to do with you."

"I beg your pardon. I have been inexcusably rude to refer to it at all. I assure you I did not mean to be probing into your private affairs," he said stiffly.

"Oh dear, I did not mean it that way," she cried contritely. "I only meant the problem had not been caused by you."

"There is a problem, then?"

"Yes, and it began many years ago. You see, when I told you I had known him only briefly as Meriel's tutor, I was not saying all of it. I . . . we . . . had a very brief . . . well, I suppose I must confess it was a romance. Then he had to go to London to take over his uncle's business and the whole affair trickled away to nothing within three months. I had not heard from him or of him since, until the day you mentioned him to us. Now he is back and it is . . . unsettling. That is all there is to the matter, really. A small thing, I assure you." She turned to him with an apologetic little smile, her grey eyes cloudy now with trouble.

He felt his heart turn over and knew all in a moment that this woman meant more to him than anything else in his life. He longed to sweep her into his arms and tell her so. Demand that she forget Leighton and the past. He was held back by that word "unsettling," which could mean any number of things, possibly that she was indeed falling in love with the scoundrel again or, worse, had loved him all this time. He wondered if Miss Armytage was aware that the fellow had married Miss Gotobed not three months after his arrival in London? It was clear that Leighton had not been as deeply involved in their "romance" as had been Miss Armytage. Max had a sudden vivid image of his own fist smashing viciously into Leighton's straight, delicate nose with satisfyingly bloody results.

What he did was to reach out to cover her clasped hands

where they rested on her knees, for a brief moment. Long
enough, he hoped, to express his understanding and sympathy.
She flashed him a grateful smile and after a moment said,
"You were right, Sir Max, the problem is lighter already,
just for being able to be honest. I dislike equivocation with
my friends. Now, let us talk of something more cheerful. The
Assembly will be held on Monday. Will you go?"

"Will you?" he countered.

"Oh, of course. Meriel will be back and would not dream
of missing it. She arrives this afternoon."

"Then I will go. Will you stand up with me for at least two
dances?"

"With the greatest pleasure, sir. Which will you have?"

"The first and the waltz," he said decidedly.

She laughed, secretly gratified, though she knew it would
have been much better had he danced those with Meriel. "If
you are sure, very well."

"And will you have supper with me also?"

"I will, but I fear I shall become very unpopular with the
ladies of Upper Chyppen."

"How so?"

"They will feel I am having more than my share of your
company. You see, we are so small a society here, and it is
rare for us to have two gentlemen to entertain, and there is an
unwritten agreement that in such cases we must all be equitable.
The rule is less strict when the guest is female."

"Well, since there are two of us, let Leighton satisfy them.
He enjoys it."

She eyed him curiously, for there had been more than a
hint of bitterness in those last words. He was aware of her
scrutiny, but did not meet her eyes. He wished he had not
spoken in that way. It would not be helpful to her in her
trouble to be snide at Leighton's expense. If he was going to
speak, it should be openly and not coloured by his own
feelings. He could not, however, divulge the information he
had. He bit his lip in vexation. To divert her he suggested
that she drive.

"And I will teach you how to swing the end of your whip
back and catch it in the same hand. It is all the crack now,
and anyone with the least pretensions as a whip must be able
to do it." She accepted eagerly.

By the time they reached Upper Chyppen she had become

quite expert and was executing the trick with a gay little
laugh as they passed Morgan driving Arabella Cole's landau with
her beside him. Arabella flashed a blinding smile, while
Morgan tipped his hat ironically. Sydney and Max acknowledged the greetings and then they were past. They did not see
the scowl directed at them by Arabella over her shoulder.

Mrs. Maplethorpe and Mrs. Dobbs, standing before the
greengrocer's, did so, however. "Our Miss Cole is not best
pleased at the turn of events," observed Mrs. Maplethorpe.

"No. So I noticed. Sir Max is the better catch, so no doubt
she would prefer to trade places."

"Oh, do you think so? I wonder. Mr. Leighton calls upon
her very often, and is not turned away. I just happened to be
passing, you see, and observed it," Mrs. Maplethorpe hastened to add.

"And Sir Max? Does he call also?"

"Not that I have seen."

"That will be it, then. She wants to claim both as admirers—
you know how she always likes to hold court as the reigning
belle. However, *I* have seen Sir Max driving towards Elmdene
several times, and this is the second time I have seen him
with Miss Armytage driving through the town."

"Do you tell me? Miss Armytage! That will certainly put
someone's nose out of joint!"

"Well, it is all most interesting. I do not remember when I
have been more entertained!"

Morgan was also entertained. He was amused to observe
Arabella's crossness when she saw Westbrook driving Sydney again. He knew she was much put out by Westbrook's
indifference and he suspected she might be entertaining some
hopes of becoming Lady Westbrook. Good luck to her, he
thought, though he would not have wagered any money on
her chances. Meanwhile he was perfectly willing to add a
little excitement to her life so long as she understood there
was no hope of her becoming Mrs. Leighton. He did not
mind driving about with her if she wished to show the town
that she had an admirer, but he would make no other commit-
ment beyond that.

As for Sydney, a little of the treatment he gave to Arabella
might be effective. He had only to stay away a day or two
and Sydney would become all complaisance with him. He

knew, in spite of the way she held him at arm's length, she was already in the way of thinking of him as an admirer, and if he should miss a day calling on her, she would feel mistreated. Women were very possessive, bless 'em. Yes, he would just stay away—say, not see her again before the Assembly Ball Monday night—and he would vouch for it she would be watching the door eagerly, fearful he would not ask her to stand up with him.

Cheerfully he whipped up the horses, drove out of town until he was well past Elmdene Grange, where he pulled into a secluded copse of trees and kissed Arabella bruisingly for a time. He knew the rougher his embraces the better she liked it.

Meriel, seated beside the poker-faced Mabel in Lady Divers' carriage, happened to pass just at that moment on her way from Bath to Elmdene, and through an opening in the branches caught the briefest glimpse of two figures in an open carriage in passionate embrace. She saw only the man's back clasped by two feminine arms, and over his shoulder, a bronze leghorn straw bonnet with large yellow cabbage roses quivering agitatedly. Who on earth could that be? she wondered. Then she forgot it and sank back into her reverie. Would he write? It would be heavenly to have a letter from him, but he might not think it proper to write without her papa's permission. He would come, he had said, and he would, she knew. She must just be patient and not fret.

They turned in at the gates and her heart leapt with joy at the sight of her home, and there was dearest Sydney running out the door . . . and darling Papa smiling benignly behind her. Meriel tumbled out of the carriage almost before it came to a full stop and flung herself into Sydney's arms to embrace her enthusiastically, talking and laughing excitedly in a way so unlike her usual self Sydney was moved to exclaim, "Goodness, child, are you feverish?"

Meriel released her to fling herself upon her papa with equal fervour. He kissed her and patted her back, very well pleased. "Well, well, dear girl, you have missed us, eh?"

Eventually they went inside, and Sydney sent Mabel back to the ministrations of Lizzy and the carriage to the stables. Then she went upstairs with Meriel to help unpack and hear all about Bath and Lady Divers.

"I suppose she is enjoying her usual state of health," she said, shaking out a gown and hanging it away.

"Yes, very much the same as always. But I went to the Pump Room every day with Mabel and read or sketched during the afternoons."

"Lord, how can you bear it, darling? I would be quite distracted by boredom. Why, what is this?" She turned from the open case, shaking out from its folds of tissue paper a froth of white spangled gauze.

"Oh, is not it the loveliest thing? It is a ball gown given to me by my godmother. And see, Syd, there is one for you also. Is she not kind?"

Sydney stared in astonishment too great for speech. Lady Divers had given Meriel presents many times, but this was her first gift to Sydney. The gown was of peach-bloom silk, with gold cord edging the low, round neckline and the short sleeves, puffed in the French fashion. The tiny bodice was bound at the very high waist with a gold cord rope ending in tassels that reached nearly to the hem. The long straight skirt ended in four Vandyked flounces bound also in gold cord. It was the most elegant gown Sydney had ever owned.

Meriel insisted she must try it on at once. It was found to be the least bit loose, and Lutie was called to take note of the necessary alterations. Then Meriel's gown was inspected and accessories discussed.

"Well, I cannot imagine what prompted Lady Divers to such generosity, but I am certainly grateful, and promise not to think of her as a hypochondriac ever again," Sydney vowed fervently. "Just the same, it is too bad of her never to make the least push to entertain you, or arrange for you to meet interesting people. Why, if you had had the opportunity to wear that gown to an Assembly in Bath, you might have caught a duke!"

"But I do not want a duke," Meriel laughed, blushing.

"How can you know if you never meet one? I suppose there was the usual collection of old dodderers at the Pump Room?"

Meriel hesitated. Not only was she bursting to confide in someone, she most desperately longed to tell Sydney, for there had never been any secrets between them, and this was the most important thing that had ever happened to Meriel. To withhold this news made her feel guiltily deceitful. Dear

Sydney, who was like a mother as well as a beloved sister, who was always so understanding and wise, and who would be so happy to share this joy. Oh Lord, Edward could not have known what he was asking when he made her promise to say nothing. She should have explained about Sydney to him. He would surely have understood and agreed that Meriel must tell her own sister. Still, she had promised to say nothing to anyone, and she could not go back on her word, especially to darling Edward, who trusted her.

She could not, however, bring herself to be entirely untruthful to Sydney, so she equivocated by saying, "For the most part, though there was one younger man there for several days."

"Good heavens, do you tell me so?" Sydney laughed. "Was he alone?"

"Yes . . . well, no . . . with his mother, actually."

"Oh. Well, it must have been a relief to see a face without wrinkles." Sydney was not impressed. She knew the type of young man who accompanied his mother to watering places. He would be either delicate himself, suffering a myriad of mysterious ailments all carefully nurtured by Mama to keep him dependent and out of the clutches of preying females, or an overly stout young man devoted to an ailing mother and much given to the discussion of the meals he had consumed and the resultant digestive difficulties. "But never mind, darling, just think how you will dazzle Upper Chyppen Monday night. I am sure Sir Max will appreciate such a gown as well as any duke."

"Oh yes, Sir Max. I had forgotten about him. Oh, Sydney!" She suddenly flung her arms about Sydney's neck and burst into tears.

Sydney was too shocked to speak for a moment. Meriel was not given to such displays and she could only suppose she was not well. She felt her brow and cheek carefully. Not feverish, certainly. "My darling girl, what on earth is wrong? Are you unhappy about something?"

"Oh no! It is just . . . just . . . oh, Syd, I love you very much and . . . and . . . I am so happy to be home . . ." Then she fished out her handkerchief and wiped her eyes and began to laugh. "How foolish I am. There—it is all over and I must change for dinner, I suppose."

She knew Sydney was looking at her strangely, and she disliked dissembling in this way, but when Edward came, it would all be clear at once, and Sydney would forgive her. It would not be very long to wait.

15

The Armytages were kept from church the next morning by a violent rainstorm that lasted well past midday. Meriel, who had been quite looking forward to a reunion with old friends, especially Cassie Maplethorpe, was disappointed, but did not fret too much, knowing she would see her the following evening at the Assembly. She settled down in the drawing room to finish reading *Emma* while Sydney at the pianoforte worked on a new piece of music Meriel had brought her from Bath.

When in the midafternoon the rain gradually ceased and the clouds began shouldering each other towards the horizon to allow a watery sunlight to break through, Sydney declared she must have exercise or she would scream. The girls donned their high pattens and cloaks and bonnets and set off down the drive. Halfway to the gates, however, Sydney suggested they walk instead to the pond. Meriel was agreeable to this plan, and they turned back.

Sydney had realized there was every possibility that others, feeling restless after the pent-up morning, would take advantage of the clearing weather to hurry out on visits to the friends they had missed at church. She had no wish to see anyone today, particularly not Morgan Leighton, nor even Sir Max. Her emotions craved rest from the turmoil roused by both gentlemen, a return to the quiet and peace they had known before their advent, when she and Meriel could spend whole days in amicable companionship with nothing more stirring to contemplate than dinner with the Maplethorpes.

The two sisters tramped along together through the wet

grass to the summerhouse, and when Meriel saw the boat she immediately wanted to row about the pond. They bailed out the rainwater and set out. Sydney told her sister of all the various social events that had taken place during her absence, bringing Morgan's name in casually as being the cause, along with Sir Max, of all the activity.

"Oh, and I missed meeting him by only a day! How did you find him, Sydney? Has he changed?"

"Well, yes and no. He is more confident now. He was only a green boy really when we knew him before, just down from university and hardly out in the world at all. His years in London and success in business have added assurance and polish."

"Do you like him as well?"

"As well?" Sydney was suddenly wary.

"Oh, sister, you know what I mean. You liked him *very* well when he was my tutor. You would blush and drop your eyes every time he looked at you. I was so afraid you were going to marry him and leave us, and I did not like him as a husband for you."

Sydney stared at her, surprised yet again by how observant Meriel really was, in spite of the fact that she herself told people often that Meriel was not so woolly-minded as her daydreamy aspect led them to believe. How had she hoped to hide such feelings as she had experienced then from Meriel, though she *was* only seven years old at the time? Now she could only answer humbly, "No, darling, I do not like him so well."

"I am glad of that," Meriel answered simply, and said no more.

When they returned to the house they found there had, surprisingly, been no callers, but the Maplethorpes' coachman was waiting for a reply to a message from Cassie. She begged the girls to come to them tomorrow morning to spend the day and attend the Assembly from the Maplethorpe house. They were also entreated to stay the night afterwards if they would like to do so. Cassie said she longed to see her dearest Meriel, and her mother joined her in urging them to come.

"Lovely!" Meriel exclaimed. "Shall I write her that we will?"

"Do you go, dearest, and I will come from here."

"Oh, Syd, can not we both go?"

"Well, you know how Papa is. If we leave him, he will decide to stay at home, and I think he does not go out enough. If he must escort me, he will go, and you know he does love dancing and company in spite of the way he grumbles sometimes."

So it was decided, and Meriel dashed off an acceptance to Cassie, which the coachman carried away. The next morning Meriel was driven to Upper Chyppen, chaperoned by her new ball gown, carefully folded into silver tissue and wrapped round with a sheet, on the seat beside her.

When Tom, the coachman, returned, he brought Sydney a posy of coral-coloured roses in a golden holder. She was puzzled for a moment as to who could have been so well acquainted with her gown as to have chosen so perfectly, until she opened the accompanying card. It was signed only "Papa."

She rushed to the library to thank him. Though he had declared that he was too old to be going to balls the day before when he learned of her arrangements, he had been secretly pleased, and had sent Tom to the flower shop in Upper Chyppen with precise instructions for colour and holder. Meriel's posy had been delivered to her at the Maplethorpes' and was white roses in a silver holder.

He was waiting, very spruce in a deep-plum-coloured coat, silver brocade waistcoat, and white satin breeches, when Sydney came down to join him for an early dinner before they left for town. He stared at her without speaking for several moments, his throat constricting and tears very near the surface. She looked so radiant, her grey eyes sparkling, a flush of colour in her cheeks exactly matching the peach-bloom of her gown, and her pale ash-blond hair shining almost silver in the candlelight.

"My dear child," he said, swallowing the lump in his throat, "how very beautiful you are."

"Now I know you love me truly," she quipped with a laugh.

"Child, you must not get into the way of thinking you are plain. With a sister like Meriel, it can be an easy habit to get into, I know. But there are different kinds of beauty, and yours is just as appealing. You look very like my own dear mother, bless her, who was accounted a beauty in her day. You have the same colouring, and you are dainty and grace-ful as she was."

"Thank you, darling Papa. For that you will have to stand up with me tonight. Now, shall we dine? It is only a very light meal, I warn you, but there will be supper later, remember." She took his arm and led him to the dining room, made too uncomfortable by his compliments to want to continue the discussion. She knew she looked well, that her gown became her, but it was far too late in life to start thinking of herself as a beauty. Such a role would not suit her.

Because of her father's worry about promptness, they were among the first arrivals at the Assembly Rooms and suffered the penalties of the unfashionably early. They met all their elderly neighbours, who had come only to watch and who wanted to assure themselves of comfortable seats out of draughts, and were given all the latest bulletins on the specific ailment of each one, as well as the current state of affairs of all their children and grandchildren. Mr. Armytage enjoyed this very much, but for Sydney it was something of a trial. She was relieved as the room began filling with people, and was not displeased to see the young girls and matrons staring openly and in most cases enviously at her elegant gown. She was glad she had taken time this morning to write Lady Divers a heartfelt letter of gratitude, and also silently blessed Meriel, who she knew had chosen the silk with an artist's eye as to what would best become her sister.

Sydney kept her eye on the door for the arrival of the Maplethorpe party, eager to see the effect her sister's entrance was bound to have on the entire company. She saw the Coles enter, Arabella in grass-green satin trimmed with purple, which Sydney was aware was the newest colour rage among the fashionable, but which did nothing at all to enhance Arabella's rather florid complexion and pale blue eyes, in Sydney's estimation. Arabella's yellow hair was parted in the middle and pulled into bunches of ringlets over each ear, and she wore a diamond tiara. People were naturally staring at so startling a vision and she was very much aware of it, preening and throwing her head about in a pretense of great amusement at something her brother was saying. He had actually just complained that his slippers were pinching and he hoped there were whist tables set up, since he was not of a mind to dance tonight. She informed him sotto voce, while smiling brilliantly up at him, that he was not to leave her side until she was assured that every dance was promised, since if any were open he would be required to stand up with her.

He stopped mulishly. "Now, look here, Bella, you cannot expect a man to dance with his own sister. Make myself a laughingstock," he protested in a voice loud enough to be heard by a number of people, who wasted no time in passing on this amusing tidbit to their less fortunate neighbours. Arabella pinched his arm viciously and propelled him down the room.

Sir Max could be seen entering now, Morgan Leighton lounging along slightly behind him, both looking very much the London gentlemen in their black coats and white Melton-cloth waistcoats, black for evening coats not being a style that had reached Upper Chyppen as yet. They progressed across the room straight to where Sydney stood with her father chatting with the Bidlake twins seated beside the fire. They both fluffed up their feathers and smiled archly over identical fans at the handsome gentlemen, hoping everyone noticed they had the honour to be greeted before everyone else.

After this duty was done, the men both turned admiring eyes on Sydney, both wondering at the same time if the other had sent her the posy and wishing he had thought to do so. Max managed to get in the first compliment, telling Sydney he had never seen a more elegant gown in all his years in London, nor one that became the wearer better. He then turned, somewhat reluctantly, to greet Mr. Armytage, leaving Sydney to Morgan. He saw that Morgan moved very close to Sydney, but could not hear what he said to her.

"Well, whatever I say will sound very lame after such a fulsome compliment, but I am sure in any case that you cannot be unaware that you outshine every woman in the room, Sydney, my dear," he said to her in a low, intimate voice.

"Ah, do not speak too hastily, Mr. Leighton," she returned lightly, withdrawing from him the least bit. "We are not all assembled as yet."

"It will not matter. You are very lovely tonight and are bound to be the belle of the evening. Dare I hope you have a dance left for me?"

"Oh, a great many are unengaged, I fear."

"The first?"

"No, that is . . . er . . . taken."

"The waltz?"

"That also," she replied, hoping she would not blush.

"Then I must have the second and the first after supper. I suppose it is too much to hope that you are free for supper?"

"No . . . I mean . . . yes . . . oh dear"—she laughed—"how difficult it is to answer a question posed in that way. Well, I must try again. I am engaged for supper, sir."

He was not at all pleased to find her so sparkling, so apparently happy, with no visible indications of irritation with him for his neglect of the past two days, but he only shrugged with his lazy smile. "Of course, and it serves me right for arriving so late tonight. I should have engaged you days ago."

"Er . . . ah . . . good evening, Leighton," said Claiborne from behind them with false bonhomie, clearly uncomfortable. On his arm, hanging back slightly so it would seem her brother had dragged her somewhat unwillingly up to the group rather than the other way around, was Arabella, making a great play with her fan.

Morgan turned. "Ah, Cole . . . good evening. Miss Cole, your servant." He bowed. She dropped him a small curtsy, greeted the rest of the group, and turned back to Morgan. "I am so glad of the rain yesterday to freshen the air, are not you, Mr. Leighton? Dancing can be so uncomfortable if it is too warm." She waited expectantly for him to request the pleasure of standing up with her, but Morgan, though he understood her very well, would not rise to her cue. It was much more amusing to wait and see what she would do next. Her smile became a little set, but fortunately she was saved by Tristan Foxx, who came tripping up to join them. He made an elaborate leg to each of the ladies in turn, then greeted the men, running an expert eye over their coats. "Weston made that up for you, I'll wager," he said knowingly to Max, who only bowed in acknowledgment. Then Tristan turned to Sydney, hands clasped ecstatically. "My *dear* Miss Armytage, your gown! The cut! The fabric! The colour! You can only have had such a gown from Paris, I vow! *Exquise! Très exquise!*"

"Dear Tristan, he takes such a great interest in ladies' gowns, do you not, Tristan?" Arabella explained sweetly.

Warned, Tristan said, "And you, enchantress! So this is the surprise you have been hatching up with your dressmaker, you naughty girl!'' He suppressed an inward shudder at the dreadful grass-green gown, and tried to look admiring, though no torture devised by man could have extracted a compliment from his lips in front of witnesses. He had his pride!

Arabella seemed satisfied and exclaimed, ''I *knew* you would love my surprise. Ah, here are the musicians! Not like the grand balls of London, eh, Tristan? Still, I do adore dancing at any time.''

Not daring to ignore this hint, Tristan cried, ''Oh, tell me you have saved *something* for me, dear Arabella. Surely you gentlemen have not been so selfish as to engage her for every dance?'' He looked around pleadingly at Sir Max and Morgan. Max shifted uneasily, then gravely requested the pleasure of a dance with Arabella. Morgan, with a barely suppressed grin, did the same.

Arabella tossed her head skittishly. ''Well, now, let me think if I have anything left. I think you may have the first, Sir Max, and—''

''Forgive me, Miss Cole, I am sorry to be unable to accept, though I thank you. I have already—''

''Oh, then the second,'' she interrupted hastily, ''and Mr. Leighton the first. Oh, then you, Tristan, shall be next. Oh dear, I shall be danced off my feet, I see.''

Claiborne, who had stood with oxlike patience through all this, brightened visibly. ''Well, Bella, now you won't need me for a partner after all, ha-ha,'' he boomed jovially. ''I'll be off then to find the card room. Ladies, 'servant . . . gentlemen . . .'' He bowed and took himself off as rapidly as his pinching slippers allowed.

Arabella began chattering at once to cover this humiliating gaffe, vowing to comb her brother's hair with a joint stool when they reached home this night. ''Tristan, do you remember when my dear aunt, Lady Boxton, told Prinny to his face that his corsets creaked so loudly she could hardly hear what he had to say, and he . . .?''

But Tristan was not listening. He was staring at the door, eyes wide with disbelief. ''Good God,'' he said simply. Everyone turned to follow his gaze, causing those near them to do the same, and gradually the movement spread over the entire room, creating a moment of stunned silence.

In the doorway was Meriel, glowing in a shimmering radiance created by herself alone. Her gown of white gauze glinted with silver embroidery in a pattern of acorns and leaves about the neckline and hem. Her riotous black curls had been smoothed back to fall from the crown of her head in a cascade down her back with a wreath of silver leaves and seed pearls, exposing the perfect cameo of her features and setting off the long almond shape of her dark eyes. Her lips curved up in a beginning smile of anticipated pleasure and her cheeks were flushed with rose. She was a vision of pure enchantment.

Even Sydney was caught in the spell of her beauty and gasped softly. Max turned to look down at her, then smiled and held out his arm. When she placed her hand on it he patted it lightly, then led her forward to join her sister. Their movement seemed to wake the room from its trance and slowly people began to turn away and speak to one another.

Only Morgan remained rooted, no longer aware of anyone else in the room beyond the girl in white. She cannot be real, he kept repeating to himself. He felt as though he had been struck from behind, still in that state of shock one experiences at such a time, dazed and unable to comprehend what could have happened.

He finally became aware of a voice buzzing beside him and that someone was tugging his sleeve. He turned and stared blankly at Arabella, who seemed to be asking him something. He muttered, "Yes, yes, of course," and walked away at once, straight across the room to the girl.

Sydney and Max had reached Meriel and were greeting her and the Maplethorpes behind her. There was a confused few moments as young men seemed to come from every direction to surround and besiege Meriel. Morgan elbowed his way through unceremoniously, ignoring the surprised stares at his rudeness, finally reaching Sydney's side.

"Miss Armytage, you must introduce me to your friend," he demanded.

"Why, Mr. Leighton, of course. But you know her already. It is Meriel, my sister. Meriel, you remember your former tutor?"

Meriel, tall and slender, turned slowly away from the young man who was beseeching her to promise him two dances. She regarded Morgan curiously for a moment before she held out her hand. "How do you do, Mr. Leighton. Welcome back to Upper Chyppen," she said dutifully, before withdrawing her hand from his overly firm clasp and turning back to the importunate young man.

"Miss Meriel," he said loudly, causing her to turn her head to him in surprise, "I claim the privilege of our old acquaintance to request that you stand up with me for the first set." He no longer remembered, nor cared, that he was engaged for it already to Arabella.

"Why, I thank you, sir, but I have just promised it to Mr. Milbanks," she said calmly, causing that young man to gape and turn beet red in gratification, for he had indeed requested it, but she had not yet said yes. "Perhaps the fourth set, if you care for it."

Morgan bowed. "With the greatest pleasure in the world, my dear . . ." But she had already turned away again. He backed away, unable to bear watching her talking and laughing with other men while he stood by, ignored.

In a very few moments Meriel's entire evening was accounted for, and Cassie and Sydney had benefited from this congregation of dancing partners as well. Then the master of ceremonies was asking Sir Max to honour the company by leading the first dance, the musicians were playing the opening strains, and Sydney found herself being led out onto the floor to the unaccustomed place of honour at the head of the line of dancers who began to form up.

"Well, Miss Armytage, you and your sister have thrown every woman in the room into the shade tonight."

"It is flattering of you to suggest that I have any part in it. I think the credit must all be Meriel's."

"She is without doubt a pretty young girl and I am sure you must be very proud of her, but I believe you share the honours."

She refused to drop her eyes in a pretense of missish confusion at his compliments, but she was confused and could think of nothing lighthearted to say to turn the conversation. She felt a blush mounting up her neck. He saw that he had embarrassed her and kindly changed the subject. "Are your Assemblies always so well attended?"

Somewhere in the middle of the line of dancers Arabella was experiencing an envy so sharp as to be painful. She felt slighted and misused. Sir Max should have saved the first dance for her, Lady Boxton's niece, who surely deserved the honour more than Sydney Armytage, who had no titled relatives to her name, but who had yet somehow managed to usurp Arabella's rightful place. To further exacerbate her temper, Morgan had not come to claim her as the music had struck up and she had been forced to ask Tristan to escort her to Morgan, who was found at last standing against the wall, arms folded, glowering across the room to where Mr. Milbanks was leading Meriel onto the floor. He had ignored their presence until Arabella hissed, "Morgan, have you lost your mind? You did request this dance of me, I believe."

Without a word of apology, nor, indeed, any word at all, he had led her out and they had taken their places. He was still silent. "I *hope* I shall not be required to seek you out each time," she snapped.

"Each time?" He looked at her blankly.

"The waltz and supper. You surely cannot have forgotten so soon?"

"I . . . I cannot seem to recall . . ."

"How *very* flattering! I asked you if I should save them for you and you said yes, of course."

"Oh . . . oh, certainly," he replied, while cursing himself silently for not having thought to ask Meriel to take supper with him when he had the chance. By now she would be bound to have promised it to one of these half-fledged oafs. How could she bear them to touch her with their great callused fists? How could she *bear* it? Oh God, she was as out of place here as a princess in a pigsty! She should be seen in London . . . Paris . . . Vienna! All the glittering capitals of the world would fall at her feet. He could see himself entering a ballroom with her on his arm, royalty crowding around to be introduced to her, the beautiful Mrs. Leighton! They would travel, she would have only the best. He began to dream of what it might be like to possess her. Oh, dear Lord, so this was what it was like to fall in love? He had always jeered at the idea, never believed he wanted to love. How wrong he had been.

"You are making a complete laughingstock of yourself, staring at that schoolgirl in such a way," hissed Arabella.

"What? Was I staring? I was not even aware of her, my mind was so far away," he protested, his mind suddenly snapping back to his present situation with alarmed wariness. He must not allow this vixen to guess his feelings. Not before he had his love secure, for Arabella was capable of going to her . . . telling her . . . Oh God! She must not!

He resolutely set himself to exercise his mechanical charm and was shortly rewarded by seeing Arabella relax as the suspicion slowly faded from her jealous eyes.

Presently the set came to an end, and by concentrating, he remembered that he was next to dance with Sydney. Very well. That too would end, and then the next, and then he would be with Meriel! He had only to be patient.

16

"That gown is monstrously becoming to you, Sydney, my dear," Morgan said as they moved through the figures of the dance. He was tinglingly aware of the white-gowned figure to his left, moving in a glowing aura which he ached, mothlike, to be drawn into. So rare, he thought, so perfect, like a divinity from another universe. He used every ounce of self-control to prevent himself from looking at her again. Soon. Soon, now, he warned himself. He managed to smile into Sydney's eyes with a simulation of warmth and admiration.

"Thank you, Mr. Leighton," she responded, though not to the smile.

"And the flowers, so exactly right. Now, which of your admirers is so fortunate as to have you carry his favour?"

"My father, Mr. Leighton."

"How kind you are to relieve my anxiety. Here I have been cursing myself all evening for not having thought of it myself, and cursing the man who did. But you are always kind to me, though I do not deserve it." He tilted his head to one side and surveyed her face in his intimate, practiced way. He no longer really cared who had sent her the flowers. None of that mattered anymore, but she was another who must suspect nothing. He wondered, briefly, if it was possible she had confided anything of their past romance to Meriel, but felt sure she had not. Sydney was a woman who would prefer to suffer in silence, keep up a brave front. Besides, he would have seen something—condemnation?—in Meriel's eyes when they met if she knew anything of the story. As it was, there had been only . . . indifference. He felt a sharp physical pain in his midsection at the realization of her indifference and nearly gasped aloud. Careful!

He forced a smile and continued his gallantries until the set had finished and he returned Sydney to her father. He wanted very much to stand someplace quietly and watch his beloved through the next dance until he could claim her, but did not dare allow himself to do so. People might notice and wonder, especially Arabella, who seemed to be watching him continuously. He approached Cassie, and when he found she was not free, led out Mrs. Maplethorpe, not really caring with whom he stood up. Years of practice brought inanities automatically to his lips. The set went on interminably and he seemed to be moving through water, each step taking twice as long to accomplish as was usual. It ended, at last, and he led Mrs. Maplethorpe off the floor, bowed, and said something that caused her to laugh girlishly before he turned away. Now.

He made his way to Meriel where she stood beside her father, surrounded by a jostling group of young men, cool, smiling pleasantly, turning to her father repeatedly to include him in the conversation. All the other faces were blurs to Morgan. Were they so to her too? Would she *see* him? Look at him with something more in her eyes than they held for the men around her? He must make sure she did. He pushed his way through. "Miss Meriel. Our dance, I believe."

She turned, nodded, smiled, turned her head to answer some remark from a lovesick boy gazing at her with calf eyes. How she could bother with them! He longed to tell them all to be gone. Instead, he turned to Mr. Armytage, complimented him on his daughters, on their beauty, their gowns, their flowers, and his taste, wondering all the while why the music was taking so long to begin.

Then the opening strains called the dancers to the floor for a quadrille and he held out his arm. She nodded all around, excused herelf to her father, and placed a long, slim, white-gloved hand on his arm. "I cannot tell you how impatiently I have awaited this moment," he murmured as they took their places, bending a meaningful look into her eyes.

"Ah, the quadrille—yes, I too like it very much," she replied, looking about in her slow, unhurried way, smiling at Cassie, then with even more enthusiasm as she saw her papa leading Sydney onto the floor. "Oh, look! Dearest Papa, he also loves the quadrille. He taught Sydney and me to dance it."

"How fortunate for the rest of us," he said, trying vainly to catch her eye.

"Oh, he is a famous dancer," she continued. "I have saved my waltz for him, though he does not know it yet."

"You break my heart, fairest! Say you will change your mind and allow me to dance it with you." He knew he sounded too desperate, too pleading, but could not prevent himself.

She gazed at him levelly, reminding him of Sydney, except the eyes were not clear, readable grey, but dark, enigmatic pools that told him nothing of what she was thinking, and causing him to lose the thread of what he was saying. Then her eyes flicked away indifferently. "I mean . . . ah . . . what I mean is . . ." He faltered like a tongue-tied schoolboy. "How I wish you were saving it for me. The waltz is my favourite dance of all."

Her eyes returned, thank God, and he smiled into them, tilting his head to the side in his most intimate way. She said, meeting his eyes squarely, "So it is mine, but I will only dance it with someone I love."

It was like a little stab of cold steel to the heart, and his mouth opened and closed soundlessly in pain. Then, wait, he told himself. Wait, and be patient with her. We have only met now really, and she does not know me. She thinks I am like all those others. She is used to tongue-tied schoolboys gazing at her in adulation, though she is only just out of the schoolroom herself. But she is vulnerable at this age, so easy to reach if one sets about it properly. I must not be one of those fawning boys, but show her I am a man of the world, sophisticated, a man who can teach her, lead her.

"Are you still partial to geography, Miss Meriel?" he said teasingly.

"Not really. I think I was only partial to it as compared to sums."

"Yes, I remember you did not care for mathematics. However, that is not a subject with which a beautiful woman need fill her head, but geography can be romantic, full of adventure. Paris, Venice, Cairo! Do not those names conjure up romance in your mind?"

"Yes, actually they do."

"I knew it! You are a woman who should see all those faraway places, who could appreciate them."

"You have travelled, Mr. Leighton?"

"Yes. Mostly for business. India, the Orient, the Caribbean. I could show you all the most exciting places, mysterious, intriguing scenes, cities that must be experienced by a mind open to adventure."

"I think you have misread me, sir," she said placidly. "I am not in the least adventuresome. I like only to read of those places, I should not care to go. I prefer Upper Chyppen to anyplace else in the world."

Was she simple-minded, he wondered, or artful beyond any woman he had ever encountered? She seemed to lead him on until he walked slap into the face of her indifference. She never blushed or dropped her eyes, even in pretense, as most young girls are taught to do. He was torn between the desire to shake her or snatch her into his arms and kiss her. He only smiled and said, "Yes, it is a lovely part of England. I always remembered my days here. That is why it came so readily to mind when Sir Max spoke to me about wanting a country place."

"Ah, that was well done of you, sir," she exclaimed, her eyes, at last, lighting up with enthusiasm. "He and Papa have hit it off so well. I do not remember when Papa has taken so to a man. It has given him a whole new interest in life."

Her papa! Was that all she could think of? Dear God, could he only reach her through her father? But wait . . . Westbrook? Could it be she had set her cap for a title? No, surely she had not seemed to treat him with any degree of particularity. On the other hand, that might be part of her plan to bring him up to scratch.

Then the dance came to an end and he was forced to lead her back to her father, who was talking to Westbrook. They both turned to greet Meriel, and Morgan watched, narrow-eyed, but could see nothing in her or Westbrook's demeanour to give him pause, and was reassured. Westbrook was to stand up with her next, it seemed, and throughout, Morgan watched, as he danced with a girl whose name he could not remember, but saw nothing out of the ordinary in Meriel's behaviour to Westbrook. She seemed entirely at ease, certainly, and laughed more than she had with himself, but there were no languishing looks or missish coyness.

Now who? he wondered, bowing to the girl. Oh Lord. Arabella. He looked about, and there she was, across the room, staring at him demandingly. He went reluctantly to join her, and she took his arm possessively.

"There you are at last. I was wondering if you would remember me. Have you been busy turning all these silly girls' heads? Oh, do not bother to deny it, I know your ways too well." She laughed. "Come, shall we stroll about the room until the music begins?"

They strolled. He forced himself to attend to her, smiling, mouthing meaningless words, eyes straying down her figure. He was all too successful, and she began to lean against his arm, and her breath quickened. When they passed an empty alcove, she suggested they sit out the dance and talk. He knew very well what she meant. She loved the excitement of being made love to with suggestive looks and words before a roomful of people. He shuddered, walking on deliberately, saying he had been too much looking forward to their dance to give it up. Saying anything to avoid the possibility of having to sit with her for Meriel to see.

Then the music began. Oh God! The waltz! And there *she* was, glimmering and sparkling, curtsying to her papa, laughing up at him adoringly in a way Morgan would gladly have died for to have her look so at him.

Sydney walked onto the floor with Sir Max, her heart suddenly beating very hard. The waltz, she thought ecstatically, so lovely, so dreamy, yet exhilarating at the same time. Sir Max bowed charmingly as she dipped a curtsy to him, and she wondered if he wished it were Meriel there before him. She had watched them as they had danced together, Meriel more animated than she had been all evening, he talking and laughing. Was it possible Meriel was beginning to see how truly attractive and estimable he was? There was no denying they made a dramatically handsome couple, nearly of a height, both dark and fine-boned. Sydney had been aware of the many speculative glances directed upon the pair as they moved about the floor.

"We shall have no trouble making the rest look to be the merest amateurs, Miss Armytage," Max said.

Her thoughts were wandering, so she did not take his meaning at once. "I . . . beg your pardon?"

"We are old hands at this." When she continued to look blank, he explained, "We have waltzed together before."

"Oh," was her witty reply.

"Now, that is a devastating set-down," he commented with a grimace. "You had forgotten."

"No! Oh no, I had not, I assure you. It was only . . . my mind was on something else."

"Another set-down," he said with mock resignation. "I see I shall have to be much more amusing if I am to hold your attention."

"Oh, please do not think . . ." she cried, flushing in consternation.

He relented and smiled. "I will not tease you, my dear. Now, tell me what you were thinking of."

"Of Meriel," she began, and then halted, realizing she could not tell him what she had been thinking. "She is . . . dancing with Papa, and he looks so proud. Is she not enchanting?"

"Yes, and a pretty-behaved child as well, which I make no doubt she learned from you."

"Oh, there was little to teach her. She has always been so sweet and biddable and—"

"Now, Miss Armytage, we begin," he stopped her, taking her hand and putting the other to her waist. "One does not speak of others while one waltzes. One only thinks of oneself and the music . . . and perhaps one's partner." With that he swung her into step and then they were whirling away down the room, swaying to the lilting music, his eyes fixed upon her own, and she did forget everything—or almost everything. The music she heard, and beyond that knew only his hands holding her and his dark eyes smiling down into hers. She was mesmerized, floating, happier than she had ever been in her life. This moment, she thought happily, this man . . . Then suddenly she was afraid of what she might be showing him and shifted her gaze over his shoulder, resolutely refusing to meet his eyes except glancingly through the remainder of the dance.

Max was puzzled. For a time she had seemed all his, even

seemed to be aware of the love he could not keep from expressing in his eyes as he looked at her, and then she seemed to withdraw, fascinated by something behind his back. As they revolved, he saw, among many other couples, Meriel and Mr. Armytage, and then Leighton with the Cole woman. Could that have been it? The sight of Leighton? Did she wish it were herself in Leighton's arms? It was too unbearable a thought to believe.

Leighton did not look to be enjoying himself. Serve him right for becoming entangled with such a creature. Had he signalled his distaste somehow to Sydney? Max gave it up, since he could not know. If she loved Leighton, she did, and there was little to be done about it. But that was still to be proved, he thought, brightening, and the game is not yet won. I will be damned if I give up so easily.

They left the floor with Meriel and Mr. Armytage and decided to all go down to supper together. They were joined by the good-looking boy with the moon-calf eyes who claimed Meriel was promised to him for supper, and who nearly fell down in his scramble to retrieve the fan she dropped.

Morgan, with Arabella clinging to his arm and chattering to Tristan on her other side, entered the supper room to see Meriel, seated between Westbrook and some clod-footed yokel, laughing up at Westbrook, her dark eyes sparkling, her mouth curved deliciously to reveal her pretty white teeth. Morgan felt faint with his desire for her, and jerking his arm away from Arabella, muttered, "Excuse me, the heat, must have some air," and pushed his way blindly back up the stairs through the crowds, leaving Arabella and Tristan staring blankly after him.

"Well, really!" Arabella exclaimed, her bad temper returning full force. "I cannot account for such rudeness! I shall certainly have something to say to him about such behaviour!"

"Come and have some iced champagne, Bella, and lower your voice unless you care to have everyone know something is wrong," counselled Tristan, too tired suddenly for tact.

"I beg your pardon?" she said haughtily.

"Oh, come along, do. Do you want everyone to watch you fly into the boughs? Put a good face on it and come along. I cannot think why you must behave so stupidly."

"I should be more careful in how you speak to me, if I were you, Tristan," she said icily.

"I warn you not to threaten me any further, Bella, or I shall leave you at once, and then who will take you to supper?"

"Do so if you dare," she hissed furiously.

"Do not tempt me, I beg you. I also know a thing or two that I will wager you would not be best pleased to have bruited about. Besides, I think my credit is good enough to refute anything you might say of me, and I am much cleverer than you, my pet."

It was a draw, and after only the slightest pause she took his arm with a tinkling laugh and they proceeded to the table.

Meriel decided not to stay the night with the Maplethorpes after all. "Cassie is a darling, but she will want to discuss all her partners before we sleep, and I should have to prop my eyelids open with sticks to stay awake," she confided to Sydney. Actually, Meriel wanted to be alone to think about Edward and what it would be like to dance with him. She had not had the opportunity all evening to really *think* about him.

So she drove home, her head on her papa's shoulder, listening to Sydney and Papa discuss the evening. When they were upstairs, Sydney came to tuck her in and sat down for a moment on the side of the bed, smoothing the black curls back in a way that Meriel loved. Her eyelids began to droop.

"Did you enjoy yourself, darling?"

"Oh yes, it was lovely," Meriel answered sleepily.

"And who was your favourite partner?"

"Oh, Papa . . . and Sir Max. You were right, Syd, he is such a charming man. I am glad," she murmured approvingly, hoping Sydney *would* take this man, who was so right for her.

Sydney sat very still for an instant, then bent to kiss the silken cheek, bid her sister good night, and went back to her own room. Well, she thought, in bed at last, staring into the darkness, it is beginning, I suppose. She will learn to love him—how could she help it? Any more than he could help loving her, and they will make a fine couple. Meriel could not hope to find a better husband, so kind, so sensitive to one's every mood, so handsome. Sydney felt tears slipping silently down her temples to soak into her hair and the pillows, as a wave of such misery overcame her she wanted to howl aloud.

Dear Lord, why has this happened to me? I cannot . . . I

will not allow myself . . . I must not even think in such a
way. But it was too late, and she knew it. She had fallen in
love with Sir Max herself—the man she would soon be
calling brother. How has this happened? How have I *let* it
happen? Thank God no one can possibly know. How could
they, when I have only learned of it myself. But no one *shall*
know; I shall make very certain of that.

17

When Sydney came down for breakfast the next morning,
Mr. Armytage was before her, eating ham with hearty appetite.
He tweaked her gently about being a lie-abed. "You young
people have no stamina. A night of dancing does you in,
while a man of my years only feels stronger for the exercise.
Where is Meriel?"

"I peeked in, but she has not stirred. I told Lutie to let her
sleep as long as she would. Do you think she is quite herself,
Papa?"

"Well, she is not the self who left here a child," he
surprised her by observing.

She thought it over for a moment and then said, "I believe
you are right, though I would never have thought of it in that
way. To me, she seems more . . . well, present, I suppose.
How odd. It would seem that something has happened while
she was away, yet she says her visit was very much like all
the others." She leaned over to kiss the top of his head and
moved around the table to take her seat.

"Good God! What is that on your head, Sydney?"

"It is a cap, Papa," she said lightly, trying to ignore the
leaden ball in her chest.

"Well, I wish you will take it off."

"Why, it is a very pretty cap, Papa."

"It is ridiculous and not at all suitable for a girl."

"I am not a girl, Papa."

"You are very little past it, and if you persist in trying to make yourself look older than you are, you will only succeed in making me feel older than I am."

"Oh, Papa, surely it cannot—"

"Take it off, my dear, to please me," he coaxed.

She calmly removed it and placed it beside her plate and drank her chocolate. When he picked up his papers and mail and said he would be in the library, she picked up the cap again and set it carefully on her head. She did not wish to make her father unhappy, but she felt sure he would cease noticing it after a day or two. A nearly sleepless night had resulted in a resolve to turn herself firmly away from her recent frivolity and back to her household duties, and to remind herself she would wear that symbol of the end of girlhood, the cap. She was seven-and-twenty and must begin behaving as what she was. If one rode out with gentlemen, or went driving with them, or waltzed with the abandon of an eighteen-year-old, one could expect to put oneself into the way of developing unsuitable romantic notions and causing oneself, in the process, a great deal of senseless pain.

People might already be whispering about her, talking of mutton pretending to be lamb, or laughing slyly about the spinster's last desperate effort. She shuddered. It would not do. It would not do at all to make herself such a figure of fun. Why, Sir Max himself might get wind of the gossip, and what he would think of her, she could not bear to dwell upon. He would not laugh at her, for he was too kind for that, but he might pity her, which was infinitely worse! He would be sorry to think that the attentions he had paid her as a compliment to Meriel had been so wrongly interpreted.

She had been horrified to discover these feelings in herself for the man she had hoped Meriel might marry, and especially now that she was convinced Meriel was beginning to look upon him with special favour. It might be somewhat premature as yet to begin planning the wedding, but surely there was little room for doubt that they were attracted to each other, and given time, it would all come about as she had originally hoped. It was too bad that she had allowed this to happen to herself, but it was not irreversible. She would simply keep herself very busy and not think of . . . of . . . him at all in such a way, and eventually it would cease to be painful.

These righteous but dismal musings were interrupted by
Lizzy, who came to tell her that a gentleman had called
and she had put him in the drawing room. Sydney started
up from her chair in a panic. Sir Max!

"Who . . . is it, Lizzy?"

"A Mr. Milbanks, miss."

Sydney sank back, relieved and disappointed. "Oh, yes,
for Miss Meriel. Well, I will go along in a moment. Thank
you, Lizzy."

"You're not lookin' yourself, quite, this morning, miss,"
observed Lizzy, "like you had the headache."

"No, no. I am fine."

"You didn't eat none of that toast," Lizzy said accusingly.

"No, I could not. I . . . am not hungry. That will do,
Lizzy."

Sydney forced herself to finish her chocolate and allowed
her heart to resume its usual pace before she rose and went to
the drawing room. Mr. Milbanks rose at once, as red-faced
and awkward as ever.

"G-good morning, Miss Armytage."

"Good morning, Mr. Milbanks. Will you not take a seat?"

"Yes . . . well . . . thank you. A b-beautiful morning."

"It is indeed. Did you enjoy the Assembly last night?"

"Oh, *very* much," he agreed. "I . . . I thought . . . I
hoped . . . I . . ." He halted. She smiled kindly. "The thing
is . . . I know Miss Meriel likes to ride, and I thought . . ."
He halted once more, looking desperately at her.

"You came to invite her to ride with you," Sydney finished for him. He nodded vigourously. "That is very thoughtful of you, but I fear my sister is not yet downstairs."

His face fell. "Oh." There was silence while he contemplated this unhappy news.

Lizzy came in to announce, "Mr. Hillsborough, miss."

The good-looking young man with the love-struck eyes
entered and stopped in mid-stride when he saw Mr. Milbanks.
They eyed each other with hostility for an instant before the
newcomer turned to survey the room, and, finding no Meriel
in it, turned politely to Sydney. "Miss Armytage, I hope you
will not mind my calling so early."

"Not at all, Mr. Hillsborough. Are you acquainted with
Mr. Milbanks?"

The two young men, who had known each other all their

lives, nodded distantly at one another, and it was left to
Sydney to make polite inquiries and unoriginal comments on
the weather for quite ten minutes without the least help from
either of them. She wished she could knock their heads
together sharply and leave them. Then the drawing-room door
opened again to Lizzy, who, eyes twinkling, announced,
"Mr. Leighton, miss."

Morgan entered with a rush, the light dying out of his eyes
when he saw the two young men. Then he turned, with his
usual smile in place, to Sydney.

"My dear Miss Armytage, how well you are looking this
morning after your night of dancing. It is obvious it agreed
with you very well."

Since she knew she was looking far from her best, she
decided she would ignore this compliment. "Allow me to
introduce Mr. Milbanks and Mr. Hillsborough to you."

The young men jumped to their feet, and all three bowed
perfunctorily. Sydney went to tell Lizzy to fetch her father
from the library. She simply did not want to cope with all this
today.

"Well, Miss Armytage, I never thought to find you in on
such a glorious day," Morgan began. She turned to him,
grateful that he, at least, seemed to have something to say.

"It is a lovely day to be out, I agree."

"Perhaps I might persuade you to come for a ride with
me."

"I thank you, but it is not possible today," she replied
firmly.

He hid his relief with a little moue of pretended disappointment. "Ah, well, I will not press you, then. Perhaps Miss
Meriel will . . ."

The other two men sat up to attention at his words, both
mouths open to press prior claims, when Mr. Armytage came
in. Leaving him to greet the callers, Sydney excused herself
and sped out of the room.

She hurried at once to Meriel's room and found her dressed,
but seated before her mirror, brushing her hair in a state of
trance, a blissful smile curving up her lips.

"Thank heaven you are dressed. The drawing room is
filled with young men all set to take you riding. You must go
down at once."

"Who is there?"

"Mr. Milbanks, Mr. Hillsborough, and Mr. Leighton."

"Oh. I do not think I care to ride today. I was going to the summerhouse to paint."

"Well, you cannot until you have got rid of all your callers," Sydney declared firmly, taking the hairbrush from her sister's limp hand and attacking the tangled black curls ruthlessly.

"Ouch! Has Sir Max not called?"

Sydney's hand halted for the barest second, and then continued. She had known she was right about Meriel's feelings. "No."

"That is good."

"Why?"

"Well, I would not want him to see *me* in a cap."

"Since he is hardly likely to in any case, it does not signify," Sydney replied tartly.

"Oh, Sydney, you are pulling," Meriel protested. "What is the matter with you this morning? And why on earth are you wearing that ridiculous thing on your head?"

"Never mind me. It is you we must worry about. There, that will have to do." She tied back the glossy curls with a ribband and pulled Meriel to her feet. "Now, go along down and deal with those young men before they begin snarling at one another."

"You can hardly call Mr. Leighton a *young* man," Meriel protested as Sydney pushed her out the door. "Where are you going?"

"Fishing," Sydney replied succinctly, stepping into her room and firmly closing the door. She swiftly changed into her old cotton gown, tied her straw bonnet on, and hurried silently down the back stairs. As she ran towards the summerhouse, she heard another horse cantering up the drive, and a quick glance over her shoulder revealed Sir Max before he was cut off from her sight by the house. She hurried on, more determinedly than ever. She took her pole, stepped into the boat, and rowed vigourously out to the far bank.

After an hour it became apparent the fish were not inclined to be interested this morning, but she sat on, trying to sink into that suspended state of mind between sleeping and waking that used to come so easily. Peace evaded her, however, and at last, when the sun was nearly overhead, she began to row back. As she came closer, she saw that Meriel was sitting in the summerhouse calmly painting.

"There you are at last. I thought you had fallen asleep out there," she commented, looking up briefly.

"Did you ride?"

"No. I said I was too tired, so we all sat about talking of nothing. It was not very pleasant, really. Mr. Milbanks and Mr. Hillsborough were rude to one another and Mr. Leighton only glowered the whole time. Sir Max came in right after I came down—you really should have waited, Syd. He, at least, was very pleasant."

"That was nice for you."

"He seemed disappointed not to find you there."

"He is always the soul of courtesy."

"He inquired for you with great particularity."

"He is all kindness and consideration."

Meriel studied her curiously, never having seen her sister in this sort of mood. What could be troubling her? Perhaps she had no interest in Sir Max after all, and he was besieging her with unwelcome attentions, though it was difficult for Meriel to imagine so kindly a man behaving in a way that would be unpleasant to any woman. She tried again: "He charged me to tell you that he hoped you would feel able to come riding with him tomorrow."

"I am planning to do out the linen cupboards with Lutie tomorrow, so you will have to go without me."

"He did not invite *me*, and surely you could do the linen cupboards another time."

"But I plan to do them tomorrow," Sydney replied inexorably. "Now, what are you painting?"

"The pond, with you in the middle of it in the boat. You know, Sydney, I have been thinking, we have not entertained this summer. Why do we not have a picnic down here?"

"Oh Lord, Meriel, I do not—"

"Do say yes, Syd! I think I shall go mad with boredom. The days seem to pass so *slowly*!"

Sydney's eyes widened in astonishment at this impassioned outburst. "Do you tell me so? And you are at home but three days! Can you mean you find Upper Chyppen dull after the gaieties of Bath?"

"Oh, well . . ."

"I seem to remember a girl who wanted everything to remain just as it is forever."

"Did I? How foolish one can be sometimes. Oh, Sydney!" Meriel suddenly jumped to her feet and ran out onto the grass to stare up into the sky.

"What, my love? What is it?" Sydney was now distinctly alarmed.

"Oh, nothing, really. Just . . . restless," Meriel said with a sigh.

Sydney capitulated. "You are right. I think a picnic would be just the thing. Come, sit down again and we will make a list of who is to be invited."

Max and Morgan rode back together. The two young men had galloped off and were now out of sight. After a time Max said, "You seem preoccupied today, Leighton."

"Do I?" Morgan straightened, the frown smoothing away between his brows. "How boring for you. Sorry. Thinking of the business. I suppose I should be thinking of returning to London to see what is happening." He had, of course, no intention of leaving, especially *now*, and he expected Westbrook to protest politely.

Max had no great enthusiasm for it, but did the best he could. "Surely the whole thing runs without you by this time?"

"Yes, you are right. I worry unnecessarily, I suppose, and I should hate to miss all this fine weather. Kind of you to insist."

Max would not have characterized his comment as insistent, and thought glumly that the fellow might have protested a bit more. He found that Leighton did not improve with acquaintance and that the more he knew of him, the less he liked his company, but short of leaving for town himself, he could think of no way to dislodge a guest who was not inclined to go. Smoky sort of fellow, that was for sure, not at all as he had seemed in London.

They reached Upper Chyppen and parted company. "I must pay my respects to Miss Cole," Morgan explained.

Arabella was waiting for him in her drawing room, crossly jabbing a needle into a piece of mangled-looking embroidery.

"Why, my dear, how domestic you look," Morgan exclaimed jovially, crossing to bow before her. She barely looked up, jabbing again with great inaccuracy.

"Ah, you are recovered, I see," she commented acidly.

"Yes, thank you. Your concern touches me deeply. May I sit down?"

She gave him only a cold look, but he sat down beside her anyway. "You seem uncommonly out of sorts this morning, Bella. Would you prefer me to take myself off and not bother you?"

She tossed the embroidery aside. "How could you have walked away and left me alone in that way last night? It was too humiliating."

"But, my dear, I felt suddenly quite unwell, and Mr. Foxx was with you, so I knew you would be well taken care of. I do apologize for my abruptness, but I found I could not face the sight of food. A touch of the headache all evening, you see, though I tried not to show it. Can you forgive me?"

"Well, I must admit you were behaving most peculiarly all evening. You should have said something."

"I could not bear to spoil your evening, my love. Come, let us forget it," he coaxed, taking her hand.

"Well," she conceded, much mollified, "but you must promise never to treat me so again."

"Never."

She leaned forward, eyes closed, mouth raised for a kiss of forgiveness, and he had nothing to do but oblige her. He blanked his mind and forced himself to forget that he was suffering with love, and after a time began to enjoy the favours at hand. He could not deny that Arabella could excite him when she put her mind to it.

18

Max had returned, by now, all of the calls that had been paid, as was proper, upon him as a newcomer, including all those who had found him out and left their cards. All, that is, except for the one he owed Miss Cole and her brother. He was aware that they had every right to be offended by this slight, if they should feel so, since they had been his first callers, but he had always found himself so disinclined to the visit that he put it off again and again.

He was riding now into Upper Chyppen and decided he could postpone the visit no longer. He had just come from Elmdene, where he had found, as he had the previous day, that Miss Armytage was mysteriously unavailable. Yesterday she had been "out" and today "not downstairs," as Meriel had rather vaguely informed him. He had sat politely chatting with Meriel and Mr. Armytage for the proper half-hour and come away dissatisfied. Nor had he been best pleased to pass Leighton in the driveway, though there was some satisfaction in knowing that the fellow would not see Miss Armytage either.

Thus in a mood of disgruntlement he decided he might as well get this long-overdue call over with. If he had been in a good mood, he would no doubt have found some further reason to delay.

He was shown into the drawing room and left to wait. But not for long. Arabella came hurrying in, her face wreathed in a happy smile, her hands extended in welcome. He was somewhat startled at creating such an effect, as well as not quite knowing how to deal with both of her hands. He did not feel they were well enough acquainted for him to take both of them, so he took one, bowed over it briefly, and released it.

She seated herself to one side of a sofa, but he pretended not to see her gesture indicating he should sit beside her and took a chair facing her. "I hope I will have the pleasure of seeing your brother also, Miss Cole."

"Oh, he is about someplace. I told the footman to inform him that you were here. He is sure to be along in a moment."

Max wondered briefly about the "footman," for he had been shown in by a maid. It seemed unlikely the household would include footmen when there was no butler.

"How very fortunate that I decided not to drive out with Mr. Leighton this morning, or I should not have been here to receive you," Arabella said brightly.

"Most fortunate," he agreed politely.

"Yes, I told him he was very selfish to expect me to come out with him every day. He was not best pleased and does tend to pout when he cannot have his way, so that I was forced to point out to him that I am fortunate in having a large circle of friends who have equal call upon my time. One must be fair in these things. And you know, there are so many calls on my time from all my dear friends, it is nearly impossible for me to keep up with my household responsibilities. Of course I am blessed with the ability to manage a large staff easily, so I do manage to keep things running smoothly. It must be difficult for you, poor man, having no wife to run your household for you."

"I have an extremely competent housekeeper," he replied.

"Ah, of course you do, and so have I! I would not have one who was not competent, but these women must be overseen to keep them up to snuff, I have found, and only another woman knows how to do that. We are trained to it, as you men are not. Now, do admit I am right, dear Sir Max."

"I am sure you are, Miss Cole," he replied, wishing Claiborne would come in so the subject could be changed.

"I must say I find it surprising that such a man as you has not married long ago. Have you given the matter any consideration, sir?"

"Well, I suppose every man thinks of it from time to time . . ." he began uneasily. Really, this was a most uncomfortable situation. It surely was not proper for an unmarried woman to receive a gentleman alone in this way. Cole should engage a companion for his sister, or take in a female relative—or at least make sure to be available himself.

"And hopes to avoid it as long as possible, I make no doubt," she riposted with a merry laugh. "But you all must come to it in the end when you want some comfort and order in your lives at last. I vow, I doubt Claiborne will marry at all so long as I remain at home. I have told him he had best set about finding himself a wife soon, for I cannot be at his command much longer. I have longed this age to set up my own household and have someone dearer than a brother can ever be to take care of," she confessed shyly.

He coughed. "Yes, I am sure . . . ah . . . that is . . . ah . . . as it should be, Miss Cole."

"And you must long for the same thing, Sir Max, though you may not be aware of it yet. I am always right about these things. I am very sensitive, you see, to the unexpressed longings of others, and I knew at once about you. I think you expressed your need for a wife when you had the urge to take a large house and settle down after your years of rattling about alone in London. Am I not right?''

"It may very well be so," he agreed cautiously. Then he rose to his feet. "I thank you for receiving me, Miss Cole. Please tell your brother I was sorry not to have seen him.''

"Oh, you must not rush away so soon! Claiborne will be devastated to miss you." She came to him and held his arm as though she would keep him there by force.

"I regret that it is necessary—other calls to make, you see," he said firmly, restraining an impulse to run.

He turned away and walked determinedly to the door, while she followed, still protesting that he must stay and meet Claiborne. He made his escape at last.

Good God, he thought, the woman is a menace. Does she treat Leighton to these long speeches about marriage? How can he bear it? Of course, I suppose there is an appeal there of sorts, even though it is not in my style. Still, he must be aware that the woman means to marry. Max thought he had never seen such an exhibition of determination in all his life. He could almost feel sorry for her to be in such a situation. How dreadful for women to have nothing else offered to them in life and to be forced to wait for the whim of a man for even that. He remembered, suddenly, Miss Gotobed, or rather Mrs. Leighton, just such another as Miss Cole, although infinitely less attractive. What a misery she must have made life for Leighton. How ironic it would be if he were to be caught again by the same sort of desperate woman.

Morgan, in the meantime, had no thoughts at all about Arabella. His only thought from the moment he had wakened had been to somehow spend some time alone with Meriel today. He had been happy to see Westbrook leaving as he had arrived at Elmdene, and even happier to find Meriel alone with her father when he was shown into the drawing room. He felt he could not have borne watching those young clods ogling her adoringly for another day.

He greeted her with a courtly bow and a touch of formality for the sake of Mr. Armytage, and then set himself to make the agreeable to the old gentleman to disarm his daughter. If her father was so important to her, then he would make sure she saw that he appreciated her father also. After twenty minutes of respectful attention he turned to Meriel to ask if she and Miss Armytage would care to ride.

"Thank you, but my sister is not available today," she replied with finality.

She obviously was not allowed to ride out with a gentleman unaccompanied. Very well. In a way he was glad to learn this, for at least it meant she would not be out alone with any other man either. "A pity to waste so fine a day," he said agreeably, "but perhaps we might walk in the grounds. Would you care for that, Mr. Armytage?"

"No, thank you, sir, but do you go along if you like, Meriel, my dear. It will do you good to take some air after a morning mewed up in the drawing room." Mr. Armytage was perfectly sanguine about leaving his daughter alone with Leighton, for it was very clear to him that she had not the least interest in him.

Morgan rose briskly to his feet before she could reply, and after an uncertain look at her father, she rose also. At last they were alone, strolling along through the shrubbery, and he was feverishly searching in his mind for the best way to take advantage of the moment. He did not anticipate failure, for nothing in his previous encounters with women had prepared him to do so, but this was too important to him to just plunge in and perhaps frighten her and make her wary before he had made his impression. He had never *cared* so deeply about anyone before, so he was not exactly sure what line to take. Apart from this, she was not like any girl he had ever met. Not only was she so beautiful as to seem unreal, she had a fey quality he could not quite grasp. She was so . . . so still! Yes, that was it. He had never met a woman of such serenity, such composure. One might almost say placidity, except that surely those dark eyes held the promise of passionate depths to be explored; he could not be mistaken about that, he was sure.

"It is an unexpected gift to be alone with you, Miss Meriel, and walk along quietly like this. You are usually so surrounded by admirers."

"It is pleasant to be quiet," she agreed.

"Yes, I am sure it must be a blessing from time to time for a beautiful woman to experience a few moments of peace to refresh her spirits with the contemplation of nature," he plowed on doggedly.

"Oh"—she laughed—"I spend a great *deal* of my time contemplating nature. I like to paint, you see."

"I should have guessed it from those long, sensitive artist's hands!" She made no comment to this, so he continued, "This shrubbery walk is well-laid-out. It must have taken years to grow to such a height."

"My great-grandfather planted it for his wife. She, poor soul, died before she had any use from it, but my grandmother and my mother have enjoyed its protection on windy days, and now so do Sydney and I."

"And how perfect a picture you make here. How Gainsborough or Lawrence would envy me my model if only I could paint you as you are now."

"You enjoy art, Mr. Leighton?"

He nearly ground his teeth in frustration. She blandly ignored every compliment and so unerringly picked up the impersonal in his every sentence to comment upon that it could not be done in innocence. She was as clever as she could stare; there was no longer any room for doubt on that score. A clever little minx, with a great deal of experience already in defusing the most ardent declaration. Her suitors must tear their hair at such tactics, which undoubtedly led them to even greater excesses.

That was her purpose, of course! How stupid he had been not to have caught on before! Ah, women with their little games. How ingenious they were. Very well, slyboots, he thought fondly, if you want to play that way, we shall.

"I appreciate a work of art in whatever form I see it, Miss Meriel, which explains why I cannot take my eyes off you when I am privileged to be in your presence."

"You are right that art takes many forms, and it is good to be able to appreciate that. Some can appreciate only the obvious, a sunset or a beautiful vista, while there is as much art in the structure of a leaf if one will but see with understanding."

"But the greatest work of all is the human form, and you, Miss Meriel, are a masterpiece of creation."

"I am not sure the human being *is* the greatest work of art, but of course, that is a matter of taste, I suppose. Well, Mr. Leighton, this has been a most interesting discussion. Thank you for calling and accompanying me in my walk. Will you like to see my father again before you leave?"

"Why, no . . . I . . ." He looked about, surprised to find they had reached the front of the house.

"I will bid you good day, then," she said with a polite smile, executing a perfect little curtsy. She turned then and walked unhurriedly up the steps and into the house without a backward glance, and in a moment the door had closed behind her.

He was left on one foot, as it were, with no chance to take her hand in farewell, much less to press the lingering kiss on it he had been so much looking forward to, nor even to take proper leave with a last compliment. By the Lord, she had not even waited to hear him say good-bye! For a moment he was gripped by a rage so intense he trembled. His fists clenched and he fantasized boxing her saucy ear smartly. He stalked around to the stables and called loudly for his horse, then rode off fuming silently.

Meriel thankfully closed the door behind her. She was aware that she had been less than courteous to a guest in treating him so brusquely, but she found him so cloying she had not been able to bear another moment of his company. She much preferred the awkwardness of Mr. Milbanks and Mr. Hillsborough. There was an honesty about them that was almost refreshing when compared to the calculation of Mr. Leighton's elaborate compliments, the awareness he had of his own good looks. Oh yes, she had to admit he was a man who would be considered handsome by most girls, though for her he was still too dainty of feature, especially when compared with darling Edward, the strong planes of whose face projected manliness and strength. Oh, how she would draw him and paint him when they were wed at last. Darling Edward, beloved Edward, her heart sang, and she held out her hands as though shaping them about his face. Her eyes closed and she could almost feel the bones of his face. After a moment she could bear it no longer and opened her eyes and started up the stairs to find Sydney.

She was at the back of the upper hallway in the linen cupboard as she had said, surrounded by stacks of linen, neat and pale, the absurd cap still firmly in place.

"Shall I help you, Sydney?"

"No, thank you. I am counting sheets, and mathematics was never your strong subject. I am making a pile of those that need mending, and needlework is another weak point of yours.''

"Goodness, you are cross. I think you must be tired and had best leave it now for Lutie to finish.''

Sydney relented a bit. "I am sorry, dearest. You are right. I am cross, though I do not know any reason why I should be so.''

"It is the cap,'' Meriel declared firmly. "I noticed it at once. You have been in a bad temper since you put it on yesterday. I should take it off at once if I were you.''

Sydney smiled. "What nonsense you talk, you silly girl, but you cheer me up. It is the linen, I expect, that has depressed me—so bland, and perfect, and inexpressive. Now, what have you been doing?''

"Well, Papa and I received first Sir Max, who was quite put out to find you not there, and then Mr. Leighton came and we walked in the shrubbery. I really think you should have come down, Sydney.''

"Well, I cannot always be sitting about idly entertaining visitors, so you must take some of the burden. Did you enjoy your walk?''

"No.'' This came out very decisively, causing Sydney to look up from her linen list in some apprehension.

"Did he . . . was he . . .?''

"He did and he was! What a boring fellow he is. I cannot think how you can bear his company, Sydney. Of course, I am sure he was different as a young man, but he seems to have picked up some displeasing habits in London.''

"Tell me . . . what did he do?'' Sydney asked faintly, her mind reeling with visions of Meriel fending off physical advances.

"Oh, he pays one tiresome sorts of compliments and then stares into one's eyes in a way I am sure he thinks irresistible, and tilts his head to one side in a way I am convinced he must practice before his glass every morning, feeling himself ever so charming. It is all most repellent. One longs to say something quite rude to depress his pretensions.''

Sydney could not help being amused in spite of the lowness of her spirits. It was so telling a picture of him, and so devastating a commentary. She might have known Meriel would have seen clear to the bottom of him at once. And she was right, of course, there was something a little too prac-

ticed about his mannerisms now. Well, at least she need have
no fears of her sister succumbing to the wiles of Morgan
Leighton! It was beyond anything that he should be attempting to begin a flirtation with Meriel, but somehow she could
only pity him.

19

Mr. Armytage had entered into the plans for a picnic with
more enthusiasm than his daughters had expected. He was
proud of Elmdene Grange, and most particularly of the summerhouse he had designed and caused to be built, as well as
the landscaping that had been done all the way around the
pond, affording beautiful vistas from every point as one
circled the water. Walks had been laid out to meander through
woodlands, small open glades, flowering shrubbery, and
flowerbeds, and over delicate bridges spanning the small,
tumbling stream that fed the pond. At appropriate places
marble benches had been placed for a more prolonged contemplation of the scenery. It was altogether an enchanting place
and Mr. Armytage was more than willing to show it off to his
neighbours.

Everyone they knew had been invited, for once they started
on the list, it had seemed impossible to leave anyone out
without causing offense, even the Coles and Tristan Foxx,
though Sydney hoped she would not be obliged to spend
much time in their company herself, if they accepted their
invitations.

They did, of course, for no power on earth could have kept
Tristan from such an event, and he persuaded Arabella that if
she stayed away she would be the only person of the gentry who
would do so, and that she would derive much more pleasure
from the day than she could possibly receive from refusing
the invitation. She allowed herself to be persuaded, though as
they both knew, she had had no intention of staying away.

She also allowed herself to be swayed by him in the matter
of the gown she declared she must have for the affair, and he
successfully lured her away from a violent pink silk by
extolling the good fortune that was theirs in finding a celestial-
blue muslin that so exactly matched her eyes. He also succeeded in dissuading her from excessive trimmings and ruffles,
so that she looked quite lovely, he thought, though showing a
great deal more bosom than he thought necessary, or even
proper for an afternoon to be spent in the open air. He rather
spitefully hoped she might suffer from sunburn. Serve her
right!

They set off together, however, in good spirits, leaving
Claiborne to come by horseback, and formed part of a proces-
sion of carriages all making their way to Elmdene Grange. It
was a pleasant drive, for the day was clear and sunny with
only a light breeze.

The drive was filled with carriages all the way down to the
gates, so that it took some time for them to reach the house.
Mr. Armytage and Meriel waited to greet their guests at the
steps and directed them around the house to the path leading
to the pond. There people milled about admiringly, greeting
one another with great cheer, while children of varying ages
chased one another about, not heeding their anxious mothers'
calls to keep away from the water. It was a scene very
pleasing to the eye, though Arabella was less than pleased
when she saw that Sydney, busy laying out rugs and pillows
on the grass, had as her assistant Morgan, who followed her
about diligently.

Max was also watching them, for he had offered to assist
her earlier and been coolly requested to attend to some of the
elderly guests who were looking about for chairs. He was
perfectly happy to do anything that would please her, but he
could not understand why she refused to meet his eyes. He
had not seen her, except for brief glimpses, since the night of
the Assembly. He had been over and over every moment of
that evening and could find no incident or word spoken to
give him an indication of the source of her displeasure with
him. He longed for just a moment's privacy with her to ask
her, but she had proved too elusive. He had hopes, however,
that today would provide him with a chance. In the meantime,
he was puzzled, and somewhat hurt, that she had accepted
Leighton's help and refused his own. He saw Arabella wav-

ing to him, clearly expecting him to come and greet her. He settled the Bidlake ladies on a bench and said he would return in a moment.

Meanwhile Arabella sailed straight up to Sydney and embraced her enthusiastically as though they were long-separated bosom bows, to Sydney's bewilderment. Max caught her wondering eye and he raised an eyebrow quizzically, and before she could catch herself she had felt a little laugh bubbling up. Then she remembered and looked away hastily. She asked Arabella to excuse her but she must attend to other arriving guests, and bustled away. Arabella held out her hand to Morgan before he could follow Sydney, and he bowed over it and asked her how she did. She then greeted Max and asked him to find a chair for her, for of course she could not be expected to sit on the ground. She not only thought it not befitting her station in life, she was also aware of not being lithe enough to assume such a position with grace, much less regain her feet with dignity intact. Max led her to one of the chairs that had been carried out from the house, and she requested Morgan to find a pillow for her. When she was at last comfortable, she managed to retain them both in conversation for quite some time before first one and then the other was called away to greet arriving friends.

Arabella looked about and noticed that all the young people not strolling about were seated on the rugs, while she and a number of elderly ladies and gentlemen were the only people occupying chairs. She jumped to her feet at once and strolled about looking for Tristan. She would have preferred Max or Morgan to take her for a walk, but Max had returned to the Bidlakes, while Morgan was now following Meriel about with a stack of drawing books. Several of the young ladies had decided to show off their skills at sketching, and Meriel was passing out materials. Arabella noticed that Sydney was on the dock with some young men who wanted to try their hand at fishing. Really, Arabella thought contemptuously, these Armytage girls will do anything. One would think they had no servants to serve their guests.

She finally located Tristan in the summerhouse, where he had found a book of Meriel's drawings and was inspecting them with great interest. Arabella made her way to his side. "Come, Tristan, I think I should like to go for a walk," she demanded peremptorily.

"A moment, dear lady," he replied absently, holding up the pad to inspect a drawing of a bewhiskered old gentleman. "She really is quite talented, the little Armytage. That is old Beddoes, I'd stake my life on it. Do look, Bella."

"Oh, really, Tristan, I have no interest in looking at amateur . . . Why, yes, you are right, how charming," she cooed, her irritation breaking off in mid-sentence. He looked up to see that Meriel had come up the steps to fetch more chalk.

"I hope you do not mind our seeing your drawings, Miss Meriel?" Tristan asked. "I was just saying you are exceptionally talented. This can only be old Beddoes. Where did you take his likeness?"

Meriel looked embarrassed, and said nervously, "Why, those are all people I saw in the Pump Room in Bath when I visited my godmother there recently." She wondered if she could possibly get it from his hands without appearing rude, for in a moment he would come to the pictures of Edward!

"Ah, Bath, of course. He does go there every year for his gout. Look at this woman, Bella, does it not remind you of your aunt, Lady Boxton?"

"My aunt is not so stout as that, surely, you naughty thing," Arabella protested with a laugh.

"She weighs a great deal more than is good for her health," replied Tristan, continuing to turn the pages.

Meriel's heart was racing and she was torn between the desire to flee before they could see Edward's likeness and her own reaction to it, for she felt she could not help betraying herself, and her need to remain in case they should recognize him and speak of him. Oh, the joy of hearing him spoken of admiringly. That he could be spoken of in any other way was, of course, impossible.

"Wait, Tristan! Turn back," Arabella suddenly exclaimed in excitement. "No, not there, another page. There! That is Trevillion. Never tell me *he* was in Bath?" She turned inquiringly to Meriel, who felt the colour staining her cheeks.

"Who? Oh yes, you are right, it is Trevillion, the handsome devil, and you have got him to the life, Miss Meriel," Tristan said.

Cassie came up to join Meriel and wanted to see the picture also. "Who did you say he is? He is very attractive."

"It is Edward Trevillion, Earl of Devitt, Miss Maplethorpe,"

Arabella informed her loftily, "one of my dancing partners at my come-out in London," she added recklessly, staring down Tristan's mocking glance, "though I find it hard to picture him in Bath, of all places. Was he alone?"

"With . . . with his mother, I think. Excuse me, I must take these chalks to Miss Tremont." She turned and fled. Only Tristan noticed that all the colour had drained from her face, and wondered about it.

Meriel forced herself not to run, for that would call attention to herself that she did not want, but she walked as fast as possible through the throngs of guests, reached the house, and at last the safety of her own room, where she sat down on the bed and stared blindly ahead. Her hands were clasped so tightly together the knuckles had turned white. "The Earl of Devitt" rang brassily through her head, making, for the moment, all other thought impossible. How long she sat unmoving, she did not know, but slowly she became aware of where she was and of the sound of talk and laughter drifting through the open windows, and with it came pain.

She began to pace furiously about the room, unable to sit still while her heart ached so much. Oh, Edward, why did you never tell me? How can you have let me believe you would come to me, when you knew it could never be so?

The tears welled up and rolled unheeded down her cheeks. He would not come, of course. They could never marry. He would never be allowed to make such a marriage. His family had no doubt arranged a marriage for him while he was still in leading strings, as was the custom in most great families of title. He could not be allowed to marry plain Miss Meriel Armytage of Elmdene Grange with a dowry of five thousand pounds. She knew this as surely as she knew anything. What she could not understand was why he had allowed her to believe that he would.

She remembered his eyes, looking so straightly into her own, and hope revived momentarily, but then she remembered his mother, an autocratic-looking lady, even formidable, who would never countenance such a marriage for her son. Even the few glances Meriel had spared her in Bath had shown her to be a proud, stiff-necked sort of woman who would have no trouble demolishing any plans in short order that did not meet with her approval.

Meriel suddenly saw Edward in her mind's eye so clearly

she cried aloud and clapped a hand over her mouth. His face
appeared to her, close, as it had been when he had held her,
his eyes telling her that he loved her. He had been sincere
. . . oh, he had! He loved her at that moment as much as she
loved him, and she had no doubt that he still loved her.
However, the obligations of a great titled family would make
themselves more apparent again once he was out of her
presence and back in his own milieu. He would realize, or it
would be pointed out to him, that a man in his position could
not follow the dictates of his heart in so important a matter as
marriage. His family would not hesitate to insist that he owed
it to his family name and prestige to sacrifice his personal
desires for the greater glory of the Devitts. He would be
forced to submit, though his heart might break.

Would his heart break, as hers was now doing? She thought
she could feel hers quite literally cracking, and the pain was
nearly unbearable. Oh, dearest Edward! She did not want him
to suffer this way! But even as she thought this, she knew it
to be untrue. I do want him to suffer! I do . . . I do! I could
not bear to think he was not suffering, for that would mean he
had not meant any of the things he had said, and she could
not believe that. He had meant it, he had loved her, but he
could not come to her and she must learn to accept it and live
with it. He would write, of course, to explain to her that it
was impossible, much as it hurt him to admit it. Such a man
as Edward would never be so cruel as to disappear from her
life without a word of explanation. That was a cruelty she
would never credit him with though he did bow to his family
and give her up.

Oh, if only she had known all this, she would never have
allowed herself to lose her heart. She would have realized the
impossibility of any happy ending for them and held aloof.
Ah, why do I say such things, even to myself? I know it is
not true. I fell in love with him as I drew his likeness, before
I ever spoke to him, and had we never met, I would still be in
love with him. The tears trailed slowly down her cheeks as
she stared drearily out the window, surprised to find the sun
still bright and the sky still cloudlessly blue when there was
no joy left for her in the world. My love, my love!

Then she heard footsteps coming along the passage and
moved quickly to her washbasin, poured water into it, and

when the door opened, raised a dripping face to Sydney, who stood there.

"Dearest, is anything wrong? Papa sent me to find you. He said he saw you hurrying into the house and thought you looked pale."

"It was . . . it is only that I was too warm—all that rushing about. I just came to bathe my face. I feel better already." She patted her face dry and went to her dressing table to brush her hair.

"Perhaps you should lie down for a bit," Sydney suggested worriedly, torn between concern for her sister and her unattended guests.

"No fussing, now, Syd. I am perfectly well. Come, we will go down again together." She took Sydney's arm and they went downstairs. Meriel felt perfectly in control of herself, though so cold all over from the chill coming from the small block of ice where her heart had been that she wondered if her face would crack if she smiled, or even if she *could* smile. She felt that she must somehow get through this day without anyone guessing anything, and then she would be able to manage anything. She longed to throw herself into Sydney's arms and cry her heart out and be comforted, but knew she could not allow herself that luxury now, with guests swarming everywhere. She must just wait—and get through this day.

20

Arabella dragged Tristan away for a walk about the pond and they strolled slowly along the path, Arabella twirling her parasol and admiring everything cheerfully. Then Tristan remarked that Meriel's sprigged-muslin gown today was very fetching, and she begged to differ with him, saying to her mind it was insipid, and as for Sydney's daffodil lawn, it was not a becoming colour for her.

"To my mind it is a most becoming colour for her," he said definitely.

"I think I may safely say my taste in such matters must be better than yours, Tristan," she informed him.

"Not if you insist on wearing grass green," he returned with asperity. "That really was too bad of you, Bella."

"It happens to be the very latest colour and all the rage in London."

"That may be, but it still does not suit *you*."

After that there was silence and they marched at a quicker pace. When they reached the far side of the pond she declared she must rest on a bench there and they sat down. Before them at the edge of the water the boat rested, half out of the water on the bank where someone had evidently rowed across and abandoned it.

"Oh, Tristan, look! You can take me back across in the boat." She imagined herself lying back in the boat, trailing a hand in the water, the very picture of allure.

"Not for anything in the world. I would have blisters before we were half across."

"But I am so tired. I cannot walk all the way back," she pleaded coaxingly.

"Then you must row yourself, my dear, for I cannot."

She pouted and said no more, for when he spoke in that tone she knew there was no moving him. Then she saw Morgan coming along looking from side to side as though searching for someone. Me, she thought; he must be looking for me! She called out and waved her parasol at him. He halted abruptly and half-turned, as though to retreat. Then he shrugged and came ahead slowly.

"Were you wondering what had become of me, sir?" she said with a melting glance.

"Er . . . yes, of course. Hello, Foxx."

"Mr. Leighton! Just the fellow we need. How opportune of you to come along at the very moment you are needed, like a knight in armour come to rescue the damsel in distress," Tristan cried out, causing several people walking past to stop in amusement.

"Distress? I do not—" Morgan began.

Tristan rushed on. "Yes, yes, dear fellow. Here is poor dear Miss Cole unable to walk another step and the boat lying there as though *sent* to take her back to the other side! And then you appear as if by magic to perform the deed of valour!''

"You might have taken her yourself, I suppose," Morgan muttered, conscious of the interested audience.

"Ah, it distresses me to deny the Fair One anything she desires, but I fear my strength is not equal to such exertion."

Arabella took matters into her own hands by rising and walking to the boat, where she simply waited very grandly for one of them to behave as a gentleman. Tristan only smiled benignly, and Morgan had nothing to do but follow her, though he was furious at this interruption, for he had been searching fruitlessly for Meriel for at least three-quarters of an hour, and with each moment that passed, ever more hideous explanations for her disappearance presented themselves to him, all involving her in some sort of dalliance with another man.

He helped Arabella into the boat and stepped in himself as Tristan came forward obligingly to push them off. Morgan began to row, while Tristan stood on the bank waving his handkerchief gaily and wishing them bon voyage.

"Ah, how exquisitely lovely it is. Mr. Armytage has truly made a showplace here. Is it not heaven to glide along in the sunshine beneath a blue sky on a summer day?" Arabella enthused, lying back as she had planned and trailing her fingertips in the water.

"All very well for you, I suppose, so long as you do not have to do anything but sit there," Morgan grumbled, much put upon.

"How can you be so ill-natured on such a day? Come, smile at me, my dear. Perhaps later we can steal a moment to visit that interesting little copse of trees I saw as I walked around," she offered with a meaningful smile. He did not respond. Now, what is the silly boy sulking about? she wondered. She prudently remained silent for a time, and the next time he looked at her, she smiled tentatively. He smiled back halfheartedly.

She does make an attractive picture, he thought, drawn despite his obsession with Meriel. His expression softened. She was encouraged to speak again.

"Do you know, Morgan, what Mrs. Dobbs said to me before? I was never more astonished, and I could not think

where to look. I am sure I must have blushed to the roots of
my hair.''

"What did she say?"

''Oh, the silly woman said she hoped she would be wishing me happy very soon. She was only fishing, of course.''

''Did she have anyone definitely in mind, or was it just a
general blessing?''

Arabella looked hurt. "Well, of course she meant you, my
dear.''

''What? Damned snoopy old besom!''

''Please do not use such language before me, Morgan. And
I cannot think why you must be so abusive. After all, she was
only saying what many must be thinking. Your attentions
have been so marked, I am sure anyone might think—''

''They may think what they like, but you would be best
advised to disabuse them of such ideas.''

She stared at him in shock for a moment; then the tears
sprang into her eyes. ''Oh, you are hateful! How can you be
so beastly to me?''

They were nearing the opposite bank, and he forced himself to speak calmly. ''Arabella, I think you must admit that I
have never said anything that could give you cause to believe
my intentions included marriage.''

''Not in words, but I naturally supposed you must—''

''No, my dear,'' he interrupted firmly, ''we have enjoyed
a pleasant flirtation, a few embraces which I am convinced
you enjoyed as much as I, no promises given or asked.''

She did not reply, but sat up stiffly, dipped her umbrella so
that it came between them, and they continued the remainder
of the way in a stony silence. Arabella's thoughts were a
chaos of hurt, injured dignity, anger, and vows of vengeance,
while Morgan was wondering where Meriel was and, more
important, who she was with.

Cook had been preparing food for a week and had outdone
herself. Lutie and Lizzy, with the help of several young men
and girls from the village, were now to be seen carrying
platter after platter of food out from the house, and soon
several large tables set up in the summerhouse groaned under
their loads of food and drink. Guests began to draw around
the tempting display, appetites sharpened by a day in the
outdoors, abandoning fishing poles and drawing pads and
hurrying around from the far side of the pond. For a consider-

able time there was a great bustle as plates were filled and places found on the rugs and cushions, and the maids moved about serving the elderly.

The westering sun lit up the scene obliquely, creating even more magical effects, and the soft, scented air fanned heated faces soothingly. Gradually a hum of contentment settled over the company; even the shrill voices of the children were stilled by good food and exhaustion.

Morgan, with exquisite courtesy, found a chair for Arabella and brought her a plate of food. He even sat on a pillow at her feet and made polite conversation to which she refused to respond by so much as a look. He was perfectly content to have it so, for he could watch Meriel as she flitted here and there through the crowd, bringing napkins, refilling glasses and plates. There was no point in attempting to be with her, for she was never still a moment, but at least she was in his sight now and unattended by anyone else, and there was still the possibility of snatching a few moments alone with her.

The moment never came. As the sun disappeared behind the belt of trees surrounding the area and the first hint of twilight began to steal over the day, parents began collecting sleepy children and making ready for departure, and Meriel was busier than ever collecting wraps, fans, toys, and lost gloves. There was soon a general exodus, and soon only the servants remained to clear away.

Max and Morgan, who had ridden over together, were the last to leave. Morgan had managed to kiss Meriel's hand in farewell, but only as she stood between her father and sister. She had not even looked at him as his lips touched her ice-cold fingers, indeed, seemed hardly aware of any of them, her eyes being wide and unfocused. It was not in the least satisfying, but he could do nothing more about it. He mounted his mare and waited as Max said a last word to Mr. Armytage and came to put a foot in the stirrup of his mount.

At that moment Meriel soundlessly slipped to the ground. There was one brief instant of shocked silence as they all stared in disbelief; then Sydney cried out and Mr. Armytage started forward. But Max was there before both of them. He stooped, lifted her easily, and carried her towards the door. Sydney rushed ahead, saying she would bring restoratives, and Mr. Armytage directed Max into the drawing room, where he helped Max to dispose her tenderly on a sofa.

Morgan slid quickly down from the saddle to follow, his first thought of himself as he cursed the bad fortune that had led him to be already mounted and Max not. *He* should have been the one to carry her in his arms! He hovered over the sofa indecisively as Sydney rushed in, pushed him aside summarily, and knelt at Meriel's side to wave a vinaigrette beneath her nose. Lizzy came with a glass of hartshorn and water, but they were unable to administer it. Nothing availed, and Meriel lay there still and white and lifeless, like a sleeping ice princess.

"Papa, what can it be?" Sydney cried frantically. "What should we do?"

"I think she should be put into her bed and the doctor summoned," Mr. Armytage replied. "Sir Max, perhaps you would carry her upstairs, and if you would be kind enough, Mr. Leighton, please go to the stables and tell Tom to ride into Upper Chyppen and fetch Dr. Kenmore."

"I . . ." Morgan began, but then realized the impossibility of changing the order of things as well as the impropriety of even suggesting such a thing at such a moment. " . . . will, of course, fetch him myself, sir," he finished, and with a curt bow hurried out to spare himself the sight of Westbrook lifting her into his arms again.

Meriel was carried upstairs, and then Max went back down to wait with Mr. Armytage and offer what comfort his presence could give. Sydney, with the help of the frightened maids, undressed Meriel and put her into a nightdress. It was like dressing a doll, so limp and lifeless were the lolling limbs and head. When she was tucked beneath the sheets, Sydney, hands trembling and face nearly as white as the one on the pillow, bent pleadingly over her, whispering distractedly, "Meriel, oh, dearest, please! Speak to me!" and holding the vinaigrette under her nose.

Why had she not insisted Meriel lie down earlier when she had found her in her room? For all the slender delicacy of her looks, Meriel was in reality very healthy and rarely ill. It seemed unlikely, now Sydney thought of it, that Meriel could have been so overcome by heat. Why, the day had not even been so warm as to warrant it. Sydney thought she had never known such terror in her life as she experienced as she tried vainly to rouse her sister. Surely it was not normal to remain unresponding for so long? Oh God! Why did I not *make* her lie down?

Though it seemed endless hours, Dr. Kenmore, thin and dour, actually arrived thirty minutes after Morgan had set off to fetch him. He walked briskly upstairs and set about examining his patient, while Sydney told him of her negligence earlier in the day and begged him to tell her what was wrong with Meriel.

Dr. Kenmore checked pulse and heartbeat and asked, "What happened? Some shock, say? Anything disagreeable?"

"Nothing! Nothing at all. It was a perfect day and everyone seemed to enjoy it. She kept very busy, of course, perhaps she did too much after she came back downstairs. She was pale, but she said it was only that she was overwarm. Oh, why did I . . . ?" She began to cry.

"No tears, if you please. Won't help her or you. Now, what are you up to, Miss Meriel?" He began massaging her arms and administering light slaps to her cheeks, scolding her all the while as he would a recalcitrant child, and after a few more moments Meriel's eyelids began to flutter and then she looked up uncomprehendingly into the doctor's face. Then her eyes moved to Sydney and she said, "Sydney! Oh, Sydney!" It was a mere whisper of sound, but it held such heartbreak it caused even Dr. Kenmore to clear his throat and pat her cheek comfortingly.

"Well, now, little girl, you have managed to frighten your family out of their wits. Raise her up, Lizzy, and give her some of that hartshorn and water . . . slowly, mind! Miss Armytage, if you could step outside with me . . ."

In the hallway she looked up at him with wide, frightened eyes, sure some awful news was about to be imparted. He unbent sympathetically and took her hands to pat them reassuringly. "Don't take on so, child, she will be all right. Very healthy young woman. I think, you know, something must have happened to her today that shocked her profoundly. Try to get her to tell you all about it—it will help her more than anything to talk about it. None of that stay-quiet-and-rest nonsense."

"But what on earth can have happened? And why was she able to go on all day before she succumbed?"

"The mind is a great mystery, so I have no answer. Sometimes one can continue to behave normally after a fatal injury to the body. The mind perhaps does the same. When the necessity for her to perform was over, it all came back full force and it was so unacceptable the body obligingly rang down the curtain on it, so to speak, allowing her to escape into unconsciousness. Now, send those girls away and stay with her for a time, try to find out what is on her mind. I will leave some laudanum drops to give her tonight to make sure she sleeps."

"How long should I keep her in bed?"

"Oh, a day or two, if she is inclined. But I would not encourage that, if I were you. She is not really ill, you know. I will come around early tomorrow to take a look at her."

"Thank you, Dr. Kenmore."

"I will go down now and reassure your father . . . and take those anxious young men away with me."

Sydney returned to Meriel's room, sent the maids away, and sat down on the bed beside her sister. She picked up one of the cold hands and looked with loving anxiety into the unnaturally white face. "Darling, what is troubling you? Can you tell me about it?"

Meriel's eyes filled with tears, and Sydney picked her up and cradled her in her arms, rocking her slightly, holding her close and murmuring endearments. Meriel began to sob, her cries so harsh and deep they quite frightened Sydney. For a time it seemed Meriel would not be able to stop, but the sobs waned from exhaustion finally, and presently she sighed wearily and began, brokenly, to tell Sydney everything: her meeting with Edward, their glorious mornings together, their rapturous declarations of love, and finally of his proposal and promise to come to Elmdene Grange and speak to her father.

"Meriel! My darling girl! But why did you not tell me?"

"He asked me not to say anything to anyone until he could tell his mother about it. I did so want to tell you, Syd, but I had promised him I would not."

"But, darling, this is wonderful news! I do not mind your little secret, I promise you. Surely you have not worried about this so much it has made you ill?"

The dark eyes filled with tears again as Meriel began to tell Sydney what she had learned today from Arabella Cole, and how she had realized at once what it meant. "He will never be allowed to marry *me*, Sydney! They will not let him! They will make him marry someone very grand."

"Meriel, you cannot know that. You have simply leaped to conclusions that you cannot know to be true!" But even as she said it, Sydney could not help feeling that Meriel was probably right. It did seem improbable that he would be allowed to marry so far beneath his station. Not that the Armytages had any reason to be ashamed of their lineage. They had been accounted gentlemen of breeding and scholarship for many generations, though always country people who lived quietly and were, for the most part, undistinguished as far as titles and honours went. They were humble folk indeed when compared with the great Trevillion family, whose Devitt earldom had been theirs for many hundreds of years. Sydney remembered hearing about them from someone.

Meriel could not be comforted. "No, I know it cannot be, though I am not sure how I am to bear it. I wish he had told me about it himself. I might never have let myself grow to love him so, had I known, for I would know it could not be." There was so much pain in her voice that Sydney was not sure she herself could bear it.

"I will not allow you to think in this way. He has asked you to marry him. He cannot be so lost to all honour as to allow his family to persuade him not to do so. I will not believe it. I feel sure he will come, as he promised."

Meriel only looked at her sadly and shook her head, then fell back to her pillows tiredly. "You need sleep, dearest, and tomorrow things will not look so bleak. Dr. Kenmore left some drops for you, and you must take them at once."

She bustled about preparing the medicine, administered it, and with a last hug and kiss on the pale cheek, took herself off, just making it to the hallway before the tears began streaming down her own cheeks. She brushed them away impatiently and made her way to the library, where she knew she would find her father waiting for her. He rose at once and came across the room, looking anxiously into her eyes. Now it was Sydney's turn for comforting, and she laid her head wearily on his chest and cried while he held her close, not asking her any questions until she had finished. When the crying turned to sniffs and hiccoughs, he handed her his handkerchief and asked if she had learned what was bothering her sister. Sydney told him the story.

"And if you could hear her, Papa! She is suffering so

much! Do you think he could possibly be so dreadful as to cry off?''

"I cannot tell you that, dear girl. They are a very great family, very old and proud and rich as Croesus. I have never been personally acquainted with any of them, but I have heard it is so. I think it is possible they would have planned a much grander alliance for the boy.''

"Yes, I knew it must be so. Poor Meriel! What are we to do?''

"Now, really, Sydney, this is not like you to give way to despair. Miss Cole said he was the earl, which means his father is dead and he has come into the title and can, presumably, do as he likes. Had he been only the heir, his family might have been able to have their own way. While it is possible they will object, there is no reason to lose all hope that he means to do exactly as he has said he would do.''

"Yes, you are right, I suppose,'' Sydney answered dispiritedly, for in spite of her father's words she could not but feel that it would all end unhappily for her sister, "though how I am to convince Meriel, I do not know. Nor even whether I should encourage her to hope at all. What if she does so and he does not come after all? Will it not be doubly unbearable for her? Perhaps he will forget her when he returns to his grand family and—''

Mr. Armytage laughed. "My dear, do you think any young man could so easily forget Meriel once having fallen in love with her? No, no, I feel quite sanguine about the matter. He will come. I must go and search out my *Debrett's* and see what I can learn of the family. Do you know, I am not entirely sure I even approve of such a marriage for Meriel. She is so used to a simple country life. Well, well, I suppose if she loves him I must not stand in the way.'' He kissed her absently and turned away to the bookshelves, and she took herself to bed, trying to derive some modicum of comfort from his confidence in the situation. She looked in first upon Meriel and found her sleeping heavily under the influence of the laudanum. No trace of colour had returned to her face, but at least she was resting. Perhaps tomorrow Papa would speak to her and things would seem less hopeless to Meriel.

She made ready for bed, so tired she felt she could not bear to even remove her gown. When she was able at last to sink into her pillow, however, she found her mind trudging round and round the problem again, unable to let it go. If there had only been something she could have done to comfort Meriel, she would not now be feeling so helpless, but she knew she had had nothing of real assurance to offer and Meriel had heard the doubt in her voice. She had never been able to bear to see Meriel cry, though heaven knew she had rarely done so in her life. Meriel had always been so good-natured and even-tempered, so easily soothed out of childish hurts. But this could not be termed childish, nor could her hurt be eased by hugs and kisses from her sister.

To think of Meriel falling in love with a man who turned out to be a great lord. It was like a novel, the sort Meriel liked, where such wildly improbable events were commonplace. Had there been nothing in the man's manner or dress to indicate his grand station?

Then it slowly came to her that Meriel was not, could never have been, falling in love with Sir Max, and before she could stop it, a slow dawn of renewed hope spread through Sydney's mind, until abruptly she realized how foolish she was being. Nothing had changed. Meriel might not ever love Sir Max, but that would not change his feelings for her. And if the worst should happen and Edward Trevillion not come to claim her, Meriel might, in time, be able to find some comfort in Sir Max's steady devotion.

Sydney forced her hopes back behind the barriers she had earlier erected and berated herself roundly for even having such selfish thoughts while her sister suffered so dreadfully. She finally surrendered to exhaustion and sank into an uneasy sleep, from which she kept starting awake in alarm, each time forced to rise and check on Meriel before she could try to sleep again. She woke at last, so little refreshed it was difficult to believe she had been to bed at all.

Meriel was awake when she went in, staring out the window at the bright day dawning. "I was so sure it would rain today," she said as Sydney came in.

"Darling, how are you this morning? I think you had a good sleep."

"Yes. I am well. I will get up soon."

"You will do no such thing. Dr. Kenmore says you are to rest in your bed today, and I mean to see that you do so. Perhaps this evening, if you feel up to it, you can dress and come down for dinner."

"No," Meriel replied, "I will get up. I am not ill, and I cannot lie here all day with nothing to do but think."

Sydney knew she would feel the same, and besides, she heard the inexorable tone in Meriel's voice that meant she would have her own way despite every protest. "Very well, my love, if Dr. Kenmore says you may. He will be here soon. Now, I will go down and order some breakfast for you."

She went away unhappily, not the least comforted by Meriel's assurance that she was not ill, not when it was delivered in that colourless, dispirited way. She thought perhaps she would after all prefer tears. This resignation was not at all a relief.

Dr. Kenmore arrived an hour later and found Meriel physically recovered enough to get up if she liked, even telling her she would be better for some exercise. While he was with her, Max and Morgan rode up to inquire about her. Sydney went down to reassure them and thank them, but firmly denied Morgan's insistent request to see her later in the day, perhaps take her for a drive.

"I do not expect her to be able to receive anyone for several days, Mr. Leighton, though I thank you for your kind thought. Now, if you will forgive me, I must return to her."

Max took the hand she held out and looked down anxiously into her eyes, noting the dark shadows of weariness around them. He longed to pull her into his arms and hold her comfortingly, but there was something so impersonal in her regard he could not even think of a warm word to say. He realized there was little he could do for her now beyond taking himself and Morgan away, so he merely bowed and left, pulling the resistant Morgan with him.

21

A week passed with agonizing slowness and enormous anxiety at Elmdene. Meriel's mood remained despondent. She was like a beautiful statue of marble, cold, pale, unsmiling, as though a light had gone out inside her. Mr. Armytage talked to her, as serenely confident as he had been with Sydney the first night, but she could not believe him, and seemed disinclined to discuss the matter any further, nor to want kind words or sympathetic looks. It was difficult for those around her to carry on as though nothing had happened while she sat so silently unhappy in their midst, but she shrugged away all comforting embraces and would not respond to any attempts to reassure her. After the second day, Sydney and Mr. Armytage ceased all efforts in that direction, seeing that it did not help her, and fearing to make matters worse by their anxious solicitude.

She was, however, very little with them. She rose early every morning and rode alone for hours. Sydney had offered to ride with her, but Meriel had said since she left the house at dawn she would not dream of asking her sister to rise at such an hour. She returned at midday only to change out of her habit and set off again on long walks about the grounds, never venturing beyond the gates, or to the pond to pace around and around or row herself tirelessly about on the water. She did not paint or sketch, nor even read. Her need was simply for physical activity. She ate her dinner, and evidently worn out by exercise, went to her bed very early and, so far as Sydney could judge, slept. Sydney's ear felt permanently cocked in the direction of her sister's bedroom, ready to go to her at once if there were any sounds of crying. But there were none.

She could not be persuaded to come down to greet any callers, even Cassie Maplethorpe, and indeed she was rarely in the house when they came, so it was left to Sydney to receive them and reassure them she was fully recovered, and to treat their probing for causes as offhandedly as possible. Since Max and Morgan came every day, Sydney was forced to see Max whether she would or not, and though they were never alone together, it was wearing just the same to be so continually on her guard. Some days she felt so unequal to it she sent Lizzy to tell her father he must receive them alone.

All the while, her worry about Meriel grew, and while her sister slept, Sydney found herself less and less able to do so, until by the end of the week Mr. Armytage gently pointed out to Meriel that her sister was looking very tired and perhaps Meriel could assist her by taking the burden of receiving visitors onto her own shoulders, since most of these were young men who called expressly to see Meriel.

The next morning Meriel made sure to return from her prebreakfast ride in good time to change her gown and tidy her hair and take her place in the drawing room. Her suitors found little joy in her presence, however, for while she was polite and responded kindly to all their inquiries, she was not the girl they had all fallen in love with. In a day or so the visitors began to thin out in the drawing room. Meriel was also very restless, pacing about the room aimlessly, and generally suggesting they all walk in the gardens. Morgan and Mr. Milbanks were her usual escorts. Max always stayed behind with Mr. Armytage in the hopes that Sydney would come in, but she did not.

After several days Mr. Milbanks failed to appear one morning and Morgan was finally rewarded with the opportunity to be alone with her that he had awaited for so long. He tried, as they paced along the path around the pond, to resume his previous tone with her, paying her ever-more-elaborate compliments and loverlike effusions, sure she understood him very well, and taking her silence for acceptance of his suit. But after a time the complete lack of response unnerved him to the point of desperation. They had now circled the pond completely and arrived back at the summerhouse, and he was not sure how much longer he could count on having her to himself. When she turned towards the path leading back to the house, he clasped her arm to detain her.

She looked at him then, but her look was one of such polite and disinterested inquiry that he rushed wildly into speech. "I cannot stand this any longer! Why must you go on pretending this way? You are teasing me, I know, but it is past bearing any longer. You must know I am nearly mad with love—''

She held up a hand warningly. "No, Mr. Leighton . . . please do not . . . you must not . . .''

"But I must. I . . . You must listen to me. I adore you . . . I . . .''

She looked horrified and tried to pull her arm from his clasp, but he became even more excited by her resistance and with an exultant little laugh pulled her into his arms, his lips seeking hers. Her head flailed from side to side to avoid him, and she struggled frantically. She finally managed to get her arms up between them and shoved him with all her strength, so that he staggered back. She turned and ran—eyes wide and unseeing—straight into Max's arms!

He had strolled out when Mr. Armytage suggested he follow the other couple. "I think Mr. Leighton may have developed a *tendre* for Meriel, Sir Max, you understand? Just now she is in a . . . ah . . . rather delicate mood, and I should not like Mr. Leighton to . . . ah . . .''

Max had hastily assured him he understood and would be happy to oblige. He also had been rather perturbed by Leighton's recent attitude towards Meriel. His previous manner with women had seemed based on lighthearted flirtations, but with Meriel he appeared brooding, angry when other men were near her. It was difficult for Max to accept that Leighton had at last succumbed to love, but if Meriel continually spurned his advances, he could very well be in the grip of an obsession to add her to his list.

Not that Max had had many thoughts to spare for Leighton's feelings this past week. Even his own anxiety about Meriel, as well as his puzzlement about the cause of her strange malady, had taken second place to his worry about his own problem. Sydney continued to elude him, and even when in his presence would not meet his eyes or unbend in her manner. He felt that if she would only grant him a few moments alone he could get to the bottom of her attitude, explain away whatever was troubling her, or, best of all, declare himself. He had been on the point of speaking to her father for permission to address her, when suddenly these walls had been thrown up between them by her. Even now, as he walked along, eyes on the ground, hands in pockets, he

was considering the advisability of confiding his dilemma to
Mr. Armytage. The old gentleman liked him very well, Max
knew, and could perhaps question Sydney about her feelings.
She surely would confide in her own—

He heard running footsteps, looked up, and jerked his
hands out of his pockets just in time to catch Meriel as she
ran full tilt into him. They stood speechless with shock
staring at one another as he steadied her by the arms.

"Good Lord, child, you nearly had me down!" he gasped,
with a laugh. Then he saw the wild look in her eyes and
exclaimed, "Why, what is wrong? Has something frightened
you?"

"He . . . he . . ." She shuddered and seemed unable to go on.

Max glanced over her shoulder to see Morgan just emerging from the belt of trees surrounding the pond. He stopped
when he saw Max, and hastily turned and disappeared.

"Was it Leighton?" Max asked softly, guessing what had
happened. She nodded dumbly. He pulled her arm through
his own and began to walk her slowly over the grass back to
the house. "Be calm, my dear, it is over now, and I promise
you I shall see to it that it does not happen again." Meriel
held his arm tightly, staring up at him with gratitude.

Sydney was going up the stairs and glanced out the stair-
well window to see them below her, strolling along, Meriel
leaning trustfully against him, gazing up into his face. Sydney continued up the stairs, but she could not erase the sight
of them from her mind, especially the way his head had bent
so solicitously over her and the way he was patting the hand
holding his arm. Sydney sighed unhappily. Yes, of course it
was bound to be so, she thought, the poor child is so unhappy
and it is often the case that in such a state of mind one will
turn to a stranger for comfort he cannot accept from his family.

Max is too sensitive a man to press his suit now, knowing
how unwelcome it might be, though of course he cannot
know what the problem is. But he will offer strength and
kindness now when she needs it the most, and eventually, if
our fears about Edward prove true, she may come to sense
the warmth and caring of his devotion and accept him.

She found herself in her room standing before her glass,
staring into her own reflection unseeingly. Her eyes focused
and she studied the image before her, seeing the fine lines at
the corners of her eyes, the—surely?—deeper etching of the

lines from nose to mouth, the tiredness apparent in her whole
expression. Suddenly, in an access of fury, she tore the
ruffled, beribbanded cap from her head and flung it across the
room and then threw herself facedown on her bed and sobbed
her heart out.

She sat up at last, wondering why, if a good cry was
supposed to be restorative, she felt so dull and dreary. She
stared at the cap on the floor, a mere scrap of lace and lawn,
symbol of all she could not allow herself to dream of. Then
she rose, bathed her swollen eyes in cold water, and looked
into the mirror. Why must one look so ugly when one cries?
Now I shall have to remain in my room for an hour until the
redness is gone.

She picked up the offending cap and smoothed it out and
set it back on her head with finicky precision.

Max walked Meriel back to the house, talking soothingly
of anything he could think of. Before saying good-bye he
assured her he would make sure Leighton did not bother her
again. "However, in light of what has happened, it might be
as well if you did not go about so much alone, or at least had
a less volatile escort than Mr. Leighton. I hope you look upon
me as a . . . brother"—he bent an inquiring eye at her, and
she nodded, understanding his meaning—"and will make use
of me if you need me—for instance, if you care to ride."

"I always go—but very early—at sunup," she said.

"I will be here tomorrow morning," he promised.

When Meriel went upstairs, Max reentered the house to
seek out Mr. Armytage and inform him of this plan and of
what had happened between Meriel and Leighton. Mr.
Armytage approved and was grateful to him for his thought-
fulness. Then Max returned home to await the arrival of
Leighton. When he heard him ride up, he stepped into the
hall and invited him to accompany him to the library.

"I suppose the silly girl came babbling all sorts of nonsense to you," Morgan began, taking the offensive at once.

"She told me nothing, being in too much shock to speak at
all, but I hope I am not such a cloth-head I cannot guess what
happened."

"A great to-do about very little. I may have lost my head,
but you know she is so damned beautiful any man could be
excused for . . . well, in any case, it was nothing so serious."

"The girl has not been well, but I suppose you have not noticed that," Max returned icily.

"Seems well enough to me. Doesn't talk much, but then, she's always been a deep 'un, not giggling and chattering like most of them do."

"You were there when she fainted—"

"Oh, women faint at the least thing. Probably laced too tight or something," Morgan returned carelessly. "Right enough now, by the looks of her."

"Well, she is not, as anyone who truly cared for her would see. I must ask you for your word that your behaviour will not be repeated while you are a guest in my house."

"Oh, now, see here, Westbrook—"

"Your word, Leighton," Max repeated, his voice hard with barely suppressed anger.

"Of course you may have it if you insist. Ask your pardon, I'm sure."

Almost any gentleman in such a situation would have at least offered to leave, if only as a gesture, but it was clear Leighton was not going to do so. There was little Max could do, short of requesting him to leave, a drastic action in the face of his apology and his word, however flippantly it was offered.

The next morning he and Meriel rode out in the clear pure dawn air, speaking hardly at all, galloping for miles through fields and country lanes. She rode intently, her eyes fixed straight ahead, hardly aware of him, he thought. He let her lead by a head or so, unwilling to intrude his presence into her need for silence. She led him, finally, to the hilltop he had first visited with Sydney. She slid down from her saddle without waiting for his assistance, and walked her mount to the tree, tied it up, and sat down on the mossy rock without looking at him. He followed suit, but did not sit beside her until she looked around, saw him standing there, and indicated that he should.

The sun had now cleared the horizon and slanted across the rising mists, lighting up here and there the trees rising like grey-green umbrella tops from the clouds of whiteness. They watched in silence as the mist submitted to the sun's insistence and began to vanish in wisps. The warm rays reached them where they sat and began to draw damp, green woody scents from the earth. If only he could share such a moment with Sydney, he thought longingly.

Meriel said, not looking at him, "It is wonderful, is it not? So much . . . larger than anything else. It helps me to understand the smallness of my own . . . concerns."

"Yes, it is cosmic, awesome even. But for me, so much so that it is too far out of my comprehension, if you take my meaning. It will go on forever without my help, or even my appreciation if I choose not to notice it. But my concerns remain, selfishly perhaps, more important to me."

He thought she had not attended his words, she was quiet for so long. Then tears began to slide down her cheeks silently. She made no move to stop them or to hide them from him—almost, it seemed to him, she was not even aware of them. Did she come here every morning and cry like this, without a sound, as though her pain had liquefied and poured out of her without her noticing it? His heart ached with pity and he longed to comfort her, but could not bring himself to intrude on what seemed so private a grief.

So they sat side by side without speaking until the flow of tears slowed and stopped. Then she rose to her feet and started back towards the horses, taking a scrap of lace-edged linen from her habit pocket and drying her cheeks unselfconsciously as she walked, and they rode slowly back to Elmdene.

"Your sister says you have attempted to paint that view several times," he said.

"Yes," she said indifferently. "It never comes out."

"Perhaps you should try again."

"I have no inclination to paint. I think it has . . . left me," she replied quietly, and again indifferently.

He was startled. He had naturally thought a great deal about what might be wrong with her, speculated about a broken romance, hoped against a serious disease. Was it possible that all along she had been mourning the loss of an accomplishment? Well, more than an accomplishment. In her case it was a very considerable ability. But could it have been so important to her she was going into a decline over its loss? He wished he were better acquainted with the artistic personality.

"You have found that . . . ah . . . loss unbearable?" he probed gently.

"Oh no. I suppose it will return someday."

Not the loss of her talent, then, he thought. "I think you should definitely try it again," he said firmly. "Sometimes great emotional stress may blot out the desire to express oneself artistically, but quite often it can open one to seeing things in a new light. It would also, I should imagine, bring its own release to express what one is feeling through one's art.''

She pondered this for a long moment and then said, ''You may be right,'' noncommittally.

He could not read anything into her words and let the matter drop. They turned into the park gates and rode up the drive in silence.

Across the road from the gates Morgan sat astride his horse, concealed from view by a clump of tall bushes. He ground his teeth in fury to see her alone with Westbrook. So that was the way the land lay. She had been out for a title all along and was bringing Westbrook up to scratch by making him jealous of my attentions. She was toying with me, pushing me to lose my head and oblige her with actions she could run tattling to Westbrook about in order to rouse him to action before he lost her.

He had never felt so tricked and helpless in his life. He knew he would no longer be received at Elmdene Grange, for she would have been sure to have confided in Sydney. Females could never be trusted to keep anything to themselves. Men would never behave so. He'd vow Westbrook had never said anything to anyone about his confidences regarding Bella. Morgan could not even feel angry with Westbrook, though he had spoken to him in that uppish way yesterday and now was apparently dangling after the girl. Poor fellow was only dancing to her tune, as Morgan himself had done.

He felt his manhood had been diminished somehow for allowing himself to be led around by the nose by a schoolroom chit. He headed automatically for Arabella's house in town, instinctively going to one place where he could be sure of restoring his shattered confidence. Bella might be still very angry with him, and all the better if she were. Exercising his special technique would be much more worthwhile in such a case. And he would vow that by now, no matter how she behaved, she would be eager to be coaxed into forgiveness. She was sure to be missing him by now, for she was a very warm-blooded girl despite those cold blue eyes, and while she always made sure not to compromise herself absolutely, she enjoyed a bit of rough and tumble, and she, at least, could be counted on not to pretend otherwise and get all coy and missish about what she wanted. What they all wanted, if they could be brought to admit it. Women liked men to be bold and take every advantage possible. It made them feel irresistible. Oh yes, *he* knew about women.

He began to feel better about Meriel. She was only using men as they all did, or tried to do, wasn't she? His own sense of superiority became restored by thinking he understood women and could be magnanimous about them.

He still loved Meriel—at least he did so as much as he was capable of loving anyone. If it had been explained to him that he was a selfish lover who thought only of his own feelings, he would not have been capable of understanding, since his only criterion for judging the actions of others was himself. He had always thought of others solely in the light of how they affected him, and assumed everyone else did the same. He scoffed at people who professed high-minded unselfishness, for he knew they were secretly moved only by their own needs. He did not despise Meriel for what he believed was her making use of him to achieve her own ends. He admired her for her cleverness in spite of his anger, and was even more determined to have her one day.

Sydney was just coming down the stairs for breakfast when she saw Max and Meriel through the wide-open front door, ambling down the drive, not speaking but seemingly comfortable together. As she reached the bottom stair, they halted and Max dismounted to assist Meriel, who put her hands confidingly on his shoulders to be lifted down. Sydney tried to force herself to turn away, but her feet felt embedded in the stair. She watched Max take Meriel's hands and speak to her, and after a moment Meriel raised her drooping head and gave him a sad little smile. With a wrench Sydney tore her hand from the newel post and fled down the hall to the dining room.

After that she tried to avoid having to witness such scenes by coming down much earlier than usual and retreating to the back of the house or upstairs when their return was imminent. In spite of these precautions, she saw them another time when they returned somewhat earlier than usual. Meriel had apparently persuaded Max to come in for some breakfast. Meriel laid down her crop and turned to put her hand on Max's arm. "Thank you, dear friend," she said softly. He smiled and

laid the backs of his fingers against Meriel's cheek with such
ineffable tenderness that Sydney felt a lump rise in her throat.
Blind with tears, she turned back into the dining room,
wondering how it was possible for her to feel this selfish pain
at the confirmation of her hopes for Meriel's eventual happiness.

22

Edward set off for London with his mother eagerly. The
sooner he got her there and could explain everything to her,
the sooner he could be with Meriel again. His heart bounded
exuberantly in his chest at the thought of it.

The Countess of Devitt was, however, a poor traveller, and
suffered from indifferent health at all times and managed to
contract a chill that necessitated a three-day stopover on the
road until she could recover enough to continue. There was a
great deal of scurrying about every day by Lady Devitt's
abigail, by the anxious landlord, overcome by the honour of
having such great folk in his house, and by his hardworking
wife and their staff of servants, while Edward was left with
nothing to do but kick his heels impatiently in the inn's best
parlour.

They finally were able to set forth again, Lady Devitt carefully swathed in shawls to fend off the stray draught, and they
managed to gain London without further delay, where his
mother immediately took to her bed again to recover from the
ill effects of the trip, and remained there for a further three
days, sending her abigail with daily bulletins on the state of
her health and begging her son to forgive her inability to
receive him, but her condition required absolute quiet and
solitude.

On the third day, when her abigail came to inform him that
m'lady would be down for dinner that evening, Edward
received a summons from his steward. Land that marched
with his own and that he had long coveted had become

available, but the old gentleman who owned it would only deal personally with the Earl of Devitt himself. He was advised to come at once. Edward was forced to send word to his mother that dearly as he looked forward to dining with her, he was called away urgently.

He managed to conclude his business in one day, but the journey to the north of England took three days, and of course, three days to return. The two weeks he had hoped would suffice to settle things with his mother was nearly over and he had yet to speak to her. He sent a rider ahead to inform her of the day of his return and beg her to dine with him if possible.

She was out when he arrived but had left word that she would indeed be in for dinner, and he fretted away the hours till then as best he could. When his mother came down at last, he hurried forward to greet her, kissed her warmly, and held her hands.

"Well, my dear, what a nice welcome," she said with a pleased smile. "I might even believe you have missed me."

"Of course I have missed you. I am very glad to see you have fully recovered."

"I am not sure that I have."

"Nonsense. You cannot stand there looking so beautiful and claim to be ill."

"Ah, you must not try to bamboozle an old lady, Edward, especially your mother. What do you want? Pockets to let?"

He laughed and led her into the dining room, where a stately and lengthy meal was served to them, which he hardly tasted. She eyed him narrowly several times, fully aware he had something on his mind which he naturally could not speak of before the servants. The meal ran through its numerous courses and finally, as was his custom when they dined alone, he took his wine into the drawing room to sit with her.

Now, he thought, watching her settle down with a piece of needlework before the fire, now we can begin. But now the moment was upon him, he found himself strangely tongue-tied. He sipped his wine for a time, trying to marshal the proper words to begin, then gave it up to wander aimlessly about the room.

"My boy, I dislike figeting, of all things. Please sit down and get on with what you have to say to me," she said finally.

He whipped around in surprise and then laughed ruefully. "You know me too well."

"You used to behave just the same way when you wanted to confess you had broken my best piece of Sèvres china," she replied knowingly, her dark eyes, so like his own, flicking up from her embroidery at him.

"Yes. Well, I do have something to tell you. Something far more momentous than breaking a piece of china."

"My dear, you are alarming me! Please stop dithering and tell me at once."

"It is that I plan to marry soon and—"

The embroidery fell to the floor and she held out her hands to him, her face lit up with joy. "Oh, Edward, at last you and Georgina have—"

"*No!*" he shouted; then more quietly, "No, Mama, *not* Georgina." He knelt before her and took her hands. "It is someone else, someone I know you will love just as much as you have always loved Georgina when—"

"But . . . but, Edward . . . this cannot be true. It has always been meant that you and Georgina would marry."

"By you and her mother perhaps, never by us. Darling Mama, please listen to me. I—"

"And also by Georgina, Edward."

"No, never, I assure you. We have laughed about it often, but we could never feel in that way for one another."

"Ah, perhaps she allowed you to think so, but I believe I know her better than you. She is a very proud girl. If you spoke disparagingly of the idea, she would not let you see that she cared."

"You cannot be right about this, Mama," he said, but there was less conviction in his voice. "But even if you were, I surely cannot be expected to marry her just because you and she and her mother planned that I would do so when we were babies. I have never allowed you to think that I would ever marry her."

"Perhaps not in so many words, but I know you are fond of her and I always believed you would realize at last how perfect a wife she would make for you. A prestigious family, a title in her own right, a great heiress, trained from birth to manage a large estate and entertain the most distinguished families in the country, even royalty. A wife befitting the Earl of Devitt."

"I do not deny all her worthy qualities, Mama, nor that I have always been fond of her. But I do not love her as a man wants to love his wife. I love someone else and I mean to marry her!"

"Who is this girl?"

"Meriel Armytage of Elmdene Grange in Middlesex."

"Armytage? I know of no Armytages."

"Proving they do not exist, I take it."

"Do not take that tone with me, Edward!" she said sharply. "Who is her father?"

"Why . . . Mr. Armytage of Elmdene Grange."

"And that is all you know of him? He might be anybody—a farmer or even a labourer of some sort."

"He is a gentleman, I assure you."

"How can you know that?"

"I have met the daughter. A beautiful, well-mannered girl that you will fall in love with on sight, I know."

"Pooh, a pretty face. I thought you were much too sensible to be caught like that, Edward. You met this girl in Bath, I take it? No doubt she was sent there to visit a relative in the hopes of attracting some old doddard with a fortune."

"Well, she was visiting her godmother, Lady Divers," he offered propitiatingly, with a grin.

She ignored this. "And she had the great good fortune to snare a young titled man. She must be very pretty indeed, or very clever."

"She is both, though not in the way you mean. For one thing, she never went anyplace in Bath but the Pump Room. She had not met one person. She doesn't even know I have a title yet."

"Not know? Nonsense," she scoffed, disbelieving. "She will have made it her business to find out before she met you. The godmother person who introduced you will have told her."

"I never met the godmother. She is an invalid who never goes out, nor receives. We . . . we introduced ourselves, and I simply said I was Edward Trevillion."

"You must have told her more than that!"

"How could I? One cannot walk up and introduce oneself by one's title. And then . . . well, after I came to know her better, I was not quite sure she would like it."

Lady Devitt looked her disbelief, and Edward felt his

temper slipping. He managed to control it, however, and patiently set about convincing her that he was genuinely in love with Meriel, had proposed and been accepted, and meant to marry her, and hoped not to be forced to do so without his mother's blessing. After an hour she grudgingly conceded that of course she could not prevent him ruining his life if he were determined to do so. Another half-hour brought her consent to receive the girl.

"But only if I hear from Georgina's lips that you have spoken to her and that she is not heartbroken. I will not have that child treated callously in this matter, Edward."

"Well, of course I will speak to her about it. I had meant to anyway. I will call on her tomorrow."

"She is away the rest of the week, visiting in Scotland with that aunt of hers who is lady-in-waiting to the Queen Mother."

Edward groaned helplessly. There was nothing for it but to wait for Georgina to return to Town, not if he wanted his mother to accept his marriage with some degree of happiness. He could not allow her to treat Meriel coldly because of some imagined slight to her godchild, or worse, to refuse absolutely to bless the marriage. He had an uneasy feeling that Meriel might even refuse to marry him if she learned of Lady Devitt's disapproval.

So he continued in London until the end of the week in raging impatience, though innocently unaware of the direful events happening at Elmdene Grange, as well as of the fact that his nonappearance in the specified fortnight or even sooner, as he had so blithely promised, had at last destroyed the tiny flicker of hope that had persisted in Meriel's heart despite every shred of common sense she could summon.

She was sitting on the mossy rock atop the hill she loved, her sketching book open in her lap, her chalk in her hand, but only a few lines had been drawn on the paper. She had been absolutely unmoving for so long that Max, who sat some distance away in the grass, was becoming worried. He cleared his throat to attempt to recall her.

"It is now eighteen days," she said quietly, as though continuing a conversation, "so *that* is over. I shall have the letter soon, I suppose."

"My dear, I am afraid I do not quite follow," he said apologetically.

"He was to come after me in a fortnight, or perhaps sooner, he said. I knew he could not do so, of course, when I learned who he really is. But I suppose one can never quite accept the worst until one is forced to do so. No doubt I will go on this way till the letter is actually in my hands."

He rose and came over to sit beside her. He removed the sketching pad and the chalk and took her hands, pulling her around to face him. "Now. Tell me all of it," he commanded, confident she would never have spoken at all if she had not wanted to talk of it to him.

He heard her out in some astonishment. Devitt, by the Lord Harry! Why, he knew the fellow! They were both members of White's in London and had played cards together a number of times. He had always thought the lad was to marry his cousin—or was it a cousin? Some connection, in any case. The Lady Georgina Something. Everyone spoke of it as a settled thing. Was it possible the lad had been playing fast and loose with this innocent girl, trifling with her affections to while away a few boring weeks in Bath? He had seemed a straight sort of chap, but they were not on any intimate sort of footing, so Max could not be certain of his true character.

By the end of her sad recital, however, he could not help but feel the possibility existed that she was right. Whether Devitt had only been amusing himself with her, or had meant it at the time but allowed his family to dissuade him, it looked as if he were not coming.

When they had returned to the house and Meriel had disappeared upstairs, he sent Lizzy with a message to Sydney, requesting her to give him ten minutes of her time on a matter of some urgency. That ought to bring her, he thought.

She came, but was very formal in her manner, and as ungiving as always. He sat down at her bidding.

"I regret having to call you from your duties, but there is something of importance I want to discuss with you." He distinctly saw her wince, but never suspected she thought he was going to discuss his feelings for Meriel with her. He went on, "She has told me, this morning, of her . . . ah . . . affair with Devitt. I find it difficult to believe he could behave in such a way."

"You know him?"

"Yes, though I did not tell Meriel that. I propose going to London to confront him, if you will not think it unwarrantable interfering."

"For what purpose?"

"To learn his intentions."

"Yes," she said slowly, "I can understand your feeling that you must do so. If it should prove that what we fear is true, however, what can you do?"

"That will depend upon what I learn," he said grimly.

"You would not . . . would not call him out?" she asked fearfully. "Oh, pray do not—I could not bear it if . . ."

"Yes?" he encouraged, wondering if it was true that she had shown, just then, something like genuine concern for him in her eyes.

She looked down. "I would not want blood to be shed, nor, I am sure, would Meriel."

"I doubt it will come to that."

"I pray you will not allow it to do so. It could not resolve anything. Just learn what it is important for you to learn and come back safely. Meriel will need you more than ever. I hope, however, that you will be patient with her. This is not a thing she will recover from at once."

He looked bewildered. "Patient with her? Why, naturally I will be patient with her. She is a very dear girl and needs all the help we can give her at such a time."

"Of course. I knew I could count on your understanding. Now, if you will excuse me"—she rose—"will you be leaving at once?"

"Tomorrow."

"Then I will wish you a safe journey, and I thank you for your . . . feelings for my sister."

"I would feel the same about anyone dear to you, Miss Armytage," he replied, reaching for the hand she did not offer him and kissing it warmly. He left then, and she stared after him for a long time, even when the door had closed behind him. Unconsciously she held the hand he had kissed to her cheek. When she realized what she was doing, she snatched it away, fiery colour staining her face. Fool! she thought, and hurried out of the room.

23

Edward was sitting on the sofa, face to face with Georgina, and holding her hands when the drawing-room door opened to admit Peach, the butler, to announce Sir Max Westbrook. Before he could speak, Sir Max appeared behind him, very stern of countenance. His eyebrows and his mouth turned down as he saw the apparently loving couple before him. Peach allowed his tone to reflect his disapproval of such bumptiousness as he announced his name, and Edward, more than a little startled at the disapproving countenance peering over Peach's shoulder, leapt to his feet.

Georgina had been with him but ten minutes, having arrived back in Town this morning, finding his note begging her to waste no time in coming to his mother without delay, and hastening to obey. He had barely managed to convey the gist of his news to her and his mother's dictum when they were interrupted. He was not best pleased by the intrusion of a slight acquaintance, but he came forward courteously and bowed. "Well, Westbrook, good morning." He allowed his eyebrows to rise questioningly, inviting the man to state his business.

Max was more than aware of what Edward must be feeling at such a moment and supposed he knew the reason. He had registered admiringly the tall, statuesque redhead on the sofa, who had lifted a regal chin at his sudden appearance, and had few doubts as to her identity. He had also noted the drift of freckles across the perfect patrician nose and a mischievous sparkle in the bright green eyes that warmed the nobility of her awesome presence. Oh yes, there was no denying she would make a perfect Countess of Devitt. But she could not hold a candle to Meriel! Damn the fellow for a black-hearted libertine! He flicked a speaking glance at the lady and back to Devitt, clearly indicating he needed to speak to Devitt alone.

Edward misinterpreted the look. "Oh," he said, "how uncivil of me. Georgina, allow me to present Sir Max Westbrook to you. Westbrook, the Lady Georgina Debray."

She acknowledged his cold bow with a curtsy and looked interestedly from one gentleman to the other.

"Lord Devitt, I would be grateful if you could oblige me with five minutes of private conversation, though I realize you must think me unpardonably rude to intrude at such a . . . private moment." He stressed the last words with a flick of the anger he was feeling.

"Well, much as I dislike appearing discourteous, Westbrook, I am in a tearing hurry just now—pressing personal business, you see—" Edward began, wild to take Georgina to his mother and settle things so that he could set out for Elmdene before midday.

"I have just come from Upper Chyppen," Max interrupted significantly.

Edward's head jerked up. "Upper Chyppen?"

"Yes, and I have something of extreme urgency to tell you."

Edward stared at him, turning an unhealthy grey colour and putting out a hand as though to ward off the words to come. "Not . . . What has happened? She is not . . ."

"If we could be alone, sir," Max repeated with a look at Georgina.

"Oh, don't mind Georgie. I have told her all about it. She understands everything. Speak, man!"

Understands, does she? Max thought grimly. Yes, of course she does, and forgives his little peccadillo, too, I make no doubt. Not the girl to give up the title of countess easily, that one. He allowed the anger and contempt he was feeling to inform his voice. "Perhaps she does, my lord, and very fortunate for you that she can be so forgiving. There are some of us, however, who look on matters in a different light."

"Will you please tell me at once if Meriel is well?" Edward ground out, his patience worn so thin he felt he might go mad in a moment.

"That would depend on your meaning of 'well.' "

Edward started forward as though to attack this stiff-necked fellow with his fists. Georgina cried out and caught his arm. "Edward . . . wait! Sir Max, I think if you could just reassure us that the girl is not ill or injured or . . ." She hesitated to pronounce any more dire circumstances.

"She is not, madam, though I think, if you will forgive me, it would be better that I say what I have come to say to Lord Devitt in privacy."

"If you do not get on with it at once, Westbrook, I shall not answer for the consequences," Edward shouted furiously.

"Be damned to your consequences," Max returned, no less angrily, not even aware of the impropriety of his language in the presence of Georgina. "I know the whole story from her own lips, I warn you, so it does you no good to pretend you know nothing of my reason for coming, and I tell you to your face you are a despicable rogue and scoundrel to have behaved so. If you care to call me out for my words, I will be happy to give you satisfaction, sir. My seconds will call on you tomorrow."

"What is this man talking about, Edward?" came a thundering voice from the door. They all whipped about in astonishment to confront the Countess of Devitt standing there in regal outrage.

"Oh, my God!" Edward muttered, running a distracted hand through his dark hair.

"Godmama," cried Georgina, running forward to embrace her.

Lady Devitt ignored the kiss being planted on her cheek. "Later, Georgina. Who is this person, Edward?"

"Sir Max Westbrook," Edward answered resignedly. "Sir, my mother."

"Lady Devitt." Max bowed stiffly.

"What is going on here? How dare you speak to my son in such a manner, sir?" the old lady demanded, refusing to acknowledge the introduction.

"I believe your son knows perfectly well of what I speak. I must leave it to him to attempt to explain his conduct to you if he dares," Max replied severely.

"Mama, will you please wait upstairs?"

"Wait *upstairs*? I am to wait upstairs while this man charges into my home, shouting abuse and throwing out challenges to my son? I will not have it, do you hear me, sir? I will not have it!" She stamped her foot angrily, her eyes flashing fire at Max.

"Godmama, please do not upset yourself! I assure you it is only a misun—"

"Be quiet, Georgina! Edward, call Peach to show this man out at once!"

"I have no intention of leaving until I have said what I came to say to Lord Devitt, madam," Max declared harshly. "This could be done in five minutes if you would have the goodness to withdraw and—"

"What? Can I be hearing aright? Do you now dare to order me from my own drawing room?" Lady Devitt gasped, drawing herself up in awesome affront.

"Mama, please! If you will not leave, have the goodness to be quiet until we can sort this out," Edward begged desperately.

"I will not be quiet! Now, sir"—she turned to Max fiercely—"I demand to know what it is you think my son has done that could justify your making such outrageous accusations. Speak at once!"

"Very well, Lady Devitt, if you will have it so, though I warn you it not a pretty tale to repeat for a woman's ears. Your son has toyed with the affections of a gently bred girl, made promises of marriage to her, only to afford himself a few hours of amusement, when all the time he was betrothed to another. This girl and her family are friends of mine and I did what any man of honour would do. I came to learn exactly what were your son's intentions toward the girl, and I had my answer as I entered the room."

"Aha! Now I understand everything. Her family has sent you here to attempt to wring some money out of us. A fairly common sort of extortion, I believe," Lady Devitt pronounced sneeringly.

"My God, Mama! I beg you . . ." Edward cried in horror.

Max drew himself up. "You demean yourself, madam, for making such a suggestion. There *are* things that cannot be paid for with money. Your son has behaved like a libertine, no doubt acceptable behaviour in your world, but not in mine."

"How dare you say such a thing of my son?" Lady Devitt spat at him, a tigress defending her cub.

"Mama," Edward shouted, nearly ready to tear his hair with frustration, "I will answer the man if you will but have the goodness to be quiet and allow me a moment to do so."

"Edward, I strongly object to your—"

"*Mama!*" There was something in his voice that deterred his mother from further argument. Her mouth snapped shut into a thin line of outrage and disapproval and she marched over to a chair, plumped herself down, and glared at both men, her displeasure with each about equal.

"Now, sir, let us sort this thing out quietly. First . . . *what is wrong with Meriel?*"

"What would you suppose from your base, cruel actions towards her? Her heart is broken, and her family very much fear for her reason, not to speak of her health, though it grieves me to say so before your mother and your betrothed."

"Betrothed?" cried Edward.

"Oh, no, sir, you mistake the . . ." Georgina said at the same moment.

Lady Devitt chimed in angrily with another: "How dare you!"

"How dare I? I only do what any honourable man would do when he has been confronted with perfidious—"

"Wait!" Edward shouted. They all turned to him. "Sir Max, please sit down. Georgina, if you please . . ." He waved her to a chair. "Now, let us all be calm. This matter can be cleared up in a moment. In the first place, Westbrook, I am not betrothed to Lady Georgina—"

"Oh, Georgina, my dearest child, are you heartbroken? I shall never forgive him if—" cried Lady Devitt.

"No, no, Godmama, you and Mama have had your heart set on a match between us, I know, but Edward and I cannot oblige you."

"Oh, my dear, you are only saying that to be brave. I know you have always expected—"

"No, truly, I assure you that I have not. In fact, I shall hope to have you wish me happy very soon."

"But . . . who . . .?"

"Captain Wynchley. I shall follow the drum." Georgina dimpled demurely.

"But when has this all come about?" demanded Lady Devitt.

"Well, things only came to a head while you were in Bath. He—"

"Georgie," Edward interrupted with a dangerous calm, "naturally we are all perfectly riveted by your news, but if you could manage to restrain yourself until my business is settled, I would be eternally grateful."

"Selfish wretch," she responded cheerfully, subsiding.

Edward turned to the by now thoroughly bewildered Max. "Forgive all this ridiculous confusion, Westbrook. Now, if I understand you correctly, you are under the misapprehension that I, being betrothed to Lady Georgina, did . . . er . . . willfully deceive Meriel."

"Well . . . I . . . that's to say . . . yes."

"By now I am sure you have gathered that I am not engaged to Lady Georgina. Now, you tell me she is suffering from a broken heart. Why should this be so?"

"You were to come, according to her, within a fortnight to speak to her father. It is now three weeks and she has not heard from you."

"No one could deplore that unhappy fact more than I. I will not bore you with all the reasons I have been detained"—he cast an accusing glance at his mother—"but surely you cannot seriously claim she has so little faith in me that she has gone into a decline for a week's delay?"

"Actually, no. It began before that. Shortly after she returned from Bath, as a matter of fact."

"*What* began?"

"She learned by accident . . . someone recognized a drawing she had done of you . . . anyway, she learned who you really are. She became convinced you would never be allowed to marry her, and . . . well . . . collapsed."

"You see, Mama," Edward cried triumphantly, "I told you she was not marrying me for my title!"

"Oh, the poor darling," said Georgina, "and then when he did not come, she—"

"Exactly," replied Max, relieved to have it all out at last.

"You know this young woman well, sir?" asked Lady Devitt.

"Yes, and all her family. I am very fond of . . . all of them."

"You have developed a *tendre* for her yourself, I take it?"

"Good Lord, no! I am very fond of her, but not in that way."

"As well for you, in the circumstances. What sort of people are these Armytages?"

"The finest sort," he replied firmly.

"Mama, if you don't mind, I am in a hurry and I think we can dispense with all this lineage tarrididdle. Westbrook, I am going to Upper Chyppen. If you would care to accompany me, I leave within the hour."

"I will be delighted! The sooner the better!"

"Georgie, wish you happy. My regards to Wynchley. Tell him from me he must beat you soundly once a week and he will have no trouble with you at all."

"Oh, Edward, my dear. I am so happy for you, and I wish you and your Meriel every joy. When may I meet her?"

"You will meet her in a few days," announced Lady Devitt, "for I have decided that if Edward is determined on this marriage, it will be necessary for me to speak with her and her father at once. I shall travel down there and will need you to accompany me."

"Mama, there is not the least necessity for you to do any such thing. You know you do not travel well."

"Pooh! I think I know my duty. I shall be there in a few days."

"My lady, I hope you will do me the honour of allowing me to offer you my home for your stay, and Lady Georgina, too, of course," Max said.

"That is kind of you," replied the old lady graciously, looking upon him so approvingly it was difficult to believe the venomous exchanges between them had really taken place.

"But I cannot accept, Sir Max," said Georgina, "dearly as I should love to. Wynchley is only in London a few weeks and he is engaged to dine with all our relatives and then we must be introduced to all of his. I could not leave Town now."

"You disappoint me gravely, Georgina. Surely these things could be postponed in view—" began Lady Devitt outrageously.

"No, Godmama, not even for you," Georgina replied, laughing.

"But I shall need someone to accompany me! Edward—"

"Not for anything in the world, Mama. I have delayed long enough for you," he said firmly.

"If you will allow me, Lady Devitt, I will stay in London and escort you to Upper Chyppen myself when you are ready, though I hope it can be within two days at most."

"I could not possibly be ready in less than three days."

"Three, then," he conceded affably.

"If that is settled, I will bid you all good-bye. If I am to be there by tomorrow, I must leave this instant." Edward kissed his mother and Georgina, shook Max warmly by the hand, and with a wave strode quickly out the door.

Max hurried after him. "Devitt, you will stay with me also, of course," he called after Edward, who was disappearing rapidly up the very grand staircase, taking the steps two at a time. "I will send word to the servants to expect you."

Max returned to take leave of the ladies. Lady Devitt invited him to return and dine with her, but he declined, saying now he was in Town he would check on his business affairs and look up some cronies he had not seen since he moved to the country. "I will call for you on the fourth morning from now, dear lady, and we shall entertain each other by becoming better acquainted."

They had, as it turned out, a delightful journey together, so much so that Lady Devitt suffered less than usual when travelling and declared she thought the problem before had been boredom. Max told her, in minute detail, all he knew of Meriel and the Armytages, then listened graciously while she extolled the virtues of her son and gave him the unabbreviated history of the Trevillion family and all their illustrious connections and honours. When this topic was exhausted, he amused her by describing some of the inhabitants of Upper Chyppen.

In the course of this conversation he promised to have a number of dinner parties in order for her to meet them all.

"With, perhaps, some dancing if there are enough couples to stand up. I like to see young people dancing," she said.

"Certainly with dancing. Indeed, why should we not have a ball?" He could just imagine the ladies of Upper Chyppen when they discovered the Countess of Devitt in their midst, stunning them all with her queenly condescension. It gave him even more pleasure to contemplate how soon she was to become the Dowager Countess of Devitt.

How had Edward fared? he wondered. But there was little reason to worry, he felt. And how had Sydney taken his sudden arrival? Now that her sister's fate was settled, could he hope to see her turning to him at last? He sighed.

24

Edward had longed to leap onto a horse and ride to Meriel full out without stopping, but second thoughts had persuaded him that it would not do. He could hardly gallop directly up to her door and present himself to her father travel-stained and dirty. So he had ordered his travelling chariot to be brought round with four horses in harness, as sleek and black as the coach itself, an elegant equipage embossed with his crest on the door. A groom was sent ahead to arrange for changes of cattle at stages along the way, and, accompanied by his valet, Edward set forth within the hour as he had said he would, driven by his coachman with a second groom in the box beside him holding the yard of tin to announce their approach to inns and toll gates.

The journey, except for his mounting impatience, was uneventful, and early on the second morning, after stopping just outside to inquire the direction of Elmdene Grange of a small boy, they swept through Upper Chyppen.

Mrs. Maplethorpe and Mrs. Dobbs were abroad early and spent quite ten minutes discussing the apparition and trying to figure out the quarterings on the coat of arms on the door.

When the carriage slowed to turn into the gates of Elmdene at last, Edward leaned out the window eagerly, though for a time there was nothing to see but the well-kept drive winding along between two rows of elm trees, with pretty parkland beyond them. Then the house came into view, solid and comfortably pleasing to the eye, but with no Meriel waiting to greet him, which he had somehow expected against all reason. Then he was out and thumping the door knocker, his heart hammering nearly as loudly.

Lizzy opened the door and gaped at the handsome man in the light four-caped driving coat standing there. Beyond him she saw the very grand carriage and elegantly accoutered attendants in their black-and-cream liveries. Her mouth opened but she was speechless.

"Is Mr. Armytage at home?"

"Oh . . . yes, m'lord." Lizzy was in no doubts at all that here was a man who should be so addressed.

"Please present my card to him and ask if he could receive me," said Edward patiently.

"Oh . . . yes, m'lord," she said, not moving, too overcome to know what she was doing. He stepped forward, and she blushed, stepped back for him to enter, curtsied, and hurried away, carrying his card before her reverently on a tray. She was back in a moment to say, "Master asks you to step into the library, sir. Will I take your coat and hat?" He removed them and she laid them carefully over a chair and then led him down the hall to a tall double-leaved oak door.

Mr. Armytage came forward at once to greet his guest, his face beaming a welcome. "Well, Lord Devitt, I have been expecting you."

Edward was taken aback somewhat, having understood from Westbrook that hope had more or less been abandoned for his appearance. "You were, sir?"

"Oh, yes," the old gentleman returned serenely.

"I thought . . . Westbrook said . . . your daughter had decided I would not come."

"Oh, well, women take these fancies, and nothing will shake them, but I knew you would come."

"Well, I am pleased that you had faith, but puzzled to know how you were so sure," Edward said, smiling.

"My boy, Meriel is the image of her mother, and I know no power on earth could have kept me from her once she had said yes to me."

Edward laughed delightedly, Mr. Armytage joined in, and they shook hands heartily. "I hope I can take it, then, sir, that you will not object to our marriage."

Mr. Armytage sobered somewhat and gave him a long, straight look. "I will not say it is what I would have thought best for her before I met you. She has always lived very simply, you understand, and has not been used to very grand society, nor has she been trained to such a position. Apart from that, she is an artist and has, I believe, an artist's temperament. She is a deep, quiet sort of girl, who needs understanding."

"I think I understand her, sir. Those qualities you speak of are what drew me to her, and I will cherish them, I assure you. I spoke to Sir Thomas Lawrence when I was in London, and he is very interested in her from what I told him. He wants to see her work and has said he will find a proper teacher for her. As for the other things, they are unimportant. Meriel has no need for the training you speak of. I am surrounded by competent servants, and Meriel has better things to do with her time than order dinner or supervise the maids. You can trust me to take care of her, Mr. Armytage."

"Yes, I think I can," replied Mr. Armytage with another long look. "You have your mother's approval?"

"Yes, I have. In fact, she is coming here—I hope that will be all right. But nothing could stop her. She should arrive in three or four days. Sir Max Westbrook is bringing her."

"Ah, we shall naturally be honoured to welcome her. Now, I suppose it would be a cruelty to keep Meriel waiting another moment."

"If you please, sir. Where will I find her?" Edward breathed earnestly, blessing the man.

"I am not sure, but Sydney will know." He crossed the room and opened the door into the hall. "Oh! There you are, my dear."

Sydney had been pacing the hall since Lizzy had come rushing upstairs with the news that a very grand young gentleman had arrived in such a carriage as she had never seen the likes of and was with the master.

Sydney had stood up abruptly, spilling the lapful of ruffled petticoat she had been mending. "Who is it, Lizzy?" knowing somehow who it must be.

"I don't know, miss. He give me his card to take to Master and didn't say his name."

Sydney knew Lizzy could not read, so did not bother to question her further. She straightened her cap with suddenly shaking hands and hurried down. But the library door was closed and she could not bring herself to simply burst in. She began to pace.

When her father appeared, she rushed to him. "Papa . . . is it . . . ?"

"Yes. Come, my dear. Lord Devitt, this is my other daughter, Sydney."

" 'Edward,' if you please, Mr. Armytage. Sydney"—he

took her hand—"you are just as Meriel told me. You will not mind my calling you Sydney? I know you too well to think of you by any other name."

"I will be pleased, Edward."

"And will you also forgive me for causing your sister pain by my delay?"

"Meriel! Good heavens, what are we doing standing here talking? You must go to her at once."

"Yes," he agreed simply, wondering why these kind people kept saying that but he kept not being taken to her.

"Come, I will show you."

She led him outside and around the house and pointed. "Go straight across the grass to the path through those trees and follow it. You will see her."

He left her without a word, but she only smiled at the rudeness as she watched him cover the grass rapidly in long strides and disappear into the trees. She turned blindly away, her eyes filled with tears.

Edward rushed along the path and came upon the summer-house and the pond—and there she was, standing at the edge of the water, her back to him, unmoving.

"Meriel . . ." he breathed, barely able to speak for the constriction he felt in his throat at the sight of the sad curve of her long neck, her head drooping like a broken flower as she stared into the water.

Her head came up and she stood there another moment before she turned her head slowly to look over her shoulder. Their eyes met, but she did not move.

"Meriel . . ." he whispered longingly.

"Edward?"

"Yes, my darling."

She turned slowly, as though still unbelieving. "It *is* you?"

"Oh, my love"—he held out his arms—"will you come to me?" He felt a dreadful uncertainty at her strangeness, and a stab of fear that he was too late and she did not love him anymore.

She flew into his arms and they clung together speechlessly, almost desperately, not speaking for a very long time. Finally she whispered into his neck, "I thought . . . I was afraid . . . I was dreaming . . . imagining you there because I wanted you to be so much."

He held her away to look into her face. "Little love, you

have been crying! Oh God, can you forgive me for making you so unhappy? I never dreamed . . ."

"I . . . thought you were not coming. I thought they would not let you."

"As though anyone in the world could have prevented me, little idiot. How could you doubt me so?"

"I did not know about your title—you should have told me. I thought your mother would not . . . I *am* an idiot," she finished simply, looking up at him with her long, black almond eyes glittering with the tears she had shed before and with the happiness of the reality of his arms around her again after so long. Then he snatched her roughly against him again and his mouth came down not at all gently on hers, and everything else was forgotten.

They wandered back to the house hours later, dazed and mute with happiness, barely able to attend anything that was said to them, so oblivious of everyone around them they seemed to move within an invisible aura that magically enveloped them and set them apart, a single entity, wherever they went. Their eyes continually sought each other, and no one could be unaware of a sort of energy that flowed between them, connecting them even when in separate parts of a room. They smiled dreamily at one another, and shyly at anyone who caught their eye, as though their love embarrassed them with its glory.

Everyone in the household smiled too. Sydney had decided the servants should be informed and asked not to speak of it until after Lord Devitt's mother had arrived and the betrothal was formally acknowledged. They were pleased to be the holders of such an important secret, and even Tom, the coachman, an inveterate gossip, swore hot pincers would not extract a word from his lips. They were all proud to bursting that their Miss Meriel had caught a great lord, "though her coulda had a prince royal had her wanted 'un," Lutie declared stoutly.

The best bedroom had been made ready by the two maids under Sydney's supervision and a cot set up in the dressing room for Godey, Edward's valet, a very superior sort of servant, whom Lutie and Lizzy held in almost as much awe as they did his master. After unpacking and hanging all of Edward's wardrobe and laying out his silver-back brushes, Godey made his way to the kitchen, where he condescended to eat the very substantial meal prepared for him by Cook and served by Lutie and Lizzy, who vied for the honour. He thawed out enough to regale them with stories of the grandeur of the earl's various establishments, which left them with mouths agape in astonishment, a condition he found entirely satisfactory. He was rather amazed to find himself staying with such minor gentry, but he decided he rather liked being looked up to so worshipfully.

Sydney thought that tomorrow she would have another bedroom prepared for Lady Devitt, though when her father had told her of that formidable lady's imminent arrival she had quailed at the thought. So grand a personage, a lady Meriel had described as autocratic-looking, and one who, possibly, still disapproved of this marriage and would make her feelings apparent and frighten Meriel. Apart from this was the worry of how they were to entertain her, and whether the small staff at Elmdene would be equal to the task. Would the woman expect large, formal dinner parties every night? Would she disdain dinner partners like Squire Dobbs, for instance? Would she expect a butler and a squad of footmen to hover in attendance?

Mr. Armytage laughed at her worries when she confided them to him. "We should make ourselves fine figures of fun if we attempted to ape the ways of the Trevillions, my child. Let us be just as usual, honest folk, and she must take us as we are. Westbrook is bringing her to us and he will be bound to have told her all about us and softened her up if she needs it. Charming fellow, knows just how to go on with thorny old ladies."

Oh yes, thought Sydney, and middle-aged ladies and young ladies, too. Not that he sets out purposely to do so, as Morgan Leighton does, but only because he is so innately courteous and kind. She longed for his return even while she acknowledged that his departure had allowed her to relax her guard against his presence. But there are some discomforts one is willing to bear because the relief from them creates a void that is more painful. She found she missed him dreadfully and ached for his return, though when he was with them once more she would be back in her old uncomfortable position. She locked all these unhappy thoughts away, however, and embraced Meriel with genuine joy for her happiness.

For the most part, Mr. Armytage and Sydney were forced

to carry on the conversation between them for the rest of the day, though Meriel and Edward did respond with nods or smiles to direct questions. At dinner they made more of an effort.

Meriel said, "Edward tells me that Sir Max went to London and straightened out everything. Was that not good of him, Syd? I will be so glad when he returns so that I can thank him properly."

"Yes, darling, we must all do that. And you *do* know he brings Edward's mama with him?"

"Oh yes, and has invited them both to stay with him, though I told Edward he must stay here."

"Certainly you must, my boy," said Mr. Armytage.

"Why, Edward, of course you will stay here, and your mama also if she cares to," added Sydney warmly.

"Then I shall, thank you very much, though Mama has already accepted Westbrook's invitation."

This was the longest and most coherent conversation between them for the next two days. The lovers wandered everywhere, though they never left the grounds, and seemed equally content whether they sat together in the drawing room or the summerhouse, rowed the boat about the pond, or simply stood gazing into each other's eyes halfway down the drive.

Meanwhile Elmdene was blessedly free of callers, since everyone had decided they were best left alone until they indicated that visits would be welcomed again, and clucked sympathetically over what they termed "poor dear Meriel's decline."

Morgan fumed to himself and watched the gates every morning hoping to find Meriel riding out alone now Westbrook had rushed away so mysteriously to London for a few days. Morgan was vaguely aware of some bustle of preparation going on at Lades Hall and supposed Westbrook had sent word that he would be bringing guests home with him. Several days before, Morgan had been served an elaborate meal that he supposed had been prepared for Westbrook's return. When he did not appear, however, Morgan was glad to polish off most of it himself, his appetite unimpaired by lack of company.

He forced himself to curb his impatience at Meriel's continued sequestration, confident she would appear sooner or later, and meantime he had made it up with Arabella and they were back on their old footing. He sometimes caught her eyeing him with an unsettling intensity, "like a cat at a mouse hole," he muttered to himself, but shrugged it away, remembering that he had made his intentions very clear to her and she had gotten over all her nonsense about marriage.

He was not aware of Edward's presence at Elmdene, nor was anyone else in Upper Chyppen. Only Mrs. Maplethorpe and Mrs. Dobbs had even noticed his carriage that morning, but they supposed it to be only passing through on the way to another town. They were not to know they were living through the calm before the storm of excitement they were about to be swept up in.

25

Lady Devitt herself set off the first intimations that stirring events were in the wind when Max's carriage was bowling through Upper Chyppen and he pointed out Mrs. Maplethorpe to her. Lady Devitt immediately requested that they stop so that she could be introduced. She had declared the people of Upper Chyppen whom Max had described for her at great length were like a Jane Austen novel, and she was eager for the diversion of meeting all of them as soon as possible. He gave his coachman the order and stepped down.

Mrs. Maplethorpe came forward, all smiles, immensely gratified that he should stop his carriage to greet her. "Well, sir, we have wondered where you had got yourself. You were called away on business, were you?" she probed.

"That is it exactly, Mrs. Maplethorpe. I have brought back a guest I would like you to meet." He led her up to the open carriage door. "Lady Devitt, allow me to introduce Mrs. Maplethorpe to you."

The handsome white-haired old lady, her eyes lighted up with interest, leaned forward. "Mrs. Maplethorpe, how do you do?"

"Very well, m'lady," replied Mrs. Maplethorpe, her eyes popping a bit as she sketched a curtsy, graceful despite her amplitude. "I hope Sir Max has persuaded you to make us a long visit."

"I hope to be able to," he replied.

"Thank you, Mrs. Maplethorpe. I shall certainly stay as long as my son," she added, tossing the information to Mrs. Maplethorpe as bait, her eyes mischievous as she watched for the reaction.

"Your son, Lady Devitt? He is coming here also?"

"He *is* here. Or at least he should be here. Have you not seen him?"

"Why . . . no, m'lady. Would he be at Lades Hall, then?"

"Well, I suppose him to be, though I imagine he spends a deal more time at . . . What is the place, Max?"

"Elmdene Grange, dear lady," Max replied, his eyes twinkling as he watched Mrs. Maplethorpe absorbing this interesting information.

"Elmdene . . . Why . . . do you tell me so?" exclaimed Mrs. Maplethorpe, trying to work out the meaning of this statement, the process so clear both Lady Devitt and Max dared not look at one another for fear of laughing. "Well, fancy! I have not been to Elmdene since the picnic some three weeks ago. We had heard that dear Meriel was not well, but I suppose being an old friend of the family . . ." She paused hopefully, not sure how to go on without seeming outright nosy. Max decided the game had gone on long enough to set the cat amongst the pigeons already, and with a bow bid Mrs. Maplethorpe good day and climbed back into the carriage. Mrs. Maplethorpe and Lady Devitt exchanged courtesies and they set off on their way again and drove to Lades Hall.

Mrs. Maplethorpe went straight to Mrs. Dobbs, and by dinnertime all Upper Chyppen was aware that most distinguished visitors were in their midst and speculation was rife as to: why was the young man at Elmdene, how had he avoided the attention of all of them, and why had his mother now appeared? Only Morgan and Arabella missed the news, for he had driven her to Roxton to shop, and when they returned, she invited him to dine with her. Claiborne was out for the evening and her servants would never dream of confiding interesting gossip to her, so they remained happily ignorant for a time.

Lady Devitt declared she felt as fit as it was possible and would be taken to Elmdene at once. Her abigail protested that she should lie down for a few hours, and even Max felt constrained to second this suggestion, but she would not hear of it. She would, however, change her gown and bonnet and take a glass of wine as a restorative. She retired to the bedroom prepared for her, and descended forty-five minutes later in mauve silk, the neckline edged with a ruff of Brussels lace, and over her shoulders a French shawl of flowered Lyons silk in shades of lavender. The towering confection on her head was covered with lilac silk flowers and plumes, and Max told her she looked quite magnificent and would doubtless leave all beholders speechless. She preened a bit, well-pleased with the idea of creating such an effect. After slowly sipping her glass of wine and learning the news that Edward had sent word to the Lades Hall butler that he would be staying with the Armytages, she declared she was ready to set forth.

Max had taken the precaution of sending a groom over with a note to announce their impending arrival so that when his carriage swept up before the front steps the family and Edward were assembled there to greet them.

Edward and Mr. Armytage stepped forward together as the carriage stopped, and both assisted the lady down. She did not greet them, for her eyes were fixed on Meriel, in no doubt at all that this was her future daughter-in-law. She moved toward her, and Meriel, though pale and shaken, curtsied respectfully and kept her eyes bravely looking up into Lady Devitt's own.

Lady Devitt had set off from London prepared to find as much fault as possible, but her journey with Sir Max had put her into a much better frame of mind and she was not displeased with this first glimpse of her son's betrothed: a tall, graceful girl, startlingly lovely, and certainly showing backbone in a tense situation. However, Lady Devitt was not quite ready to show her approval, needing, though she would not have acknowledged it even to herself, her good opinion to be sought with a bit more cosseting and flattery. She could not quite rid herself of the feeling that she had been cheated of a mother's natural privilege to have a hand in finding a proper bride for her son. She satisfied the demands of the moment by holding out her hand to Meriel and saying, "Well, my dear, I am happy to make your acquaintance."

Meriel shook her hand, murmured that she was likewise pleased, and looked appealingly to Edward, who stepped forward at once.

"Mama, here is Meriel's sister, Sydney."

Sydney curtsied and smiled, not allowing herself to be intimidated by this imposing old lady. The Armytages could hold up their heads before anyone in the world. "Welcome to Elmdene Grange, Lady Devitt. You have given us all a great deal of pleasure by this visit. This is my father, who would also like to welcome you."

Mr. Armytage stepped forward, bowed profoundly, and kissed her hand gallantly. "Dear lady, I hope that in years to come Elmdene will become as familiar to you as your own home. It welcomes you, as do we all. Will you be pleased to come inside?"

This warm and clearly sincere speech went down very well, for she smiled at him most graciously and laid her hand on his arm and strolled inside, telling him that he had a very pretty property here and she would like very much to be shown over the house. This request was a blessing to the entire party, for it obviated the necessity of a stilted hour of sitting together in the drawing room, attempting awkward conversation. The discussion of mouldings and furniture put them all at ease, and by the end of the tour they all felt more comfortable and settled down in the dining room for a light nuncheon Sydney had ordered of chicken à la tarragon and new peas with Cook's fresh baked apple tarts to follow. Lady Devitt ate heartily of everything and declared she must have the recipe for the chicken for her own chef.

It was clear she considered Max as her own special *gallant*, and Sydney was grateful for the attention she demanded of him, which kept him at her side most of the day. Sydney had shaken him warmly by the hand to show her gratitude when he had arrived, but had spoken only casually to him since. She knew she must find a time before the day was ended to thank him for his efforts on Meriel's behalf, but this must be done out of Lady Devitt's hearing and, hopefully, in company with Meriel or Papa. She had studied him covertly and found his attitude, in light of what she believed his feelings to be, somewhat puzzling. Though he had greeted Meriel warmly and smiled at her speaking look of gratitude, he had not shown any of the signs of a rejected lover. He and Edward were heartily and openly friendly to each other and had clapped each other's shoulders and grinned broadly on meeting. Sydney could only ascribe his behaviour to a firm resolution not to mar the happy occasion with any sign that he was wearing the willow, another indication to her of the largeness of his heart. Her own heart felt swollen with love for him. He was worth twenty Edwards, she thought, though she liked Edward very well, and it amazed her that Meriel had not seen this.

They sat over the meal quite two hours, and even Meriel, who ordinarily spoke very little in company, was drawn on by Lady Devitt to speak enthusiastically of her father's summerhouse. Lady Devitt declared she must see it, and the entire company trailed across the grass and into the trees. After she had exclaimed delightedly that she had seen nothing equal to it and spent some time chatting there, Max said firmly that he must take her back to rest before dinner, and that all the Elmdene party must take the meal at Lades Hall with them. She allowed herself to be driven away without demur, for she was by this time feeling somewhat exhausted and quite looked forward to a nice lie-down in a darkened room.

When Lady Devitt made her entrance some hours later, the Elmdene party was already assembled and waiting for her and made an agreeable fuss over her costume, a pale grey satin embroidered with seed pearls and trimmed with much quilled lace and rouleaux about the hem. She was charmed and softened by their attentions, and dinner was an amiable and pleasant meal as a result.

She rose and led the two sisters away to the drawing room, leaving the men to their wine, and the girls clasped hands encouragingly as they followed her, both more than a little nervous to be on their own with her for the first time.

She had decided to show her approval, however, and pulled Meriel down beside her on the sofa and for a moment looked at her without speaking. "Well, my dear, I must tell you that you are a monstrously pretty girl. I do not believe I have ever seen anyone more so." Meriel blushed and dropped her eyes in confusion at this fulsome compliment, which reaction met with Lady Devitt's approval, for she patted her cheek and told her she was a pretty-behaved child as well.

"Thank you, Lady Devitt," Meriel replied breathlessly, "but I hope I shall please you as a . . . a . . . daughter."

"You please me very well, my dear. Miss Armytage"— she turned to Sydney—"your sister pleases me very well. Fetch me that box on the table there, if you will be so kind. Ah, thank you." She took the long flat velvet-covered box and said, "I brought this for you. It was given me by my own mother-in-law when I became engaged to Devitt, and has been handed down so for many hundreds of years. The Devitt pearls, you see." She opened the box and handed it to Meriel.

The long, double strand of large, perfectly matched pearls glimmered opulently from their velvet bed, the clasp a large square-cut emerald set in diamonds.

Meriel stared speechlessly at the pearls, then at Lady Devitt, then at Sydney, and back to the pearls. Then she cried, "Oh!" and threw her arms about Lady Devitt and kissed her cheek fervently, the velvet box and necklace slipping unheeded to the floor. When she sat back, Lady Devitt's eyes could be seen filled with tears and she reached for Meriel's hands and held them until she had recovered herself. Then she bent, scooped up the pearls, and said scoldingly, "There, now, careless child, you have little respect for jewelry, I see. Bend nearer now and I will put it on for you."

Sydney dropped to her knees before them to retrieve the box and watch as the necklace was clasped about Meriel's long throat, and thought surely the Devitts in all their long history had never had a more beautiful bride on whom to bestow the pearls. When Lady Devitt had finished and sat back, they both stared at Meriel admiringly and Sydney reached out to take Lady Devitt's hand and hold it to her cheek for a moment, too overcome with gratitude to her to feel in awe of the grand old lady any longer.

Lady Devitt looked down at her, pressed her hand, and said, "Dear Sydney—for I shan't stand on ceremony with you anymore, and so I warn you—I have brought a trinket for you also." She fished about in her reticule and then handed Sydney a pair of sapphire earrings. "They were given me by my papa when I was a girl, but they are too young for an old body like myself. Put them on, my dear, put them on," she added, waving away Sydney's attempt to thank her. "Max told me all about you, you see, so I knew exactly what would suit you.''

The gentlemen rejoined them, led by Edward, too eager to be back with Meriel to allow them to sit overlong, and she danced up to him excitedly to show him his mother's gift. She was radiant with happiness, and Edward, overcome with her beauty, clasped her in his arms and swung her off her feet before everyone. Her happy laugh caused them all to smile indulgently. He then went to embrace his mother and kiss her soundly.

Sydney was persuaded by Max to play for them, and soon after that the tea tray was brought in, ordered earlier than was usual by Max, who thought Lady Devitt was beginning to flag, and had no desire to have her fall ill while she was a guest in his house.

Over the teacups he told them of the plans Lady Devitt and he had devised for a ball. ''It is to be three days from now, and we are going to drive around to deliver the invitations informally ourselves, so that Lady Devitt can meet all the good citizens of the town. We stopped in Roxton to engage an orchestra, so that is taken care of, and three days should be enough time for all the ladies to furbish up their ball gowns.''

While everyone discussed this excitedly, Max drew near Sydney and said softly, ''I know how happy you must be, Miss Armytage. He is a fine fellow and will be very good to Meriel, you may be sure.''

''Sir Max, I have wanted to speak to you all day.''

''What very encouraging news,'' he replied, smiling quizzically down into her eyes.

She blushed, but continued determinedly, ''Your efforts on Meriel's behalf were unbelievably kind, and we are all very much in your debt.''

''I am glad to know it. I believe I need as much credit as I can acquire in your books.''

''Well . . . I . . . I think you need not worry about that, sir.''

''Then you are not offended with me any longer?''

''Oh! Offended?'' She held out her hand in dismay. ''Why, how could I be so . . . how could you even think . . . I assure you I have never . . .'' She halted in confusion, so anxious to reassure him that she could not think of the proper words. He murmured, "I am glad," and took her hand and held it in both his own until she shyly withdrew it.

Lady Devitt had watched this little playlet with great interest and now turned to Mr. Armytage to raise a questioning eyebrow. He smiled back rather smugly, and a slow answering grin spread over her features. Well, well, she thought, he has hopes in that direction, eh? Her frustrated matchmaking instincts revived instantly. Indeed, Max should be married. It was odd that he was not already leg-shackled. Now, Miss Sydney, let me take a better look at you. Well, no great beauty like your sister, but most appealing for all that. No longer in the first flush of youth, but Max is at least five-and-thirty himself, and the girl certainly is still of childbearing age. There is certainly a prettiness in those large, clear grey eyes, and her smile is charming, her complexion very fine. Her dowry will not be large, I think, but Max surely will not care about that, being rich enough not to have to look out for an heiress. Yes, I approve the match. I must sound him out at the first opportunity.

She found it when the company had gone and Max escorted her to her room. She stopped outside the door and gave him her hand. "It has been years since I have enjoyed a day as much as this one."

"You are pleased with your son's choice, then?"

"Yes, I am," she said definitely. "She is a dear, sweet girl. I like all the family very much. Good sound English stock. I am very much taken with the sister, you know. Very pretty young woman. Has she suitors?"

Max was not taken in by the innocent look that accompanied her question. "Oh, any number."

"Good. It is time she married. And what of you, sir?"

"I?"

"It is more than time for you to think of setting up your nurseries, Max. I do not approve of gentlemen remaining single for too long. They become as set in their ways as old maids."

"Oh, I could not agree with you more, dear lady. Now, I must let you go to your bed. Sleep well." He kissed her fingers and left her.

Well, she thought, I see I shall have to stir him up a bit. Yes, Sydney Armytage will do very well for him.

Max returned to the library for a glass of brandy and was

sitting low on his spine, his long legs extended to the fire, when Morgan returned from his dinner *a deux* with Arabella, and seeing the light, stepped into the room. Max informed him briefly of his other guest.

"A countess, by the lord! A widow, I take it," he added insinuatingly.

"Why, yes, she is," Max drawled.

"You are a sly one, Westbrook," Morgan said admiringly. "Am I to wish you happy, then?"

Max studied his brandy glass and decided he quite definitely disliked this man. "Well, perhaps not quite yet," he said at last, and then rose, bid him good night abruptly, and went to bed without telling him anything further.

26

By the night of the ball, all of Upper Chyppen was in a state of mild hysteria, even the shopkeepers and lowly folk who would not be attending. Everyone had at least seen, and been mightily impressed by, the countess. Those who had met her as she and Max delivered their verbal invitations were quite overcome by her condescension and elegance and awed to have a real countess in their midst.

The biggest item of speculation was the countess's son, who had not yet been seen and who was, so far as could be learned, staying, not with his mother at Lades Hall, but with the Armytages at Elmdene Grange. The pressing question was: why? And why had his mother come here? Where had the Armytages struck up an acquaintance with the Earl of Devitt? By now, of course, his lineage had been thoroughly dissected and all his titles and honours came quite trippingly off the tongues of the Upper Chyppians.

Arabella was referred to frequently, since a number of people had heard from Cassie that he had been a dancing partner of hers at her come-out in London. She was vague in detail, as usual, though she had indeed seen him in London on several occasions, but, alas, had never been introduced to him, much less danced with him. But she felt she might well have, and he could surely not remember every debutante he had danced with, so, nothing deterred, she had herself driven to Elmdene and was received politely by Mr. Armytage, who told her that unfortunately all the young people were out. He did not tell her they were only in the summerhouse, and after a quarter of an hour she took herself off in frustration. The rest of Upper Chyppen was more discreet and decided they could wait for the ball to see him.

Meriel wore her white gown from her godmother, since Edward had not seen her in it, and the Devitt pearls, and was even more breathtaking than she had been the first time she had worn it. Sydney wore her peach-bloom silk again because she had no other gown to compare with it and she wanted to honour Lady Devitt by looking her best. They all went to dine with Sir Max, and for the first time in two weeks Morgan set eyes on Meriel.

He was struck all over again by her beauty, for there was tonight a radiance emanating from her that belied any possible belief in the tales of her decline that had spread over Upper Chyppen. She only nodded to him when she came in and did not look in his direction or speak to him during the meal, but afterwards he went directly up to her and bowed. "Miss Meriel, I am very happy to see you recovered and among us again."

She inclined her head in acknowledgment, but still did not speak. Max came up at once and said Lady Devitt wanted her and took her away to where the countess sat enthroned on a sofa in the ballroom, resplendent in dark gold lamé with a Turkish turban of the same material fringed with gold and a dazzling diamond necklace.

Morgan cursed silently and eyed with suspicion the old lady's son, who seemed inclined to hover over Meriel. Never mind, little one, he said to her silently, I will have my dance with you. He would wait a few moments and then approach her again, and surely she would not be able to refuse to stand up with him while she sat there with Lady Devitt, who was a fellow house guest here at Lades Hall. He knew that if he could only speak to her privately for a moment he could explain to her how irresistible she was and how she could not truly blame him for losing his head that day, which he most truly repented. She could not withstand such a handsome apology. She was, by now, completely surrounded by her friends, who swarmed across the room as soon as they entered to tell her how happy they were to see her going about again, and also to make worshipful obeisance to the countess and be introduced at long last to her son. There was not, however, the usual crowd of young men about her yet, so Morgan felt he could afford to wait until there was a slackening of new arrivals.

Arabella came in with Tristan and her brother and saw Morgan at once. He pretended not to see her and turned away to engage Squire Dobbs in conversation. She knew very well he had seen her, but she refused to allow herself to become angry. She knew she was looking very well tonight and did not want to spoil her looks by frowning. She had chosen to wear white, a rich figured French gauze over white satin, and she moved across the room to the countess confidently.

"My dearest Lady Devitt, how divine to see you here! I could not believe my ears when I heard you were in Upper Chyppen. I was sorry to be out when you called, but Claiborne told me of it."

Lady Devitt turned to Meriel. "Perhaps you would introduce us, my dear."

Arabella laughed gaily. "Ah, you have forgotten me! We were introduced by my aunt, Lady Boxton. I shall write to her tonight to describe every detail of your delicious gown. I know she will want to hear about it and naturally would want me to extend her warmest regards."

Lady Devitt greeted this with a raised eyebrow and turned to Meriel again.

"Lady Devitt, this is Miss Cole," Meriel told her in some embarrassment.

Arabella gave another little laugh and dipped a curtsy as though humouring the countess's forgetfulness, before turning to Meriel to say she was glad to see the rumours she had heard of her illness could not, of course, have been true, then turned to Edward with bright-eyed interest, clearly awaiting an introduction.

"My son, Miss Cole," Lady Devitt obliged, enjoying the whole little scene very much.

"Ah! The mysterious Lord Devitt! You have been the talk

of Upper Chyppen, sir, and it was quite pitiless of you to hide yourself away this age. Shame, sir! But there, we must be forgiving tonight, since we are all gathered together for pleasure. Do you enjoy dancing, Lord Devitt?''

"Very much, Miss Cole,'' he returned politely, thinking her a handsome girl but so strangely intense, staring at one as though offering a challenge.

When she saw that he was not going to invite her to stand up with him, Arabella looked about for Tristan to assist her as he usually did, but she could not see him, and when she turned back, Edward was being introduced to another set of guests who had come up, and she had lost his attention completely. She was distinctly put out and walked away to find Morgan.

He, however, had dodged around the other way to avoid her and now made his way to Meriel, who rose at that moment and was going across the room to her father. Morgan stepped in front of her and she halted.

"Miss Meriel . . . please . . . let me tell you how sorry—''

"Please do not speak of it, Mr. Leighton,'' she said, and tried to step around him.

He moved in front of her again. "If you have truly forgiven me, please say you will stand up with me,'' he said with his most cajoling smile.

She looked up squarely at him then and said quietly, "No, Mr. Leighton, I will not dance with you.''

"Oh, but you cannot—''

"Meriel?'' Sydney had seen her sister being accosted by Morgan and had come at once to her side.

"Oh, Sydney, I was just going to ask Papa which dance he wanted me to save for him. Come with me.'' She took Sydney's arm and they walked away without a word. Morgan's hands curled into fists and he would have liked very much to smash them into something. He turned away into the room where tables had been set up to hold liquid refreshments and took a glass of iced champagne to calm himself. After two more in rapid succession he began to feel somewhat better. He heard the music strike up but stayed where he was, not really interested in dancing at the moment.

In the ballroom Max was leading out Lady Devitt to open the ball, and after a moment Meriel and Edward followed with Sydney and Mr. Armytage.

Her papa had asked her at dinner, " . . . though it is taking unfair advantage over the other lads." He had laughed.

"Thank you, Papa," she said in a low voice so she would not be overheard, "but I will not dance tonight."

"What? Not dance? Now, what is this strange bee in your bonnet?"

"I have thought about it and decided it is time to—"

"Aha! I see. All in line with this cap business and throwing yourself headlong into old age. Well, I will not have it, Sydney! It is all some nonsense that I will not countenance for a moment. Do you understand me?" He looked as severe as she had ever seen him.

"Papa, please do not—" she pleaded.

"You will do me the honour of the first set, Sydney, and if you refuse anyone else, I shall require you to stand up with me for every dance. That should be punishment enough for any disobedient child."

She had to laugh, though she knew very well he would carry out his threat, for he was like Meriel when he had made up his mind to something, never ranting or angry, just gently having his way. So when Sir Max had turned away from Lady Devitt for a moment and requested the second set and the waltz, she had not been able to refuse him under her father's steady eye. The decision she had arrived at so painfully was out the window in a matter of moments and she could not truly have said she was sorry, for much as she feared the storm of emotions that might be set off by waltzing again with Sir Max, she also knew that to sit by while that music stirred the blood in her veins and watch him sailing by with someone else would be a torment of unimaginable dimension.

So she had entered the ballroom, greeted all her friends as they arrived, and by the time the first strains of music were heard, had promised every dance in a mood of reckless abandon, caught up by her own relief to have been chivied out of her resolve, and the electrically charged atmosphere of the room. No one, so far as she could see, had declined Sir Max's invitation, and all were dressed in their best. There were, she noted, an astonishing number of new gowns, which caused her to wonder what their wearers had paid their dressmakers to get them made up in such a short space of time. People swirled continuously about Lady Devitt, dipping and bowing and eyeing her son eagerly, and the talk and laughter reached a high pitch of excitement never before equalled at any Upper Chyppen ball.

Sydney danced with her papa and then with Max, who was so attentive she did not know where to look. It was a quadrille, for which she was grateful, for the steps of the dance separated them frequently enough that she was able to regain her poise very well, and congratulated herself at the finish of it that she had managed to be coolly polite while allowing for the necessity of showing him he had not displeased her in any way as her previous behaviour to him had evidently done.

Her real dread was the waltz, for she was not sure she could keep her feelings in check under the heady influence of the music and his hand at her waist. In the meantime she danced with Edward and other gentlemen she had promised, in a state of numb suspension.

Then the moment was upon her and she found Sir Max smiling and bowing before her and gave him her ice-cold hand to be led onto the floor.

Morgan, fortified by wine, had by this time returned to the ball-room, to watch the proceedings with a small contemptuous sneer. He would not join all this foolishness, could not be bothered to make the agreeable to a set of bores and snobs, all overset by having a live earl and countess in their midst. The waltz music caught his ear and then he was riveted by the sight of Devitt leading Meriel onto the floor. Meriel, who had told him she would never dance it except with someone she loved—and then he saw the way she looked as she dipped into a low curtsy before her partner, her face raised to him, her eyes glowing, her smile . . . adoring!

Morgan swung awkwardly away from the sight and shouldered his way back to the refreshment room, where he sat down and stared blackly at the floor. Not Westbrook! Oh no, he was not grand enough for *her*! She must have an earl at least. He should have known a mere baronet would never satisfy such a coldhearted little . . .

Then he could not go on. It is no use, he thought despairingly, it is only words to fend off the truth. For he had known, at that moment he saw her looking at Devitt with her love shining out of her eyes, that he, Morgan Leighton, loved this girl as truly and as everlastingly as he had always denied was possible. That when he had first seen her and thought of

her as his wife, that had been his honest desire. One he had
covered over quickly in fear. And he had been right to do so.
To allow anyone to reach one's heart was the sure way to
court pain. He felt now as though his very soul hurt. I have
lost her, he cried silently, I shall never see her looking so at
me! Oh, how I should have loved her—she will never know
such love as I could have given her. Unable to bear the
suffering sweeping through him, he rose and asked for a glass
of champagne to swallow down the hard lump in his throat. It
remained obdurate until several glasses at last seemed to
dissolve it.

Sydney, meanwhile, was going through a sweeter torment,
the one she had feared and hoped to avoid by not dancing at
all: the warm hand at her waist, the face bent over her own
seeking her eyes steadily, the music lifting her, melting her
resolve. She tried to look away from him, but he held her
gaze so determinedly it became difficult. She finally wrenched
her eyes away for fear she would show him everything. It
was so easy to allow oneself to be carried away, the romantic
music so clearly demanded it . . . No! She tore her eyes away
from his again.

From her sofa Lady Devitt, with Mr. Armytage beside her,
was watching them with great interest. "He is very much in
love with her," she stated firmly.

Mr. Armytage did not pretend to misunderstand her. "Yes,
I have thought so for some time."

"And what of her?"

"Oh, she loves him."

"Then what are they waiting for?"

"Sydney is working through a problem she has set for
herself."

"Explain yourself, sir."

"Well, I believe she first had him in her eye for Meriel,
then fell in love with him herself."

"But surely now she sees—"

"Yes, but she thinks Max has already given his heart to
Meriel, so—"

"What nonsense! Is she so blind? Why do you not take a
hand in the affair? Tell her, if she will not see."

"Oh, she will come to it herself. I would not dream of
interfering in the course of love, Lady Devitt. So much more
interesting for them to work it out themselves. Think of the

hours of enchanting conversation it will give them later: 'Do you remember when . . . And I thought you . . . And you said . . . But then we . . .' Delightful stuff! They can spend several years of married life recounting it over and over. Would you have me deprive them of a moment of it?''

''You are a great rogue, sir,'' she pronounced severely, then spoiled it, first by smiling, then by a shout of laughter. ''Come, will you give me your arm for a stroll about the room?''

He rose and bowed gallantly. ''With the greatest pleasure in the world, dear lady.''

Arabella's evening had slowly eroded. Her opening gambit with Lady Devitt and her son had failed, Tristan buzzed about the room busily giving her less attention than she liked, and Morgan had so far eluded her entirely. She had danced a few sets, but now she was humiliatingly sitting out the waltz alone. She fanned herself vigorously in a pretense of being overcome by the exertions demanded of her on the dance floor and scanned the room carefully for Morgan. How could he behave so slightingly, not even coming to bid her welcome? Of course, he had not danced so far with anyone else, a rather cold comfort when she was forced to sit here without a partner. Even Claiborne would have been welcome, and she tried to catch his eye, but he continued talking to the vicar in his fatuous way and never looked in her direction.

Then she saw Morgan, walking carefully along near the wall. He came to a curtained alcove, pulled aside the curtain to peer in, swaying slightly, then disappeared. What on earth was the matter with him tonight, skulking about in such a fashion, and she could swear he was half-flown with wine. She rose and made her way to the alcove. It was dimly lit when she stepped inside, but she saw Morgan clearly enough. He was stretched out on the sofa!

''Good heavens, Morgan, what *are* you doing?'' she exclaimed crossly.

''Whaa . . .?'' He stared at her blearily.

''Get up at once! You cannot fall asleep here. This is a ball and you are a guest in the house. You have some obligations, you know.''

''Be damned to that,'' he replied, so slurred in his speech her suspicions were confirmed. She took his arm and pulled him into a sitting position.

"How can you be so wanting in conduct as to embarrass your host by becoming drunk?" she scolded, straightening his coat and pushing the disordered locks back from his forehead.

He heaved himself to his feet with the help of her arm and stood swaying. "Damned room spinning," he muttered, closing his eyes for a moment.

"What is wrong with you tonight anyway?"

"Nothing. Merry as a grig," he pronounced carefully, opening his eyes wide and focusing them on her with some difficulty. "Mosh . . . most . . . becomin' gown, Bella. You look fine as fivepensh."

She smiled, softening. "Very kind of you to say so, sir."

"Tha's my Bella. Can't resist old Morgan, can you?" he said, his eyes filling with drunken sentimental tears.

"Why Morgan! What is it, my dear?" she cried, astounded by the sight.

"Good ole Bella," he said, and embraced her clumsily. She tried to push him away, only too aware of the sounds of people passing just outside the curtain and likely to come in at any moment. "Come on, Bella, console me." His mouth found hers and clamped down firmly and, despite the state he was in, expertly. She melted and returned the kiss, forgetting everyone for a moment.

Suddenly the curtain was pushed aside with a rattle of rings on the pole and Claiborne was saying, "There you are, Bella, I was . . ." before he stopped and his mouth gaped open at the sight before him. Arabella tore herself from Morgan's arms and stared around in horror. Behind him she saw the wide-eyed faces of Mr. Armytage and Lady Devitt, Mrs. Maplethorpe and the vicar, among others.

"What the devil is the meaning of this, Leighton?" Claiborne blustered loudly, causing others to stop and stare.

" 'S only . . . 's only . . ." Morgan muttered.

Arabella's wits did not desert her. She had at first thought that she might kill Claiborne with her bare hands for putting her in such a position by his bungling, but just as swifly she saw the advantage. She made her decision and smiled blindingly. "It is quite all right, Claiborne, though perhaps naughty of us. Mr. Leighton has just . . . we are betrothed!" She dropped her eyes demurely.

"What? Well . . . well, I . . ." Claiborne floundered, while the attentive onlookers drew a concerted gasp. "Well, sir, is this true?"

Morgan, nearly sobered by Arabella's words, stared at him while his mind attempted to grapple with the situation. Then he thought wildly: why not? What does it matter? Nothing matters any longer: "Yes . . . yes . . . perfe'ly true, ole boy. Wish us happy," and he plumped back down on the sofa, giggling weakly, helplessly, at the trap he had allowed himself to fall into. It was really hilariously funny—a great joke on himself.

Mr. Armytage drew Lady Devitt away. "The man is drunk," he said distastefully. "I cannot care for him, but this is too bad."

"Do I take it that though you dislike him your masculine sense of brotherhood causes you to defend him? You feel he has been taken advantage of?"

"Well, I suppose he deserved it, but—"

"And what of the advantage he has taken of her? Oh, I have heard enough from Max to have guessed what was going on between them. I probably know more of it than you, and I say he more than deserved it, he owed it to her," Lady Devitt declared ringingly.

"They will make each other most unhappy."

"No doubt," returned Lady Devitt dryly, "for he is a scoundrel and she is a discontented, pushing sort of girl who could have done better for herself if she did not frighten the men away by her naked determination to get a husband. Still, she will be saved the fate of becoming the old-maid aunt to her brother's children. A terrible fate for a woman, Mr. Armytage. I cannot care for Miss Cole, but I would not wish that on her."

Mr. Armytage replied meekly that no doubt she was right. Indeed, in his heart he knew she was, but still he felt a niggling pity for Leighton that he could not feel for Miss Cole. What a dreadful life was in prospect for Leighton, he thought, for Mr. Armytage was in no doubts at all about which was the stronger of the two.

27

The ladies of Upper Chyppen had almost more interesting tidbits on their plates than they knew how to deal with, and the day following the ball a veritable hum of conversation could be heard over the town as they attempted to digest all the amazing things that had happened. Arabella's coup was rehashed until the subject had worn quite thin, but even that took second place to the reverberations caused by Meriel and the Earl of Devitt! No announcement had been made, but it was clear to all who had seen them together that one could be expected in the not-too-distant future. Our Meriel to be a countess! But there, so beautiful a girl . . . one could not wonder. How much allowance do you think he will make her? Did you *see* those pearls? They must have come from the Devitts, for the Armytages never had anything like them. Surely he will come down handsomely in the settlements—how many establishments does he keep? Naturally, he will give her her own carriage, perhaps several! Her first son will be the Viscount Somerville! Is not that astonishing to think of? Our Meriel!

Max and Lady Devitt breakfasted together only a half-hour past their usual time, mutually congratulating one another on their stamina and need for only a little sleep to feel completely restored after a night of dancing. They agreed together that the ball had been a splendid affair, and not marred at all by the behaviour of Morgan and Arabella. Lady Devitt regaled him with tales of even less savoury events she had witnessed at balls in London and Scotland, and they agreed that what had occurred had only added a last fillip of excitement to an already solidly successful evening.

"Though I shudder to think what Mr. Leighton's head will be like when he wakes up," said Lady Devitt.

"And it will not be helped by having to face the reality of what has happened to him."

"Ah, well, life has a way of springing the most outrageous surprises on one. I have been wondering a great deal about you, Max," she said thoughtfully.

"About me?"

"Well, betrothals seem to be in the air," she said with a great pretense of casualness.

"Speaking of outrageous . . ." He laughed.

"Well, one can but wonder," she continued, undeterred.

"I suppose not when one is a lady who likes to stir her finger about in everybody's stew in search of interesting bits," he teased.

She agreed, not in the least offended. "Yes, I do like to make things happen when I see they should."

"Have no fear, dear lady," he said obliquely, and refused to be drawn further.

His drawing room began filling quite early with callers eager to enlarge their acquaintance with the countess, and she enjoyed herself hugely with the ordering of their lives, not hesitating to advise them how they should go on, even in matters of estate management or the breeding of cattle. Max watched and listened in great amusement, trying to stem his rising impatience to get to Elmdene.

He was sure now, or almost sure, that Sydney returned his feelings, and why she was so reluctant to show it, he meant to find out very soon. However, it was quite an hour later before the last caller was gone and he finally could announce that he was going to Elmdene and would be happy to drive the countess there if she would not require too much time to prepare for a visit.

She studied him for a moment and then laughed mischievously. "No. I think you can handle the matter without my help, do not you?"

"I cannot think what you are talking about." He grinned, and then, kissing her cheek, strode out of the house.

Sydney was in a very strange state this morning, distrait and bemused. She had put her cap on, taken it off, and finally wandered down to breakfast with it in her hand, absentmindedly wiping her fingers on it after crumbling her toast and staring out the window, while every-

one else ate heartily and discussed the preceding evening
with pleasure.

Edward and Meriel were going to ride, and invited
Sydney to go with them, but she said she had too much to
do. They went away presently, and she continued to sit
there, her chin on her hand.

Her father rose, gathering his papers. "Do not work
too hard, my dear."

"What?"

"I said," he repeated with a smile, "do not work too
hard."

"Oh . . . yes . . . no, of course . . . I must . . ." She rose
and wandered out into the hall, where she stood for a long
time with her hand on the newel post. She felt strange and
somehow disembodied this morning, as though something
momentous had happened to her that had in some mysterious way been erased from her memory. She knew she was
behaving idiotishly, but could not seem to pull her wits together.

Suddenly she hurried up the stairs and changed quickly
into her new blue riding habit and the bonnet to match it,
with a trailing white plume. She raced along to the stable,
had her mare saddled, and rode off over the fields at a
hard gallop. Thirty minutes later she came galloping back,
turned the horse over to the groom, and trailed away
across the grass to the pond. She stood on the dock for a
long time staring into the water, and at last, despite her
resolve after she had left the ball the night before, the
memory of the evening swept back over her. Wait, wait!
she commanded herself, and stepped into the boat and
rowed for the other shore. Before she reached it, she
stopped, shipped the oars, and sat quietly and allowed
herself to remember every moment, every word they had
exchanged, every expression on his face. Not once had she
seen any signs of anything but delight with matters as
they stood between himself and Meriel. Had he realized
the folly of his feelings for her and turned . . . No! He was
not so shallow a man as that! Then had he ever felt
anything for her? Sydney thought back to the scene she
had witnessed from the window that had convinced her
that he loved Meriel. Meriel had told her about Morgan's
behaviour and how kind Max had been, but naturally
Sydney had assumed . . . But perhaps he *was* only being

kind, as naturally he would be, and when he took her out riding every day after that, it was only to protect her. I imagined everything, then, built the entire romance up in my mind on nothing at all but my own decision that they would naturally fall in love with one another.

Why? Why should I do such a thing? She thought back to their meeting in the lending library, and slowly the answer forced itself upon her. Because I fell in love with him then, at the very first sight of him, and decided it was not possible he could ever love me. I was protecting myself against that hurt by building up a romance for Meriel. Oh, how foolish I have been, for in the end I caused even more unhappiness for myself when I could no longer deny my feelings. All those miserable days of being cold to him.

And all the time . . . No, I don't know that—for sure—but at least last night . . . the way he looked at me as we waltzed! I could not have mistaken that look. I *did* not mistake it!

The joy rose in her and lifted her to her feet, and she spun around, arms raised, nearly shouting with rapture, "He—" Then she was tipped abruptly into the water. She came up dripping and gasped, "—loves me!" before she began to cough up the pond water she had swallowed. Then, laughing, she began to swim for the near shore, pulling the boat along behind her by the painter. She pulled it up onto the grass and squelched her way through the strawberry bushes to return to the house as quickly as she could go in her sopping habit. She did not see Max come out of the trees, stop before the summerhouse to stare around, before setting off along the path the other way around the pond.

He had arrived at Elmdene shortly after she had returned from her ride and gone in to Mr. Armytage.

"Well, well, my boy, good morning. How is the dear countess today? Did she not come with you?"

"No, but do doubt she will come over later."

"You must both dine here with us, or Cook will resign. She complained bitterly to me this morning that she had not yet had the honour of making a grand dinner for her ladyship."

"Very kind of you both. I am sure she will like that."

"Bang-up party last night."

"Yes, everyone seemed to enjoy it, with the exception, perhaps, of Mr. Leighton. Well, where is . . . everybody?"

"Edward and Meriel have gone riding."

"Look here, sir, I . . ." Max halted.

"Yes, my boy?" Mr. Armytage encouraged.

"I think you know what I want to say already. I love Sydney very much and want your permission to address her."

"You must already know that you have it."

"I thought you would not object. Thank you, sir. There is something else I wanted to speak about. There has been some . . . some . . . strangeness between us for a time. Do you know . . . has she ever confided her reasons for it to you?"

"No, my boy," Mr. Armytage said truthfully. "I should ask her if I were you. I am sure you will get to the bottom of it between you. Lizzy said she had seen Sydney going towards the summerhouse," he added helpfully.

"Oh. Well, then, if you will excuse me, I . . ."

"Cut right along, dear boy. Best to get these things sorted out while one's courage is up," said Mr. Armytage, waving him genially out of the room.

Max strode around the house and across the grass rapidly, but when he reached the summerhouse he did not see her, though after a moment he noticed the boat drawn up on the far side of the pond and set off on the path around the pond.

Sydney left a trail of water behind her as she rushed in the front door and across to the stairs. Her father emerged from the library just as she started up. "Good God!" he exclaimed, taking in the sopping habit and soaked hair streaming about her face. "What has happened? Did Max—?"

She spun about. "Max?"

"Why, did you not see him? He went to the summerhouse to find you."

"Oh!" She turned, hitched her skirt over one arm, and leaping down the two steps, ran out of the house. Mr. Armytage stared after her for a moment and then began to laugh uproariously.

Sydney pounded across the grass past the summerhouse and straight on along the path. When she came up with him Max was leaning over the water. He stood up with her blue bonnet in his hands, the white plume streaming water, a look of horror on his face. He whirled around when he heard running footsteps, dropped the hat, and ran forward to sweep her up into his arms. "Sydney! Oh, my God, Sydney, are you all right? I thought . . . Oh, Sydney, my darling!" He crushed her against him and she could feel his heart pounding even more loudly than her own. After a moment he held her away to look into her face. "I was frightened when I saw that hat! Your father said you were here . . . and then I could not find you . . . Ah, dearest, darling Sydney." He pulled her even closer and kissed her almost frantically, as though to make sure she was truly there. Then, in reassurance, the kiss turned into something slower and deeper as her lips softened beneath his and she began returning his kiss, shyly at first and then with more and more passion to match his own. They spent a very long time learning all the possibilities for bliss that kissing one's beloved affords.

Breathlessly they drew apart and stood gazing at one another, smiling rather idiotically. He gradually became aware of the condition she was in and held her away to look at her more carefully. "Why, Sydney, you are wet through."

"I have spoiled your neckcloth beyond repair, I fear, and made your coat terribly wet as well."

"Never mind that. What happened?"

"I fell out of the boat," she said simply.

"You fell out? But how?"

"It was when I realized . . ." She stopped, overcome with shyness, which, considering the intimacy of the kiss that had just concluded, was senseless. Still, there was much to be explored, deliciously, between them.

He tilted up her chin with one finger. "What did you realize, my darling?"

"That . . . you were not in love with Meriel," she said, equivocating only a little.

"Good Lord! What an idea! What can have put such a hare-brained thought into your head?"

"She is so beautiful," she replied, unable to confess just yet her own folly.

"Well, she is that, and naturally I enjoy looking at her, as I would do at anything beautiful, but she is only seventeen, Sydney. I have never been partial to green girls."

"No?" she said encouragingly, hoping to hear what he *was* partial to.

He obliged, his voice a caress. "I am partial to young women with hazy, fair hair and bright grey eyes and impertinent noses and lovely smiles with soft pink mouths"—he stopped then to illustrate how partial he was to soft pink mouths, and after a lazy, langourous exploration of its shape with his own lips, continued—"who like to fish and swim and play the pianoforte and drive to the inch."

"Do I drive to the inch?" she asked dreamily.

"Yes. How did you not know I loved you then—when I let you drive?"

"How could I have?"

"My greys! Do you imagine any man in the world would trust his best nags to a woman unless he were bewitched by her?" His voice was disbelieving.

"Sir Max, kiss me again," she demanded.

He complied at length and then said plaintively, "After that, perhaps you could call me simply Max. Lady Devitt does so, and I have never even kissed her."

"Max, my darling," she said obediently.

"I like that even better. Good Lord! I am forgetting entirely. You must get out of these wet clothes before you catch a chill." He bent and lifted her easily into his arms and started off for the house. She put her arms around his neck and nestled her face into his neck.

"Do you know," she confided, "this is my new habit. I had it made up after our first ride together. Do you remember? Cassie Maplethorpe was in green and I felt so drab in my old brown."

"I thought you were beautiful. I do not have any memory of what you were wearing. I remember being very jealous of Leighton."

"*Were* you? How silly. Was that when you first . . .?"

"I believe so. And when did you first . . .?"

"The bookstore, I think, when you said—"

"You were so prim and adorable, and then when—"

"What did you mean that day when—?"

". . . do you remember?

". . . and then we . . ."

The trip to the house took a very long time, with many long pauses to punctuate their memories with kisses to erase any lingering hurts they might have given one another.

Mr. Armytage had come out onto the front steps after Sydney's abrupt and dripping departure to wait for them, and watched their slow return across the grass with a complacent grin. He knew very well what their conversation was about.

More Regency Romances from SIGNET